THE COLONEL'S TONGUE WAS A MAGICIAN'S WAND

THE GILDED AGE

A TALE OF TO-DAY

BY

MARK TWAIN
(Samuel L. Clemens)

AND

CHARLES DUDLEY WARNER

IN TWO VOLUMES

VOL. I

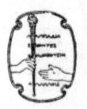

HARPER & BROTHERS PUBLISHERS
NEW YORK AND LONDON

PREFACE

THIS book was not written for private circulation among friends; it was not written to cheer and instruct a diseased relative of the author's; it was not thrown off during intervals of wearing labor to amuse an idle hour. It was not written for any of these reasons, and therefore it is submitted without the usual apologies.

It will be seen that it deals with an entirely ideal state of society; and the chief embarrassment of the writers in this realm of the imagination has been the want of illustrative examples. Ire a state where there is no fever of speculation, no inflamed desire for sudden wealth, where the poor are all simple-minded and contented, and the rich are all honest and generous, where society is in a condition of primitive purity, and politics is the occupation of only the capable and the patriotic, there are necessarily no materials for such a

history as we have constructed out of an ideal commonwealth.

No apology is needed for following the learned custom of placing attractive scraps of literature at the heads of our chapters. It has been truly observed by Wagner that such headings, with their vague suggestions of the matter which is to follow them, pleasantly inflame the reader's interest without vrholly satisfying his curiosity, and we will hope that it may be found to be so in the present case.

Our quotations are set in a vast number of tongues; this is done for the reason that very few foreign nations among whom the book will circulate can read in any language but their own; whereas we do not write for a particular class or sect or nation, but to take in the whole world.

We do not object to criticism; and we do not expect that the critic will read the book before writing a notice of it. We do not even expect the reviewer of the book will say that he has not read it. No, we have no anticipations of anything unusual in this age of criticism. But if the Jupiter, who passes his opinion on the novel, ever happens to peruse it in some weary moment of his subsequent life, we hope that he will not be the victim of a remorse bitter but too late.

One word more. This is — what it pretends to be — a joint production, in the conception of the story, the exposition of the characters, and in its literal composition. There is scarcely a chapter that does not bear the marks of the two writers of the book. S. L. c.

C. D. W.

PUBLISHER'S NOTE

AT the close of each volume will be found translations of the mottoes placed at the heads of the chapters, — selected for their appropriateness and translated by the eminent philologist, the late J. Hammond Trumbull, LL.D., L.H.D., from the various languages represented.

The mottoes themselves have appeared in all the many editions of "The Gilded Age" heretofore published, but the translations have never been made public until now, and are therefore a feature of this edition.

THE COLONEL'S TONGUE WAS A
MAGICIAN'S WAND . . W. T. Smetley Frontispiece
"THY WAYS GREATLY TRY ME,
RUTH" W.T.Smedlty

THE GILDED AGE

SQUIRE HAWKINS' TENNESSEE LANDS Nibiwa win o-dibendan aki.

Eng. A gallant tract Of land it is!

Meercraft. 'Twill yield a pound an acre: We must let cheap ever at first. But, sir, This looks too large for you, I see.

Benjonson. The Devil is an Ass.

JUNE, 18—, Squire Hawkins sat upon the pyramid of large blocks, called the " stile," in front of his house, contemplating the morning.

The locality was Obedstown, East Tennessee. You would not know that Obedstown stood on the top of a mountain, for there was nothing about the landscape to indicate it — but it did: a mountain that stretched abroad over whole counties, and rose very gradually. The district was called the " Knobs of East Tennessee," and had a reputation like Nazareth, as far as turning out any good thing was concerned.

The Squire's house was a double log cabin, in a

See Publisher's Note,

(13)

state of decay; two or three gaunt hounds lay asleep about the threshold, and lifted their heads sadly whenever Mrs. Hawkins or the children stepped in and out over their bodies. Rubbish was scattered about the grassless yard; a bench stood near the door with a tin wash-basin on it and a pail of water and a gourd; a cat had begun to drink from the pail, but the exertion was overtaxing her energies, and she had stopped to rest. There was an ash-hopper by the fence, and an iron pot, for soft-soap-boiling, near it.

This dwelling constituted one-fifteenth of Obeds-town; the other fourteen houses were scattered about among the tall pine trees and among the cornfields in such a way that a man might stand in the midst of the city and not know but that he was in the country if he only depended on his eyes for information.

" Squire " Hawkins got his title from being postmaster of Obedstown — not that the title properly belonged to the office, but because in those regions the chief citizens always must have titles of some sort, and so the usual courtesy had been extended to Hawkins. The mail was monthly, and sometimes amounted to as much as three or four letters at a single delivery. Even a rush like this did not fill up the postmaster's whole month, though, and therefore he " kept store " in the intervals.

The Squire was .contemplating the morning. It was balmy and tranquil, the vagrant breezes were

laden with the odor of flowers, the murmur of bees was in the air, there was everywhere that suggestion of repose that summer woodlands bring to the senses, and the vague pleasurable melancholy that such a time and such surroundings inspire.

Presently the United States mail arrived, on horseback. There was but one letter, and it was for the postmaster. The long-legged youth who carried the mail tarried an hour to talk, for there was no hurry; and in a little while the male population of the village had assembled to help. As a general thing, they were dressed in homespun "jeans," blue or yellow — there were no other varieties of it; all wore one suspender and sometimes two — yarn ones knitted at home,— some wore vests, but few -wore coats. Such coats and vests as did appear, however, were rather picturesque than otherwise, for they were made of tolerably fanciful patterns or calico — a fashion which prevails there to this day among those of the community who have tastes above the common level and are able to afford style. Every individual arrived with his hands in his pockets; a hand came out occasionally for a purpose, but it always went back again after service; and if it was the head that was served, just the cant that the dilapidated straw hat got by being uplifted and rooted under was retained until the next call altered the inclination; many hats were present, but none were erect and no two were canted just alike. We are speaking impartially of

men, youths, and boys. And we are also speaking of these three estates when we say that every individual was either chewing natural leaf tobacco prepared on his own premises, or smoking the same in a corncob pipe. Few of the men wore whiskers; none wore moustaches; some had a thick jungle of hair under the chin and hiding the throat — the only pattern recognized there as being the correct thing in whiskers; but no part of any individual's face had seen a razor for a week.

These neighbors stood a few moments looking at the mail carrier reflectively while he talked; but fatigue soon began to show itself, and one after another they climbed up and occupied the top rail of the fence, hump-shouldered and grave, like a company of buzzards assembled for supper and listening for the death-rattle. Old Damrell said:

" Tha hain't no news 'bout the jedge, hit ain't likely?"

" Cain't tell for sartin; some thinks he's gwyne to be 'long toreckly, and some thinks 'e hain't. Russ Mosely he tole ole Hanks he mought git to Obeds tomorrer or nex' day he reckoned."

" Well, I wisht I knowed. I got a prime sow and pigs in the cote-house, and I hain't got no place for to put 'em. If the jedge is a gwyne to hold cote, I got to roust 'em out, I reckon. But tomorrer'll do, I 'spect."

The speaker bunched his thick lips together like the stem end of a tomato and shot a bumblebee dead

that had lit on a weed seven feet away. One after another the several chewers expressed a charge of tobacco juice and delivered it at the deceased with steady aim and faultless accuracy.

" What's a stirrin', down 'bout the Forks?" continued Old Damrell.

"Well, I dunno, skasely. Ole Drake Higgins he's ben down to Shelby las' week. Tuck his crap down; couldn't git shet o' the most uv it; hit warn't no time for to sell, he say, so he fetch it back agin, 'lowin' to wait tell fall. Talks 'bout goin' to Mozouri — lots uv 'ems talkin' that-away down thar, Ole Higgins say. Cain't make a livin' here no mo',, sich times as these. Si Higgins he's ben over to Kaintuck n' married a high-toned gal thar, outen the fust families, an' he's come back to the Forks with jist a hell's-mint o' whoop-jamboree notions, folks say. He's tuck an' fixed up the ole house like they does in Kaintuck, he say, an' tha's ben folks come cler from Turpentine for to see it. He's tuck an' gawmed it all over on the inside with plarsterin'."

" What's plarsterin' ?"

dono. Hit's what he calls it. Ole Mam Higgins, she tole me. She say she warn't gwyne to hang out in no sich a dern hole like a hog. Says it's mud, or some sich kind o' nastness that sticks on n' kivers up everything. Plarsterin', Si calls it."

This marvel was discussed at considerable length;

and almost with animation. But presently there was a dog-fight over in the neighborhood of the blacksmith shop, and the visitors slid off their perch like so many turtles and strode to the battle-field with an interest bordering on eagerness. The Squire remained, and read his letter. Then he sighed, and sat long in meditation. At intervals he said:

" Missouri. Missouri. Well, well, well, everything is so uncertain."

At last he said:

I believe I'll do it. — A man will just rot, here. My house, my yard, everything around me, in fact, shows that I am becoming one of these cattle — and I used to be thrifty in other times."

He was not more than thirty-five, but he had a worn look that made him seem older. He left the stile, entered that part of his house which was the store, traded a quart of thick molasses for a coon-skin and a cake of beeswax to an old dame in linsey-woolsey, put his letter away, and went into the kitchen. His wife was there, constructing some dried - apple pies; a slovenly urchin of ten was dreaming over a rude weather-vane of his own contriving; his small sister, close upon four years of age, was sopping corn-bread in some gravy left in the bottom of a frying-pan and trying hard not to sop over a finger-mark that divided the pan through the middle — for the other side belonged to the brother, whose musings made him forget his stomach for the moment; a negro woman was busy cooking at a vast fireplace. Shiftlessness and poverty reigned in the place.

"Nancy, I've made up my mind. The world is done with me, and perhaps I ought to be done with it. But no matter — I can wait. I am going to Missouri. I won't stay in this dead country and decay with it. I've had it on my mind some time. I'm going to sell out here for whatever I can get, and buy a wagon and team and put you and the children in it and start."

"Anywhere that suits you, suits me, Si. And the children can't be any worse off in Missouri than they are here, I reckon."

Motioning his wife to a private conference in their own room, Hawkins said: "No, they'll be better off. I've looked out for them, Nancy," and his face lighted. " Do you see these papers? Well, they are evidence that I have taken up Seventy-five Thousand Acres of Land in this county — think what an enormous fortune it will be some day! Why, Nancy, enormous don't express it — the word's too tame! I tell you, Nancy "

" For goodness sake, Si "

"Wait, Nancy, wait — let me finish—I've been secretly boiling and fuming with this grand inspiration for weeks, and I must talk or I'll burst! I haven't whispered to a soul — not a word — have had my countenance under lock and key, for fear it might drop something that would tell even these animals here how to discern the gold mine that's

glaring under their noses. Now, all that is necessary to hold this land and keep it in the family is to pay the trifling taxes on it yearly — five or ten dollars— the whole tract would not sell for over a third of a cent an acre now, but some day people will be glad to get it for twenty dollars, fifty dollars, a hundred dollars an acre! What should you say to " [here he dropped his voice to a whisper and looked anxiously around to see that there were no eavesdroppers] " a thousand dollars an acre!

" Well you may open your eyes and stare ! But it's so. You and I may not see the day, but they'll see it. Mind I tell you, they'll see it. Nancy, you've heard of steamboats, and maybe you believed in them — of course you did. You've heard these cattle here scoff at them and call them lies and humbugs,— but they're not lies and humbugs, they're a reality, and they're going to be a more wonderful thing some day than they are now. They're going to make a revolution in this world's affairs that will make men dizzy to contemplate. I've been watching I've been watching while some people slept, and I know what's coming.

Even you and I will see the day that steamboats will come up that little Turkey River to within twenty miles of this land of ours — and in high water they'll come right to it! And this is not all, Nancy — it isn't even half! There's a bigger wonder— the railroad! These worms here have never even heard of it — and when they do they'll not

believe in it. But it's another fact. Coaches that fly over the ground twenty miles an hour — heavens and earth, think of that, Nancy! Twenty miles an hour. It makes a man's brain whirl. Some day, when you and I are in our graves, there'll be a railroad stretching hundreds of miles — all the way down from the cities of the Northern States to New Orleans — and its got to run within thirty miles of this land — maybe even touch a corner of it. Well, do you know, they've quit burning wood in some places in the Eastern States? And what do you suppose they burn? Coal!" [He bent over and whispered again:] "There's whole worlds of it on this land! You know that black stuff that crops out of the bank of the branch? well, that's it. You've taken it for rocks; so has everybody here; and they've built little dams and such things with it. One man was going to build a chimney out of it. Nancy, I expect I turned as white as a sheet! Why, it might have caught fire and told everything. I showed him it was too crumbly. Then he was going to build it of copper ore — splendid yellow forty-per-cent ore ! There's fortunes upon fortunes of copper ore on our land! It scared me to death, the idea of this fool starting a smelting furnace in his house without knowing it, and getting his dull eyes opened. And then he was going to build it of iron ere! There's mountains of iron ore here, Nancy — whole mountains of it. I wouldn't take any chances. I just stuck by him — I haunted him— I

never let him alone till he built it of mud and sticks like all the rest of the chimneys in this dismal country. Pine forests, wheat land, corn land, iron, copper, coal — wait till the railroads come, and the steamboats! Will never see the day, Nancy — never in the world — never, never, never, child. We've got to drag along, drag along, and eat crusts in toil and poverty, all hopeless and forlorn — but they'll ride in coaches, Nancy! They'll live like the princes of the earth; they'll be courted and worshiped; their names will be known from ocean to ocean! Ah, well-a-day! Will they ever come back here, on the railroad and the steamboat, and say ' This one little spot shall not be touched — this hovel shall be sacred — for here our father and our mother suffered for us, thought for us, laid the foundations of our future as solid as the hills!' '

" You are a great, good, noble soul, Si Hawkins, and I am an honored woman to be the wife of such a man "— and the tears stood in her eyes when she said it. "We will go to Missouri. You are out of your place here, among these groping dumb creatures. We will find a higher place, where you can walk with your own kind, and be understood when you speak — not stared at as if you were talking some foreign tongue. I would go anywhere, anywhere in the wide world with you. I would rather my body should starve and die than your mind should hunger and wither away in this lonely land."

" Spoken like yourself, my child ! But we'll not starve, Nancy. Far from it. I have a letter from Beriah Sellers — just came this day. A letter that — I'll read you a line from it!"

He flew out of the room. A shadow blurred the sunlight in Nancy's face — there was uneasiness in it, and disappointment. A procession of disturbing thoughts began to troop through her mind. Saying nothing aloud, she sat with her hands in her lap; now and then she clasped them, then unclasped them, then tapped the ends of the fingers together; sighed, nodded, smiled — occasionally paused, shook her head. This pantomime was the elocutionary expression of an unspoken soliloquy which had something of this shape:

" I was afraid of it — was afraid of it. Trying to make our fortune in Virginia, Beriah Sellers nearly ruined us — and we had to settle in Kentucky and start over again. Trying to make our fortune in Kentucky, he crippled us again and we had to move here. Trying to make our fortune here, he brought us clear down to the ground, nearly. He's an honest soul, and means the very best in the world, but I'm afraid, I'm afraid he's too flighty. He has splendid ideas, and he'll divide his chances with his friends with a free hand, the good generous soul, but something does seem to always interfere and spoil everything. I never did think he was right well balanced. But I don't blame my husband, for I do think that when that man gets his head full of

a new notion, he can out-talk a machine. He'll make anybody believe in that notion that'll listen to him ten minutes — why, I do believe he would make a deaf-and-dumb man believe in it and get beside himself, if you only set him where he could see his eyes talk and watch his hands explain. What a head he has got! When he got up that idea there in Virginia of buying up whole loads of negroes in Delaware and Virginia and Tennessee, very quiet, having papers drawn to have them delivered at a place in Alabama and take them and pay for them, away yonder at a certain time, and then in the meantime get a law made stopping everybody from selling negroes to the South after a certain day — it was somehow that way — mercy how the man would have made money! Negroes would have gone up to four prices. But after he'd spent money and worked hard, and traveled hard, and had heaps of negroes all contracted for, and everything going along just right, he couldn't get the laws passed and down the whole thing tumbled. And there in Kentucky, when he raked up that old numskull that had been inventing away at a perpetual - motion machine for twenty-two years, and Beriah Sellers saw at a glance where just one more little cogwheel would settle the business, why I could see it as plain as day when he came in wild at midnight and hammered us out of bed and told the whole thing in a whisper with the doors bolted and the candle in an empty barrel. Oceans of money in it—anybody

could see that. But it did cost a deal to buy the old numskull out — and then when they put the new cogwheel in they'd overlooked something somewhere and it wasn't any use — the troublesome thing wouldn't go. That notion he got up here did look as handy as anything in the world; and how him and Si did sit up nights working at it with the curtains down and me watching to see if any neighbors were about. The man did honestly believe there was a fortune in that black gummy oil that stews out of the bank Si says is coal; and he refined it himself till it was like water, nearly, and it did burn, there's no two ways about that; and I reckon he'd have been all right in Cincinnati with his lamp that he got made, that time he got a house full of rich speculators to see him exhibit, only in the middle of his speech it let go and almost blew the heads off the whole crowd. I haven't got over grieving for the money that cost, yet. I am sorry enough Beriah Sellers is in Missouri now, but I was glad when he went. I wonder what his letter says. But of course it's cheerful; he s never downhearted — never had any trouble in his life — didn't know it if he had. It's always sunrise with that man, and fine and blazing, at that—never gets noon, though — leaves off and rises again. Nobody can help liking the creature, he means so well — but I do dread to come across him again; he's bound to set us all crazy, of course. Well, there goes old Widow Hopkins —it always takes her a week to buy a spool of thread and trade a hank of yarn. Maybe Si can come with the letter, now."

And he did:

Widow Hopkins kept me — I haven't any patience with such tedious people. Now listen, Nancy — just listen at this:

"Come right along to Missouri! Don't wait and worry about a good price, but sell out for whatever you can get, and come along, or you might be too late. Throw away your traps, if necessary, and come empty-handed. You'll never regret it. It's the grandest country — the loveliest land—the purest atmosphere — I can't describe it; no pen can do it justice. And it's filling up every day — people coming from everywhere. I've got the biggest scheme on earth — and I'll take you in ; I'll take in every friend I've got that's ever stood by me, for there's enough for all, and to spare. Mum's the word — don't whisper — keep yourself to yourself. You'll see! Come! — rush! — hurry!—don't wait for anything!'

"It's the same old boy, Nancy, just the same old boy — ain't he?"

" Yes, I think there's a little of the old sound about his voice yet. I suppose you — you'll still go, Si? "

Go ! Well, I should think so, Nancy. It's all a chance, of course, and chances haven't been kind to us, I'll admit — but whatever comes, old wife, they're provided for. Thank God for that!"

" Amen," came low and earnestly.

And with an activity and a suddenness that bewildered Obedstown and almost took its breath away, the Hawkinses hurried through with their arrangements in four short months and flitted out into the great mysterious blank that lay beyond the Knobs of Tennessee.

CHAPTER II.

SQUIRE HAWKINS ADOPTS CLAY

TOWARD the close of the third day's journey the wayfarers were just beginning to think of camping, when they came upon a log cabin in the woods. Hawkins drew rein and entered the yard. A boy about ten years old was sitting in the cabin door with his face bowed in his hands. Hawkins approached, expecting his footfall to attract attention, but it did not. He halted a moment, and then said:

" Come, come, little chap, you mustn't be going to sleep before sundown."

With a tired expression the small face came up out of the hands, — a face down which tears were flowing.

"Ah, I'm sorry I spoke so, my boy. Tell me, is anything the matter?"

The boy signified with a scarcely perceptible

(27)

gesture that the trouble was in the house, and made room for Hawkins to pass. Then he put his face in his hands again and rocked himself about as one suffering a grief that is too deep to find help in moan or groan or outcry. Hawkins stepped within. It was a poverty-stricken place. Six or eight middle-aged country people of both sexes were grouped about an object in the middle of the room; they were noiselessly busy and they talked in whispers when they spoke. Hawkins uncovered and approached. A coffin stood upon two backless chairs. These neighbors had just finished disposing the body of a woman in it—a woman with a careworn, gentle face that had more the look of sleep about it than of death. An old lady motioned toward the door and said to Hawkins in a whisper: " His mother, po' thing. Died of the fever, last night. Tha warn't no sich thing as saving of her. But it's better for her — better for her. Husband and the other two children died in the spring, and she hain't ever hilt up her head sence. She jest went around broken-hearted like, and never took no intrust in anything but Clay — that's the boy thar. She jest worshiped Clay — and Clay he worshiped her. They didn't 'pear to live at all, only when they was together, looking at each other, loving one another. She's ben sick three weeks; and if you believe me that child has worked, and kep' the run of the med'cin, and the times of giving it, and sot up nights and nussed her, and tried to keep up her

sperits, the same as a grown-up person. And last night when she kep' a sinking and sinking, and turned away her head and didn't know him no mo', it was fitten to make a body's heart break to see him climb onto the bed and lay his cheek agin hern and call her so pitiful and she not answer. But bymeby she roused up like, and looked around wild, and then she see him, and she made a great cry and snatched him to her breast and hilt him close and kissed him over and over agin; but it took the last po' strength she had, and so her eyelids begin to close down, and her arms sort o' drooped away and then we see she was gone, po' creetur. And Clay, he — oh, the po' motherless thing — I cain't talk about it—I cain't bear to talk about it."

Clay had disappeared from the door; but he came in, now, and the neighbors reverently fell apart and made way for him. He leaned upon the open coffin and let his tears course silently. Then he put out his small hand and smoothed the hair and stroked the dead face lovingly. After a bit he brought his other hand up from behind him and laid three or four fresh wild flowers upon the breast, bent over and kissed the unresponsive lips time and time again, and then turned away and went out of the house without looking at any of the company. The old lady said to Hawkins:

" She always loved that kind o' flowers. He fetched 'em for her every morning, and she always kissed him. They was from away north somers

she kep' school when she fust come. Goodness knows what's to become o' that po' boy. No father, no mother, no kinfolks of no kind. Nobody to go to, nobody that k'yers for him — and all of us is so put to it for to get along and families so large."

Hawkins understood. All eyes were turned inquiringly upon him. He said:

"Friends, I am not very well provided for myself, but still I would not turn my back on a homeless orphan. If he will go with me I will give him a home, and loving regard — I will do for him as I would have another do for a child of my own in misfortune."

One after another the people stepped forward and wrung the stranger's hand with cordial good will, and their eyes looked all that their hands could not express or their lips speak.

" Said like a true man," said one.

"You was a stranger to me a minute ago, but you ain't now," said another.

"It's bread cast upon the waters — it'll return after many days," said the old lady whom we have heard speak before.

"You got to camp in my house as long as you hang out here," said one. " If tha hain't room for you and yourn my tribe'll turn out and camp in the hayloft."

A few minutes afterward, while the preparations for the funeral were being concluded, Mr. Hawkins

arrived at his wagon leading his little waif by the hand, and told his wife all that had happened, and asked her if he had done right in giving to her and to himself this new care. She said :

" If you've done wrong, Si Hawkins, it's a wrong that will shine brighter at the judgment day than the rights that many a man has done before you. And there isn't any compliment you can pay me equal to doing a thing like this and finishing it up, just taking it for granted that I'll be willing to it. Willing? Come to me, you poor motherless boy, and let me take your grief and help you carry it."

When the child awoke in the morning, it was as if from a troubled dream. But slowly the confusion in his mind took form, and he remembered his great loss; the beloved form in the coffin; his talk with a generous stranger who offered him a home; the funeral, where the stranger's wife held him by the hand at the grave, and cried with him and comforted him; and he remembered how this new mother tucked him in his bed in the neighboring farmhouse, and coaxed him to talk about his troubles, and then heard him say his prayers and kissed him good night, and left him with the soreness in his heart almost healed and his bruised spirit at rest.

And now the new mother came again, and helped him to dress, and combed his hair, and drew his mind away by degrees from the dismal yesterday, by telling him about the wonderful journey he was

going to take and the strange things he was going to see. And after breakfast they two went alone to the grave, and his heart went out to his new friend and his untaught eloquence poured the praises of his buried idol into her ears without let or hindrance. Together they planted roses by the headboard and strewed wild flowers upon the grave; and then together they went away, hand in hand, and left the dead to the long sleep that heals all heartaches and ends all sorrows.

CHAPTER III.

UNCLE DANIEL'S FIRST SIGHT OF A STEAMBOAT

Babillebabou! (disoit-il) void pis qu'antan. Fuyons! C'est, pai la mort boeuf! Leviathan, descript par le noble prophete Moses en la vie du sainct home Job. Il nous avallera tous, comme pilules. . . . Voy le cy. O que tu es horrible et abhominable! . . . Ho ho! Diable, Satanas, Leviathan! Je ne te peux veoir, tant tu es ideux et detestable.

Rabelais. Pantagruel, b. iv., c. 33.

WHATEVER the lagging dragging journey may have been to the rest of the emigrants, it was a wonder and delight to the children, a world of enchantment; and they believed it to be peopled with the mysterious dwarfs and giants and goblins that figured in the tales the negro slaves were in the habit of telling them nightly by the shuddering light of the kitchen fire.

At the end of nearly a week of travel, the party went into camp near a shabby village which was caving, house by house, into the hungry Mississippi. The river astonished the children beyond measure. Its mile-breadth of water seemed an ocean to them, In the shadowy twilight, and the vague riband of trees on the further shore, the verge of a continent which surely none but they had ever seen before. (33)

"Uncle Dan'l" (colored), aged 40; his wife, "Aunt Jinny," aged 30, " Young Miss" Emily Hawkins, " Young Mars " Washington Hawkins, and " Young Mars" Clay, the new member of the family, ranged themselves on a log, after supper, and contemplated the marvelous river and discussed it. The moon rose and sailed aloft through a maze of shredded cloud-wreaths; the somber river just perceptibly brightened under the veiled light; a deep silence pervaded the air and was emphasized, at intervals, rather than broken, by the hooting of an owl, the baying of a dog, or the muffled crash of a caving bank in the distance.

The little company assembled on the log were all children (at least in simplicity and broad and comprehensive ignorance), and the remarks they made about the river were in keeping with the character; and so awed were they by the grandeur and the solemnity of the scene before them, and by their belief that the air was filled with invisible spirits and that the faint zephyrs were caused by their passing wings, that all their talk took to itself a tinge of the supernatural, and their voices were subdued to a low and reverent tone. Suddenly, Uncle Dan'l exclaimed:

" Chil'en, dah's sumfin a comin' !"

All crowded close together and every heart beat faster. Uncle Dan'l pointed down the river with his bony finger.

A deep coughing sound troubled the stillness,

way toward a wooded cape that jutted into the stream a mile distant. All in an instant a fierce eye of fire shot out from behind the cape and sent a long brilliant pathway quivering athwart the dusky water. The coughing grew louder and louder, the glaring eye grew larger and still larger, glared wilder and still wilder. A huge shape developed itself out of the gloom, and from its tall duplicate horns dense volumes of smoke, starred and spangled with sparks, poured out and went tumbling away into the farther darkness. Nearer and nearer the thing came, till its long sides began to glow with spots of light which mirrored themselves in the river and attended the monster like a torchlight procession.

" What is it! Oh, what is it, Uncle Dan'l I" With deep solemnity the answer came: " It's de Almighty! Git down on you' knees!" It was not necessary to say it twice. They were all kneeling in a moment. And then while the mysterious coughing rose stronger and stronger, and the threatening glare reached farther and wider, the negro's voice lifted up its supplications:

" O. Lord, we's ben mighty wicked, an' we knows dat we 'zerve to go to de bad place, but good Lord, deah Lord, we ain't ready yit, we ain't ready — let dese po' chil'en hab one mo' chance, jes' one mo' chance. Take de ole niggah if you's got to hab somebody. Good Lord, good deah Lord, we don't know whah you's a gwyne to, we don't know who you's got yo' eye on, but we knows by de way

you's a comin', we knows by de way you's a tiltin' along in yo' charyot o' fiah dat some po' sinner's a gwyne to ketch it. But, good Lord, dese chil'en don't b'long heah, dey's f'm Obedstown whah dey don't know nuffin, an' you knows, yo' own sef, dat dey ain't 'sponsible. An' deah Lord, good Lord, it ain't like yo' mercy, it ain't like yo' pity, it ain't like yo' long-sufferin' lovin'-kindness for to take dis kind o' 'vantage o' sich little chil'en as dese is when dey's so many ornery grown folks chuck full o' cussedness dat wants roastin' down dah. Oh, Lord, spah de little chil'en, don't tar de little chil'en away f'm dey frens, jes' let 'em off jes' dis once, and take it out'n de ole niggah. HEAH I IS, LORD, HEAH I is! De ole niggah's ready, Lord, de ole "

The flaming and churning steamer was right abreast the party, and not twenty steps away. The awful thunder of a mud-valve suddenly burst forth, drowning the prayer, and as suddenly Uncle Dan'l snatched a child under each arm and scoured into the woods with the rest of the pack at his heels. And then, ashamed of himself, he halted in the deep darkness and shouted (but rather feebly) :

" Heah I is, Lord, heah I is!"

There was a moment of throbbing suspense, and then, to the surprise and the comfort of the party, it was plain that the august presence had gone by, for its dreadful noises were receding. Uncle Dan'l headed a cautious reconnoissance in the direction of

the log. Sure enough " the Lord " was just turning a point a short distance up the river, and while they looked the lights winked out and the coughing diminished by degrees and presently ceased altogether.

"H'wsh! Well now dey's some folks say dey ain't no 'ficiency in prah. Dis chile would like to know whah we'd a ben now if it warn't fo' dat prah? Dat's it. Dat's it!"

" Uncle Dan'l, do you reckon it was the prayer that saved us?" said Clay.

"Does I reckon? Don't I know it! Whah was yo' eyes? Warn't de Lord jes' a comin' chow! cfiow! CHOw! an' a goin' on turrible — an' do de Lord carry on dat way 'dout dey's sumfin don't suit him? An' warn't he a lookin' right at dis gang heah, an' warn't he jes' a reachin' for 'em? An' d'you spec' he gwyne to let 'em off 'dout somebody ast him to do it? No indeedy!"

" Do you reckon he saw us, Uncle Dan'l?"

" De law sakes, chile, didn't I see him a lookin' at us?"

"Did you feel scared, Uncle Dan'l? "

"No sah! When a man is 'gaged in prah, he ain't fraid o' nuffin — dey can't nuffin tetch him."

" Well, what did you run for?"

"Well, I — I — Mars Clay, when a man is under de influence ob de sperit, he do-no what he's 'bout — no sah; dat man do-no what he's 'bout. You mout take an' tah de head off'n dat man an' he

wouldn't scasely fine it out. Dah's de Hebrew chil'en dat went frough de fiah; dey was burnt con-sidable — ob coase dey was; but dey didn't know nuffin 'bout it—heal right up agin; if dey'd ben gals dey'd missed dey long haah (hair), maybe, but dey wouldn't felt de burn."

" don't know but what they were girls. I think they were."

" Now, Mars Clay, you knows bettern dat. Sometimes a body can't tell whedder you's a sayin' what you means or whedder you's a sayin' what you don't mean, 'case you says 'em bofe de same way."

But how should know whether they were boys or girls?"

" Goodness sakes, Mars Clay, don't de Good Book say? 'Sides, don't it call 'em de brew chil'en? If dey was gals wouldn't dey be de she-brew chil'en? Some people dat kin read don't 'pear to take no notice when dey do read."

"Well, Uncle Dan'l, I think that My!

here comes another one up the river! There can't be two!"

"We gone dis time — we done gone dis time, sho'! Dey ain't two, Mars Clay — dat's de same one. De Lord kin 'pear eberywhah in a second. Goodness, how de fiah and de smoke do belch up ! Dat mean business, honey. He comin' now like he fo'got sumfin. Come 'long, chil'en, time you's gwyne to roos'. Go 'long wid you — ole Uncle

Daniel gwyne out in de woods to rastle in prah — de ole nigger gwyne to do what he kin to sabe you agin."

He did go to the woods and pray; but he went so far that he doubted, himself, if the Lord heard him when He went by.

CHAPTER TV.

SQUIRE HAWKINS ON A MISSISSIPPI STEAMBOAT

— Seventhly, Before his Voyage, He should make his peace with God, satisfie his Creditors if he be in debt; Pray earnestly to God to prosper him in his Voyage, and to keep him from danger, and, if he be sui juris, he should make his last will, and wisely order all his affairs, since many that go far abroad, return not home. (This good and. Christian Counsel is given by Martinus Zeilerus in his Apodemical Canons before his Itinerary of Spain and Portugal.)

Leigh's Diatribe of Travel, p. 7.

EARLY in the morning Squire Hawkins took passage in a small steamboat, with his family and his two slaves, and presently the bell rang, the stage-plank was hauled in, and the vessel proceeded up the river. The children and the slaves were not much more at ease after finding out that this monster was a creature of human contrivance than they were the night before when they thought it the Lord of heaven and earth. They started, in fright, every time the gauge-cocks sent out an angry hiss, and they quaked from head to foot when the mud-valves thundered. The shivering of the boat under the beating of the wheels was sheer misery to them. But of course familiarity with these things soon

(40)

took away their terrors, and then the voyage at once became a glorious adventure, a royal progress through the very heart and home of romance, a realization of their rosiest wonder-dreams. They sat by the hour in the shade of the pilot-house on the hurricane deck and looked out over the curving expanses of the river sparkling in the sunlight. Sometimes the boat fought the midstream current, with a verdant world on either hand, and remote from both; sometimes she closed in under a point, where the dead water and the helping eddies were, and shaved the bank so closely that the decks were swept by the jungle of overhanging willows and littered with a spoil of leaves; departing from these " points " she regularly crossed the river every five miles, avoiding the " bight" of the great bends and thus escaping the strong current; sometimes she went out and skirted a high " bluff" sandbar in the middle of the stream, and occasionally followed it up a little too far and touched upon the shoal water at its head — and then the intelligent craft refused to run herself aground, but "smelt" the bar, and straightway the foamy streak that streamed away from her bows vanished, a great foamless wave rolled forward and passed her under way, and in this instant she leaned far over on her side, shied from the bar and fled square away from the danger like a frightened thing — and the pilot was lucky if he managed to " straighten her up" before she drove her nose into the opposite bank; sometimes she

approached a solid wall of tall trees as if she meant to break through it, but all of a sudden a little crack would open just enough to admit her, and away she would go plowing through the "chute" with just barely room enough between the island on one side and the mainland on the other; in this sluggish water she seemed to go like a race-horse; now and then small log cabins appeared in little clearings, with the never-failing frowsy women and girls in soiled and faded linsey-woolsey leaning in the doors or against wood-piles and rail fences, gazing sleepily at the passing show; sometimes she found shoal water, going out at the head of those " chutes " or crossing the river, and then a deck-hand stood on the bow and hove the lead, while the boat slowed down and moved cautiously; sometimes she stopped a moment at a landing and took on some freight or a passenger while a crowd of slouchy white men and negroes stood on the bank and looked sleepily on with their hands in their pantaloons pockets,— of course,—for they never took them out except to stretch, and when they did this they squirmed about and reached their fists up into the air and lifted themselves on tiptoe in an ecstasy of enjoyment.

When the sun went down it turned all the broad river to a national banner laid in gleaming bars of gold and purple and crimson; and in time these glories faded out in the twilight and left the fairy archipelagoes reflecting their fringing foliage in the steely mirror of the stream.

At night the boat forged on through the deep solitudes of the river, hardly ever discovering a light to testify to a human presence — mile after mile and league after league the vast bends were guarded by unbroken walls of forest, that had never been disturbed by the voice or the footfall of a man or felt the edge of his sacrilegious axe.

An hour after supper the moon came up, and Clay and Washington ascended to the hurricane deck to revel again in their new realm of enchantment. They ran races up and down the deck; climbed about the bell; made friends with the passenger-dogs chained under the lifeboat; tried to make friends with a passenger-bear fastened to the verge-staff, but were not encouraged; " skinned the cat" on the hog-chains; in a word, exhausted the amusement-possibilities of the deck. Then they looked wistfully up at the pilot-house, and finally, little by little, Clay ventured up there, followed diffidently by Washington. The pilot turned presently to "get his stern-marks," saw the lads and invited them in. Now their happiness was complete. This cosy little house, built entirely of glass and commanding a marvelous prospect in every direction, was a magician's throne to them, and their enjoyment of the place was simply boundless.

They sat them down on a high bench and looked miles ahead and saw the wooded capes fold back and reveal the bends beyond; and they looked miles to the rear and saw the silvery highway diminish its

breadth by degrees and close itself together in the distance. Presently the pilot said :

" By George, yonder comes the Amaranth!"

A spark appeared, close to the water, several miles down the river. The pilot took his glass and looked at it steadily for a moment, and said, chiefly to himself:

" It can't be the Blue Wing. She couldn't pick us up this way. It's the Amaranth, sure."

He bent over a speaking-tube and said:

" Who's on watch down there?"

A hollow, unhuman voice rumbled up through the tube in answer:

"am. Second engineer."

"Good! You want to stir your stumps, now, Harry — the Amaranth's just turned the point — and she's just a-humping herself, too !"

The pilot took hold of a rope that stretched out forward, jerked it twice, and two mellow strokes of the big bell responded. A voice out on the deck shouted:

" Stand by, down there, with that labboard lead !"

"No, I don't want the lead," said the pilot, " I wantj<?«. Roust out the old man — tell him the Amaranth's coming. And go call Jim — tell him.*'

" Aye-aye, sir!"

The "old man" was the captain — he is always called so, on steamboats and ships; "Jim" was the other pilot. Within two minutes both of these

men were flying up the pilot-house stairway, three steps at a jump. Jim was in his shirt-sleeves, with his coat and vest on his arm. He said:

" I was just turning in. Where's the glass?"

He took it and looked:

" Don't appear to be any night-hawk on the jack-staff— it's the Amaranth, dead sure!"

The captain took a good long look, and only said:

Damnation !"

George Davis, the pilot on watch, shouted to the night-watchman on deck:

" How's she loaded?"

" Two inches by the head, sir." Tain't enough!"

The captain shouted, now:

 Call the mate. Tell him to call all hands and; get a lot of that sugar forrard — put her ten inches by the head. Lively, now!"

Aye-aye, sir!"

A riot of shouting and trampling floated up from below, presently, and the uneasy steering of the boat soon showed that she was getting down by the head."

The three men in the pilot-house began to talk in short, sharp sentences, low and earnestly. As their excitement rose, their voices went down. As fast as one of them put down the spyglass another took it up — but always with a studied air of calmness. Each time the verdict was:

She's a gaining!"

The captain spoke through the tube:

" What steam are you carrying?"

"A hundred and forty-two, sir! But she's getting hotter and hotter all the time."

The boat was straining and groaning and quivering like a monster in pain. Both pilots were at work now, one on each side of the wheel, with their coats and vests off, their bosoms and collars wide open, and the perspiration flowing down their faces. They were holding the boat so close to the shore that the willows swept the guards almost from stem to stern.

" Stand by!" whispered George.

" All ready!" said Jim, under his breath.

" Let her come!"

The boat sprang away from the bank like a deer, and darted in a long diagonal toward the other shore. She closed in again and thrashed her fierce way along the willows as before. The captain put down the glass:

"Lord, how she walks up on us! I do hate to be beat!"

"Jim," said George, looking straight ahead, watching the slightest yawing of the boat and promptly meeting it with the wheel, " how it do to try Murderer's Chute?"

"Well, it's — it's taking chances. How was the cotton-wood stump on the false point below Board-man's Island this morning?"

" Water just touching the roots."

"Well, it's pretty close work. That gives six

feet scant in the head of Murderer's Chute. We can just barely rub through if we hit it exactly right. But it's worth trying. She don't dare tackle it!"— meaning the Amaranth.

In another instant the Boreas plunged into what seemed a crooked creek, and the Amaranth's approaching lights were shut out in a moment. Not a whisper was uttered, now, but the three men stared ahead into the shadows and two of them spun the wheel back and forth with anxious watchfulness while the steamer tore along. The chute seemed to come to an end every fifty yards, but always opened out in time. Now the head of it was at hand. George tapped the big bell three times, two leadsmen sprang to their posts, and in a moment their weird cries rose on the night air and were caught up and repeated by two men on the upper deck:

" No-o bottom!"

" De-e-p four!"

"Half three!"

 Quarter three!"

" Mark under wa-a-ter three !"

"Half twain!"

"Quarter twain! "

Davis pulled a couple of ropes — there was a jingling of small bells far below, the boat's speed slackened, and the pent steam began to whistle and the gauge-cocks to scream:

 By the mark twain !"

" Quar-ter-Ar-er-M twain!"

Eight and a half!"

" Eight feet!"

" Seven-ana-half! "

Another jingling of little bells and the wheels ceased turning altogether. The whistling of the steam was something frightful, now—it almost drowned all other noises.

" Stand by to meet her!"

George had the wheel hard down and was standing on a spoke.

"All ready!"

The boat hesitated — seemed to hold her breath, as did the captain and pilots — and then she began to fall away to starboard and every eye lighted:

" Now then!—meet her! meet her! Snatch her!"

The wheel flew to port so fast that the spokes blended into a spider-web — the swing of the boat subsided — she steadied herself

" Seven feet!"

" Sev — six and a half!"

"Sir feet! Six "

Bang! She hit the bottom! George shouted through the tube:

Spread her wide open! Whale it at her!"

Pow — wow—chow! The escape-pipes belched snowy pillars of steam aloft, the boat ground and surged and trembled — and slid over into

'' M-a-r-k twain !"

" Quarter "

"Tap! tap! tap!" (to signify "Lay in the leads.")

And away she went, flying up the willow shore, with the whole silver sea of the Mississippi stretching abroad on every hand.

No Amaranth in sight!

" Ha-ha, boys, we took a couple of tricks that time!" said the captain.

And just at that moment a red glare appeared in the head of the chute and the Amaranth came springing after them!

"Well, I swear!"

" Jim, what is the meaning of that?"

"I'll tell you what's the meaning of it. That hail we had at Napoleon was Wash Hastings, wanting to come to Cairo — and we didn't stop. He's in that pilot-house, now, showing those mud turtles how to hunt for easy water."

"That's it! I thought it wasn't any slouch that was running that middle bar in Hog-eye Bend. If it's Wash Hastings — well, what he don't know about the river ain't worth knowing — a regular gold-leaf, kid-glove, diamond-breastpin pilot Wash Hastings is. We won't take any tricks off of him, old man!"

" I wish I'd a stopped for him, that's all."

The Amaranth was within three hundred yards of the Boreas, and still gaining. The "old man" spoke through the tube:

" What is she carrying now?"

"A hundred and sixty-five, sirl"

" How's your wood?"

"Pine all out — cypress half gone — eating up cotton-wood like pie!"

" Break into that rosin on the main deck — pile it in, the boat can pay for it!"

Soon the boat was plunging and quivering and screaming more madly than ever. But the Amaranth's head was almost abreast the Boreas's stern:

" How's your steam, now, Harry?"

" Hundred and eighty-two, sir!"

" Break up the casks of bacon in the forrard hold ! Pile it in ! Levy on that turpentine in the fantail — drench every stick of wood with it!"

The boat was a moving earthquake by this time:

"How is she now?"

'* A hundred and ninety-six and still a-swelling!— water below the middle gauge-cocks!— carrying every pound she can stand ! nigger roosting on the safety-valve !"

Good ! How's your draft?"

"Bully! Every time a nigger heaves a stick of wood into the furnace he goes out the chimney with it!"

The Amaranth drew steadily up till her jack-staff breasted the Boreas's wheelhouse — climbed along inch by inch till her chimneys breasted it — crept along further and further till the boats were wheel to wheel — and then they closed up with a heavy jolt and locked together tight and fast in the middle

of the big river under the flooding moonlight! A roar and a hurrah went up from the crowded decks of both steamers — all hands rushed to the guards to look and shout and gesticulate — the weight careened the vessels over toward each other — officers flew hither and thither cursing and storming, trying to drive the people amidships — both captains were leaning over their railings shaking their fists, swearing and threatening — black volumes of smoke rolled up and canopied the scene, delivering a rain of sparks upon the vessels — two pistol shots rang out, and both captains dodged unhurt and the packed masses of passengers surged back and fell apart while the shrieks of women and children soared above the intolerable din

And then there was a booming roar, a thundering crash, and the riddled Amaranth dropped loose from her hold and drifted helplessly away!

Instantly the fire-doors of the Boreas were thrown open and the men began dashing buckets of water into the furnaces — for it would have been death and destruction to stop the engines with such a head of steam on.

As soon as possible the Boreas dropped down to the floating wreck and took off the dead, the wounded, and the unhurt—at least all that could be got at, for the whole forward half of the boat was a shapeless ruin, with the great chimneys lying crossed on top of it, and underneath were a dozen victims imprisoned alive and wailing for help. While men

with axes worked with might and main to free these poor fellows, the Boreas's boats went about, picking up stragglers from the river.

And now a new horror presented itself. The wreck took fire from the dismantled furnaces! Never did men work with a heartier will than did those stalwart braves with the axes. But it was of no use. The fire ate its way steadily, despising the bucket brigade that fought it. It scorched the clothes, it singed the hair of the axemen — it drove them back, foot by foot — inch by inch — they wavered, struck a final blow in the teeth of the enemy, and surrendered. And as they fell back they heard prisoned voices saying:

"Don't leave us! Don't desert us! Don't, don't do it!"

And one poor fellow said:

" I am Henry Worley, striker of the Amaranth! My mother lives in St. Louis. Tell her a lie for a poor devil's sake, please. Say I was killed in an instant and never knew what hurt me — though God knows I've neither scratch nor bruise this moment! It's hard to burn up in a coop like this with the whole wide world so near. Good-bye, boys — we've all got to come to it at last, anyway!"

The Boreas stood away out of danger, and the ruined steamer went drifting down the stream, an island of wreathing and climbing flame that vomited clouds of smoke from time to time, and glared more fiercely and sent its luminous tongues higher and

higher after each emission. A shriek at intervals told of a captive that had met his doom. The wreck lodged upon a sandbar, and when the Boreas turned the next point on her upward journey it was still burning with scarcely abated fury.

When the boys came down into the main saloon of the Boreas, they saw a pitiful sight and heard a world of pitiful sounds. Eleven poor creatures lay dead and forty more lay moaning, or pleading or screaming, while a score of Good Samaritans moved among them doing what they could to relieve their sufferings; bathing their skinless faces and bodies with linseed oil and lime water, and covering the places with bulging masses of raw cotton that gave to every face and form a dreadful and unhuman aspect.

A little wee French midshipman of fourteen lay fearfully injured, but never uttered a sound till a physician of Memphis was about to dress his hurts. Then he said:

" Can I get well ? You need not be afraid to tell me."

"No — I — I am afraid you cannot."

"Then do not waste your time with me—help those that can get well."

"But "

" Help those that can get well! It is not for me to be a girl. I carry the blood of eleven generations of soldiers in my veins !"

The physician — himself a man who had seen

service in the navy in his time — touched his hat to this little hero, and passed on.

The head engineer of the Amaranth, a grand specimen of physical manhood, struggled to his feet, a ghastly spectacle, and strode toward his brother, the second engineer, who was unhurt. He said:

"You were on watch. You were boss. You would not listen to me when I begged you to reduce your steam. Take that!—take it to my wife and tell her it comes from me by the hand of my murderer ! Take it — and take my curse with it to blister your heart a hundred years — and may you live so long!"

And he tore a ring from his finger, stripping flesh and skin with it, threw it down, and fell dead!

But these things must not be dwelt upon. The Boreas landed her dreadful cargo at the next large town and delivered it over to a multitude of eager hands and warm Southern hearts — a cargo amounting by this time to 39 wounded persons and 22 dead bodies. And with these she delivered a list of 96 missing persons that had drowned or otherwise perished at the scene of the disaster.

A jury of inquest was impaneled, and after due deliberation and inquiry they returned the inevitable American verdict which has been so familiar to our cars all the days of our lives—"NOBODY TO

BLAME."

The incidents of the explosion are not invented. They happened just as they are told. — THE AUTHORS.

CHAPTER V.

LAURA VAN BRUNT ADOPTED BY THE HAWKINSES

veut faire secher de la neige au four et la vendre pour du sel blanc.

WHEN the Boreas backed away from the land to continue her voyage up the river, the Hawkinses were richer by twenty-four hours of experience in the contemplation of human suffering and in learning through honest hard work how to relieve it. And they were richer in another way also. In the early turmoil an hour after the explosion, a little black-eyed girl of five years, frightened and crying bitterly, was struggling through the throng in the Boreas' s saloon calling her mother and father, but no one answered. Something in the face of Mr. Hawkins attracted her, and she came and looked up at him; was satisfied, and took refuge with him. He petted her, listened to her troubles, and said he would find her friends for her. Then he put her in a stateroom with his children, and told them to be kind to her (the adults of his party were all busy with the wounded) and straightway began his search.

(55)

It was fruitless. But all day he and his wife made inquiries, and hoped against hope. All that they could learn was that the child and her parents came on board at New Orleans, where they had just arrived in a vessel from Cuba; that they looked like people from the Atlantic States; that the family name was Van Brunt and the child's name Laura. This was all. The parents had not been seen since the explosion. The child's manners were those of a little lady, and her clothes were daintier and finer than any Mrs. Hawkins had ever seen before.

As the hours dragged on the child lost heart, and cried so piteously for her mother that it seemed to the Hawkinses that the meanings and the wailings of the mutilated men and women in the saloon did not so strain at their heart-strings as the sufferings of this little desolate creature. They tried hard to comfort her; and in trying, learned to love her; they could not help it, seeing how she clung to them and put her arms about their necks and found no solace but in their kind eyes and comforting words. There was a question in both their hearts — a question that rose up and asserted itself with more and more pertinacity as the hours wore on; but both hesitated to give it voice — both kept silence and waited. But a time came at last when the matter would bear delay no longer. The boat had landed, and the dead and the wounded were being conveyed to the shore. The tired child was asleep in the arms of Mrs. Hawkins. Mr. Hawkins came

into their presence and stood without speaking. His eyes met his wife's; then both looked at the child, and as they looked it stirred in its sleep and nestled closer; an expression of contentment and peace settled upon its face that touched the mother-heart; and when the eyes of husband and wife met again, the question was asked and answered.

When the Boreas had journeyed some four hundred miles from the time the Hawkinses joined her, a long rank of steamboats was sighted, packed side by side at a wharf like sardines in a box, and above and beyond them rose the domes and steeples and general architectural confusion of a city — a city with an imposing umbrella of black smoke spread over it. This was St. Louis. The children of the Hawkins family were playing about the hurricane deck, and the father and mother were sitting in the lee of the pilot-house essaying to keep order and not greatly grieved that they were not succeeding.

" They're worth all the trouble they are, Nancy."

"Yes, and more, Si."

" I believe you ! You wouldn't sell one of them at a good round figure?"

" Not for all the money in the bank, Si."

" My own sentiments every time. It is true we are not rich — but still you are not sorry — you haven't any misgivings about the additions?"

" No. God will provide."

"Amen. And so you wouldn't even part with Clay? Or Laura!"

"Not for anything in the world. I love them just the same as I love my own. They pet me and spoil me even more than the others do, I think. I reckon we'll get along, Si."

" Oh yes, it will all come out right, old mother. I wouldn't be afraid to adopt a thousand children if I wanted to, for there's that Tennessee Land, you know — enough to make an army of them rich. A whole army, Nancy! You and I will never see the day, but these little chaps will. Indeed they will. One of these days it will be ' the rich Miss Emily Hawkins — and the wealthy Miss Laura Van Brunt Hawkins — and the Hon. George Washington Hawkins, millionaire — and Gov. Henry Clay Hawkins, millionaire!' That is the way the world will word it! Don't let's ever fret about the children, Nancy — never in the world. They're all right. Nancy, there's oceans and oceans of money in that land — mark my words !"

The children had stopped playing, for the moment, and drawn near to listen. Hawkins said:

"Washington, my boy, what will you do when you get to be one of the richest men in the world?"

" I don't know, father. Sometimes I think I'll have a balloon and go up in the air; and sometimes I think I'll have ever so many books; and sometimes I think I'll have ever so many weather-cocks and water-wheels; or have a machine like that one you and Colonel Sellers bought; and sometimes I think I'll have — well, somehow I don't know —

somehow I ain't certain; maybe I'll get a steamboat first."

"The same old chap!—always just a little bit divided about things. And what will you do when you get to be one of the richest men in the world, Clay?"

" I don't know, sir. My mother—my other mother that's gone away — she always told me to work along and not be much expecting to get rich, and then I wouldn't be disappointed if I didn't get rich. And so I reckon it's better for me to wait till I get rich, and then by that time maybe I'll know what I'll want — but I don't now, sir."

" Careful old head ! Governor Henry Clay Hawkins ! that's what you'll be, Clay, one of these days. Wise old head ! weighty old head! Go on, now, and play — all of you. It's a prime lot, Nancy, as the Obedstown folk say about their hogs."

A smaller steamboat received the Hawkinses and their fortunes, and bore them a hundred and thirty miles still higher up the Mississippi, and landed them at a little tumble-down village on the Missouri shore in the twilight of a mellow October day.

The next morning they harnessed up their team, and for two days they wended slowly into the interior through almost roadless and uninhabited forest solitudes. And when for the last time they pitched their tents, metaphorically speaking, it was at the goal of their hopes, their new home.

By the muddy roadside stood a new log cabin,

one-story high — the store; clustered in the neighborhood were ten or twelve more cabins, some new, some old.

In the sad light of the departing day the place looked homeless enough. Two or three coatless young men sat in front of the store on a drygoods box, and whittled it with their knives, kicked it with their vast boots, and shot tobacco-juice at various marks. Several ragged negroes leaned comfortably against the posts of the awning and contemplated the arrival of the wayfarers with lazy curiosity. All these people presently managed to drag themselves to the vicinity of the Hawkins' wagon, and there they took up permanent positions, hands in pockets and resting on one leg; and thus anchored they proceeded to look and enjoy. Vagrant dogs came wagging around and making inquiries of Hawkins's dog, which were not satisfactory and they made war on him in concert. This would have interested the citizens, but it was too many on one to amount to anything as a fight, and so they commanded the peace, and the foreign dog furled his tail and took sanctuary under the wagon. Slatternly negro girls and women slouched along with pails deftly balanced on their heads, and joined the group and stared. Little half-dressed white boys, and little negro boys, with nothing whatever on but tow-linen shirts with a fine southern exposure, came from various directions and stood with their hands locked together behind them and aided in the inspection. The rest

of the population were laying down their employments and getting ready to come, when a man burst through the assemblage and seized the new-comers by the hands in a frenzy of welcome, and exclaimed — indeed, almost shouted:

"Well who could have believed it! Now is it you sure enough — turn around! hold up your heads ! I want to look at you good ! Well, well, well, it does seem most too good to be true, I declare! Lord, I'm so glad to see you! Does a body's whole soul good to look at you! Shake hands again! Keep on shaking hands! Goodness gracious alive. What will my wife say? Oh yes indeed, it's so ! married only last week — lovely, perfectly lovely creature, the noblest woman that ever — you'll like her, Nancy! Like her? Lord bless me you'll love her — you'll dote on her — you'll be twins! Well, well, well, let me look at you again ! Same old — why bless my life it was only just this very morning that my wife says, ' Colonel'—she will call me Colonel spite of everything I can do — she says ' Colonel, something tells me somebody's coming!' and sure enough here you are, the last people on earth a body could have expected. Why, she'll think she's a prophetess — and hanged if I don't think so too — and you know there ain't any country but what a prophet's an honor to, as the proverb says. Lord bless me — and here's the children, too! Washington, Emily, don't you know me? Come, give us a kiss. Won't

I fix you, though!—ponies, cows, dogs, everything you can think of that'll delight a child's heart —

an d Why how's this? Little strangers ?

Well you won't be any strangers here, I can tell you. Bless your souls we'll make you think you never was at home before—'deed and "deed we will, can tell you! Come, now, bundle right along with me. You can't glorify any hearthstone but mine in this camp, you know — can't eat anybody's bread but mine — can't do anything but just make yourselves perfectly at home and comfortable, and spread yourselves out and rest! You hear me! Here — Jim, Tom, Pete, Jake, fly around! Take that team to my place — put the wagon in my lot — put the horses under the shed, and get out hay and oats and fill them up! Ain't any hay and oats? Well get some — have it charged to me — come, spin around, now! Now, Hawkins, the procession 's ready; mark time, by the left flank, forward — march!"

And the Colonel took the lead, with Laura astride his neck, and the newly-inspired and very grateful immigrants picked up their tired limbs with quite a spring in them and dropped into his wake.

Presently they were ranged about an old-time fireplace, whose blazing logs sent out rather an unnecessary amount of heat; but that was no matter — supper was needed, and to have it, it had to be cooked. This apartment was the family bedroom, parlor, library, and kitchen, all in one. The

matronly little wife of the Colonel moved hither and thither and in and out with her pots and pans in her hands, happiness in her heart and a world of admiration of her husband in her eyes. And when at last she had spread the cloth and loaded it with hot corn bread, fried chickens, bacon, buttermilk, coffee, and all manner of country luxuries, Col. Sellers modified his harangue and for a moment throttled it down to the orthodox pitch for a blessing, and then instantly burst forth again as from a parenthesis, and clattered on with might and main till every stomach in the party was laden with all it could carry. And when the new-comers ascended the ladder to their comfortable feather beds on the

second floor — to wit, the garret Mrs. Hawkins

was obliged to say:

" Hang the fellow, I do believe he has gone wilder than ever, but still a body can't help liking him if they would — and what is more, they don't ever want to try when they see his eyes and hear him talk."

Within a week or two the Hawkinses were comfortably domiciled in a new log-house, and were beginning to feel at home. The children were put to school; at least, it was what passed for a school in those days: a place where tender young humanity devoted itself for eight or ten hours a day to learning incomprehensible rubbish by heart out of books and reciting it by rote, like parrots; so that a finished education consisted simply of a permanent

headache and the ability to read without stopping to spell the words or take breath. Hawkins bought out the village store for a song and proceeded to reap the profits, which amounted to but little more than another song.

The wonderful speculation hinted at by Col. Sellers in his letter turned out to be the raising of mules for the Southern market; and really it promised very well. The young stock cost but a trifle, the rearing but another trifle, and so Hawkins was easily persuaded to embark his slender means in the enter-prise, and turn over the keep and care of the animals to Sellers and Uncle Dan'l.

All went well. Business prospered little by little. Hawkins even built a new house, made it two full stories high and put a lightning rod on it. People came two or three miles to look at it. But they knew that the rod attracted the lightning, and so they gave the place a wide berth in a storm, for they were familiar with marksmanship and doubted if the lightning could hit that small stick at a distance of a mile and a half oftener than once in a hundred and fifty times. Hawkins fitted out his house with " store " furniture from St. Louis, and the fame of its magnificence went abroad in the land. Even the parlor carpet was from St. Louis — though the other rooms were clothed in the " rag " carpeting of the country. Hawkins put up the first " paling" fence that had ever adorned the village; and he did not stop there, but whitewashed it. His oilcloth window-

curtains had noble pictures on them of castles such as had never been seen anywhere in the world but on window-curtains. Hawkins enjoyed the admiration these prodigies compelled, but he always smiled to think how poor and cheap they were, compared to what the Hawkins mansion would display in a future day after the Tennessee Land should have borne its minted fruit. Even Washington observed, once, that when the Tennessee Land was sold he would have a " store " carpet in his and Clay's room like the one in the parlor. This pleased Hawkins, but it troubled his wife. It did not seem wise, to her, to put one's entire earthly trust in the Tennessee Land and never think of doing any work.

Hawkins took a weekly Philadelphia newspaper and a semi-weekly St. Louis journal — almost the only papers that came to the village, though Godey's Lady's Book found a good market there, and was regarded as the perfection of polite literature by some of the ablest critics in the place. Perhaps it is only fair to explain that we are writing of a bygone age — some twenty or thirty years ago. In the two newspapers referred to lay the secret of Hawkins's growing prosperity. They kept him informed of the condition of the crops South and East, and thus he knew which articles were likely to be in demand and which articles were likely to be unsalable, weeks and even months in advance of the simple folk about him. As the months went by he came to be regarded as a wonderfully lucky man. It did not 6*

occur to the citizens that brains were at the bottom of his luck.

His tide of " Squire" came into vogue again, but only for a season; for, as his wealth and popularity augmented, that title, by imperceptible stages, grew up into " Judge " ; indeed, it bade fair to swell into "General" by and by. All strangers of consequence who visited the village gravitated to the Hawkins Mansion and became guests of the "Judge."

Hawkins had learned to like the people of his section very much. They were uncouth and not cultivated, and not particularly industrious; but they were honest and straightforward, and their virtuous ways commanded respect. Their patriotism was strong, their pride in the flag was of the old-fashioned pattern, their love of country amounted to idolatry. Whoever dragged the national honor in the dirt won their deathless hatred. They still cursed Benedict Arnold as if he were a personal friend who had broken faith but a week gone by.

CHAPTER VI.

TEN YEARS LATER. LAURA A YOUNG BEAUTY

Mesu eu azheiashet

Washkebematizitaking, Nawuj beshegandaguze

Manwabegonig edush wen.

Ojibwa Nuguwioshang, p. 78.

WE skip ten years, and this history finds certain changes to record.

Judge Hawkins and Col. Sellers have made and lost two or three moderate fortunes in the meantime, and are now pinched by poverty. Sellers has two pairs of twins and four extras. In Hawkins's family are six children of his own and two adopted ones. From time to time, as fortune smiled, the elder children got the benefit of it, spending the lucky seasons at excellent schools in St. Louis and the unlucky ones at home in the chafing discomfort of straitened circumstances.

Neither the Hawkins children nor the world that knew them ever supposed that one of the girls was E» (67)

of alien blood and parentage. Such difference as existed between Laura and Emily is not uncommon in a family. The girls had grown up as sisters, and they were both too young at the time of the fearful accident on the Mississippi to know that it was that which had thrown their lives together.

And yet any one who had known the secret of Laura's birth and had seen her during these passing years, say at the happy age of twelve or thirteen, would have fancied that he knew the reason why she was more winsome than her school companion.

Philosophers dispute whether it is the promise of what she will be, in the careless schoolgirl, that makes her attractive, the undeveloped maidenhood, or the mere natural, careless sweetness of childhood. If Laura at twelve was beginning to be a beauty, the thought of it had never entered her head. No, indeed. Her mind was filled with more important thoughts. To her simple schoolgirl dress she was beginning to add those mysterious little adornments of ribbon-knots and earrings, which were the subject of earnest consultations with her grown friends.

When she tripped down the street on a summer's day with her dainty hands propped into the ribbon-broidered pockets of her apron, and elbows consequently more or less akimbo, with her wide Leghorn hat flapping down and hiding her face one moment and blowing straight up against her forehead the next and making its revealment of fresh young beauty; with all her pretty girlish airs and graces in

full play, and tfiat sweet ignorance of care and that atmosphere of innocence and purity all about her that belong to her gracious time of life; indeed, she was a vision to warm the coldest heart and bless and cheer the saddest.

Willful, generous, forgiving, imperious, affectionate, improvident — bewitching, in short — was Laura at this period. Could she have remained there, this history would not need to be written. But Laura had grown to be almost a woman in these few years, to the end of which we have now come — years which had seen Judge Hawkins pass through so many trials.

When the Judge's first bankruptcy came upon him, a homely human angel intruded upon him with an offer of $1,500 for the Tennessee Land. Mrs. Hawkins said take it. It was a grievous temptation, but the Judge withstood it. He said the land was for the children — he could not rob them of their future millions for so paltry a sum. When the second blight fell upon him, another angel appeared and offered $3,000 for the land. He was in such deep distress that he allowed his wife to persuade him to let the papers be drawn; but when his children came into his presence in their poor apparel, he felt like a traitor and refused to sign.

But now he was down again, and deeper in the mire than ever. He paced the floor all day, he scarcely slept at night. He blushed even to acknowledge it to himself, but treason was in his mind

— he was meditating, at last, the sale of the land. Mrs. Hawkins stepped into the room. He had not spoken a word, but he felt as guilty as if she had caught him in some shameful act. She said:

"Si, I do not know what we are going to do. The children are not fit to be seen, their clothes are in such a state. But there's something more serious still. There is scarcely a bite in the house to eat."

" Why, Nancy, go to Johnson "

"Johnson indeed! You took that man's part when he hadn't a friend in the world, and you built him up and made him rich. And here's the result of it: He lives in our fine house, and we live in his miserable log cabin. He has hinted to our children that he would rather they wouldn't come about his yard to play with his children,— which I can bear, and bear easy enough, for they're not a sort we want to associate with much — but what I can't bear with any quietness at all, is his telling Franky our bill was running pretty high this morning when I sent him for some meal — and that was all he said, too — didn't give him the meal — turned off and went to talking with the Hargrave girls about some stuff they wanted to cheapen."

" Nancy, this is astounding!"

" And so it is, I warrant you. I've kept still, Si, as long as ever I could. Things have been getting worse and worse, and worse and worse, every single day; I don't go out of the house, I feel so down;

but you had trouble enough, and I wouldn't say a word — and I wouldn't say a word now, only things have got so bad that I don't know what to do, nor where to turn." And she gave way and put her face in her hands and cried.

"Poor child, don't grieve so. I never thought that of Johnson. I am clear at my wit's end. I don't know what in the world to do. Now, if somebody would come along and offer $3,000 — oh, if somebody only would come along and offer $3,000 for that Tennessee Land "

" You'd sell it, Si?" said Mrs. Hawkins excitedly.

" Try me !"

Mrs. Hawkins was out of the room in a moment. Within a minute she was back again with a business-looking stranger, whom she seated, and then she took her leave again. Hawkins said to himself, 1 ' How can a man ever lose faith ? When the blackest hour comes, Providence always comes with it — ah, this is the very timeliest help that ever poor harried devil had; if this blessed man offers but a thousand I'll embrace him like a brother!"

The stranger said:

" I am aware that you own 75,000 acres of land in East Tennessee, and, without sacrificing your time, 1 will come to the point at once. I am agent of an iron manufacturing company, and they empower me to offer you ten thousand dollars for that land."

Hawkins's heart bounded within him. His whole frame was racked and wrenched with fettered

hurrahs. His first impulse was to shout—" Done! and God bless the iron company, too !"

But a something flitted through his mind, and his opened lips uttered nothing. The enthusiasm faded away from his eyes, and the look of a man who is thinking took its place. Presently, in a hesitating, undecided way, he said:

"Well, I — it don't seem quite enough. That — that is a very valuable property — very valuable. It's brimful of iron ore, sir — brimful of it! And copper, coal,— everything — everything you can think of! Now, I'll tell you what I'll do. I'll reserve everything except the iron, and I'll sell them the iron property for $15,000 cash, I to go in with them and own an undivided interest of one-half the concern — or the stock, as you may say. I'm out of business, and I'd just as soon help run the thing as not. Now how does that strike you?"

"Well, I am only an agent of these people, who are friends of mine, and I am not even paid for my services. To tell you the truth, I have tried to persuade them not to go into the thing; and I have come square out with their offer, without throwing out any feelers — and I did it in the hope that you would refuse. A man pretty much always refuses another man's first offer, no matter what it is. But I have performed my duty, and will take pleasure in telling them what you say."

He was about to rise. Hawkins said:

"Wait a bit."

Hawkins thought again. And the substance of his thought was: "This is a deep man; this is a very deep man ; I don't like his candor; your ostentatiously candid business man's a deep fox — always a deep fox; this man's that iron company himself—• that's what he is; he wants that property, too; I am not so blind but I can see that; he don't want the company to go into this thing—O, that's very good; yes, that's very good indeed — stuff! he'll be back here to-morrow, sure, and take my offer; take it? I'll risk anything he is suffering to take it now; here — I must mind what I'm about. What has started this sudden excitement about iron? I wonder what is in the wind? just as sure as I'm alive this moment, there's something tremendous stirring in iron speculation " [here Hawkins got up and began to pace the floor with excited eyes and with gesturing hands]—"something enormous going on in iron, without the shadow of a doubt, and here I sit mousing in the dark and never knowing anything about it; great heaven, what an escape I've made! this underhanded mercenary creature might have taken me up — and ruined me! but I have escaped, and I warrant me I'll not put my foot into —

He stopped and turned toward the stranger, saying: " I have made you a proposition,— you have not accepted it, and I desire that you will consider that I have made none. At the same time my conscience will not allow me to— Please alter the figures I named to thirty thousand dollars, if you will, and let

the proposition go to the company — I will stick to it if it breaks my heart! "

The stranger looked amused, and there was a pretty well-defined touch of surprise in his expression, too, but Hawkins never noticed it. Indeed, he scarcely noticed anything or knew what he was about. The man left; Hawkins flung himself into a chair; thought a few moments, then glanced around, looked frightened, sprang to the door

"Too late — too late! He's gone ! Fool that I am !— always a fool! Thirty thousand — ass that I am! Oh, why didn't I say fifty thousand ! "

He plunged his hands into his hair and leaned his elbows on his knees, and fell to rocking himself back and forth in anguish. Mrs. Hawkins sprang in, beaming:

"Well, Si?"

" Oh, con-found the con-founded — con-found it, Nancy. I've gone and done it, now! "

" Done what, Si, for mercy's sake ! "

" Done everything! Ruined everything! "

"Tell me, tell me, tell me! Don't keep a body in such suspense. Didn't he buy, after all? Didn't he make an offer?"

"Offer? He offered $10,000 for our land, and "

"Thank the good Providence from the very bottom of my heart of hearts ! What sort of ruin do you call that, Si!"

" Nancy, do you suppose I listened to such a

preposterous proposition? No ! Thank fortune I'm not a simpleton! I saw through the pretty scheme in a second. It's a vast iron speculation! millions upon millions in it! But fool as I am I told him he could have half the iron property for thirty thousand — and if I only had him back here he couldn't touch it for a cent less than a quarter of a million ! "

Mrs. Hawkins looked up, white and despairing:

" You threw away this chance, you let this man go, and we in this awful trouble? You don't mean it, you can't mean it! " •

"Throw it away? Catch me at it! Why, woman, do you suppose that man don't know what he is about? Bless you, he'll be back fast enough tomorrow."

" Never, never, never. He never will come back. I don't know what is to become of us. I don't know what in the world is to become of us."

A shade of uneasiness came into Hawkins's face. He said:

" Why, Nancy, you — you can't believe what you are saying."

" Believe it, indeed? I know it, Si. And I know that we haven't a cent in the world, and we've sent ten thousand dollars a-begging."

" Nancy, you frighten me. Now could that man — is it possible that I —hanged if I don't believe I have missed a chance ! Don't grieve, Nancy, don't grieve. I'll go right after him. I'll take — I'll

take — what a fool I am !—I'll take anything he'll give!"

The next instant he left the house on a run. But the man was no longer in the town. Nobody knew where he belonged or whither he had gone. Hawkins came slowly back, watching wistfully but hopelessly for the stranger, and lowering his price steadily with his sinking heart. And when his foot finally pressed his own threshold, the value he held the entire Tennessee property at was five hundred dollars — two hundred down and the rest in three equal annual payments, without interest.

There was a sad gathering at the Hawkins fireside the next night. All the children were present but Clay. Mr. Hawkins said:

"Washington, we seem to be hopelessly fallen, hopelessly involved. I am ready to give up. I do not know where to turn — I never have been down so low before, I never have seen things so dismal. There are many mouths to feed; Clay is at work; we must lose you, also, for a little while, my boy. But it will not be long — the Tennessee land "

He stopped, and was conscious of a blush. There was silence for a moment, and then Washington — now a lank, dreamy-eyed stripling between twenty-two and twenty-three years of age — said :

14 If Col. Sellers would come for me, I would go and stay with him a while, till the Tennessee land is sold. He has often wanted me to come, ever since he moved to Hawkeye."

•* I'm afraid he can't well come for you, Washington. From what I can hear — not from him of course, but from others — he is not far from as bad off as we are — and his family is as large, too. He might find something for you to do, maybe, but you'd better try to get to him yourself, Washington — it's only thirty miles."

*' But how can I, father? There's no stage or anything."

"And if there were, stages require money. A stage goes from Swansea, five miles from here. But it would be cheaper to walk."

" Father, they must know you there, and no doubt they would credit you in a moment, for a little stage ride like that. Couldn't you write and ask them?"

'* Couldn't you, Washington — seeing it's you that wants the ride? And what do you think you'll do, Washington, when you get to Hawkeye? Finish your invention for making window-glass opaque?"

" No, sir, I have given that up. I almost knew 1 could do it, but it was so tedious and troublesome I quit it."

was afraid of it, my boy. Then I suppose you'll finish your plan of coloring hen's eggs by feeding a peculiar diet to the hen?"

"No, sir. I believe I have found out the stuff that will do it, but it kills the hen; so I have dropped that for the present, though I can take it up again some day when I learn how to manage the mixture better."

" Well, what have you got on hand — anything?"

Yes, sir, three or four things. I think they are all good and can all be done, but they are tiresome, and besides they require money. But as soon as the land is sold "

"Emily, were you about to say something?" said Hawkins.

"Yes, sir. If you are willing, I will go to St. Louis. That will make another mouth less to feed. Mrs. Buckner has always wanted me to come."

" But the money, child?"

"Why, I think she would send it, if you would write her — and I know she would wait for her pay till "

" Come, Laura, let's hear from you, my girl."

Emily and Laura were about the same age — between seventeen and eighteen. Emily was fair and pretty, girlish and diffident — blue eyes and light hair. Laura had a proud bearing and a somewhat mature look; she had fine, clean-cut features, her complexion was pure white and contrasted vividly with her black hair and eyes; she was not what one calls pretty— she was beautiful. She said:

" I will go to St. Louis, too, sir. I will find a way to get there. I will make a way. And I will find a way to help myself along, and do what I can to help the rest, too."

She spoke it like a princess. Mrs. Hawkins smiled proudly and kissed her, saying in a tone of fond reproof:

" So one of my girls is going to turn out and work for her living! It's like your pluck and spirit, child, but we will hope that we haven't got quite down to that, yet."

The girl's eyes beamed affection under her mother's caress. Then she straightened up, folded her white hands in her lap, and became a splendid iceberg. Clay's dog put up his brown nose for a little attention, and got it. He retired under the table with an apologetic yelp, which did not affect the iceberg.

Judge Hawkins had written and asked Clay to return home and consult with him upon family affairs. He arrived the evening after this conversation, and the whole household gave him a rapturous welcome. He brought sadly-needed help with him, consisting of the savings of a year and a half of work — nearly two hundred dollars in money.

It was a ray of sunshine which (to this easy household) was the earnest of a clearing sky.

Bright and early in the morning the family were astir, and all were busy preparing Washington for his journey — at least all but Washington himself, who sat apart, steeped in a reverie. When the time for his departure came, it was easy to see how fondly all loved him and how hard it was to let him go, notwithstanding they had often seen him go before, in his St. Louis schooling days. In the most matter-of-course way they had borne the burden of getting him ready for his trip, never seem-

ing to think of his helping in the matter; in the same matter-of-course way Clay had hired a horse and cart; and now that the good-byes were ended he bundled Washington's baggage in and drove away with the exile.

At Swansea Clay paid his stage fare, stowed him away in the vehicle, and saw him off. Then he returned home and reported progress, like a committee of the whole.

Clay remained at home several days. He held many consultations with his mother upon the financial condition of the family, and talked once with his father upon the same subject, but only once. He found a change in that quarter which was distressing; years of fluctuating fortune had done their work; each reverse had weakened the father's spirit and impaired his energies; his last misfortune seemed to have left hope and ambition dead within him; he had no projects, formed no plans — evidently he was a vanquished man. He looked worn and tired. He inquired into Clay's affairs and prospects, and when he found that Clay was doing pretty well and was likely to do still better, it was plain that he resigned himself with easy facility to look to the son for a support; and he said, " Keep yourself informed of poor Washington's condition and move-ments, and help him along all you can, Clay."

The younger children, also, seemed relieved of all fears and distresses, and very ready and willing to look to Clay for a livelihood. Within three days a

general tranquillity and satisfaction reigned in the household. Clay's hundred and eighty or ninety dollars had worked a wonder. The family were as contented, now, and as free from care as they could have been with a fortune. It was well that Mrs. Hawkins held the purse — otherwise the treasure would have lasted but a very little while.

It took but a trifle to pay Hawkins's outstanding obligations, for he had always had a horror of debt.

When Clay bade his home good-bye and set out to return to the field of his labors, he was conscious that henceforth he was to have his father's family on his hands as pensioners; but he did not allow himself to chafe at the thought, for he reasoned that his father had dealt by him with a free hand and a loving one all his life, and now that hard fortune had broken his spirit it ought to be a pleasure, not a pain, to work for him. The younger children were born and educated dependents. They had never been taught to do anything for themselves, and it did not seem to occur to them to make an attempt now.

The girls would not have been permitted to work for a living under any circumstances whatever. It was a Southern family, and of good blood; and for any person except Laura, either within or without the household, to have suggested such an idea would have brought upon the suggester the suspicion of being a lunatic.

CHAPTER VII.

COL. SELLERS' SCHEMES FOR MONEY-MAKING

Via, Pecunia! when she's run and gone
And fled, and dead, then will I fetch her again
With aqua vitae, out of an old hogshead!
While there are lees of wine, or dregs of beer,

I'll never want her! Coin her out of cobwebs,
Dust, but I'll have her! raise wool upon egg-shells,
Sir, and make grass grow out of marrow-bones,
To make her come!
Ben Jon3o*.

BEARING Washington Hawkins and his fortunes, the stage-coach tore out of Swansea at a fearful gait, with horn tooting gayly and half the town admiring from doors and windows. But it did not tear any more after it got to the outskirts; it dragged along stupidly enough, then — till it c^me in sight of the next hamlet; and then the bugle tooted gayly again, and again the vehicle went tearing by the houses. This sort of conduct marked every entry to a station and every exit from it; and so in those days children grew up with the idea that stage-coaches always tore and always tooted; but they also grew up with the idea that pirates went

(82)

into action in their Sunday clothes, carrying the black flag in one hand and pistoling people with the other, merely because they were so represented in the pictures: but these illusions vanished when later years brought their disenchanting wisdom. They learned then that the stage-coach is but a poor, plodding, vulgar thing in the solitudes of the highway; and that the pirate is only a seedy, unfantastic " rough," when he is out of the pictures.

Toward evening, the stage-coach came thundering into Hawkeye with a perfectly triumphant ostentation— which was natural and proper, for Hawkeye was a pretty large town for interior Missouri. Washington, very stiff and tired and hungry, climbed out, and wondered how he was to proceed now. But his difficulty was quickly solved. Col. Sellers came down the street on a run and arrived panting for breath. He said:

" Lord bless you — I'm glad to see you, Washington— perfectly delighted to see you, my boy! I got your message. Been on the lookout for you. Heard the stage horn, but had a party I couldn't shake off — man that's got an enormous thing on hand—wants me to put some capital into it — and I tell you, my boy, I could do worse, I could do a deal worse. No, now, let that luggage alone; I'll fix that. Here, Jerry, got anything to do? All right — shoulder this plunder and follow me. Come along, Washington. Lord, I'm glad to see you! Wife and the children are just perishing to look at F*

you. Bless you, they won't know you, you've grown so. Folks all well, I suppose? That's good — glad to hear that. We're always going to run down and see them, but I'm into so many operations, and they're not things a man feels like trusting to other people, and so somehow we keep putting it off. Fortunes in them ! Good gracious, it's the country to pile up wealth in ! Here we are — here's where the Sellers dynasty hangs out. Dump it on the doorstep, Jerry — the blackest niggro in the state, Washington, but got a good heart — mighty likely boy, is Jerry. And now I suppose you've got to have ten cents, Jerry. That's all right — when a man works for me — when a man — in the other pocket, I reckon — when a man — why, where the mischief is that portmonnaie !—when a — well now that's odd — Oh, now I remember, must have left it at the bank; and b'George I've left my checkbook, too — Polly says I ought to have a nurse — well, no matter. Let me have a dime, Washington, if you've got—ah, thanks. Now clear out, Jerry, your complexion has brought on the twilight half an hour ahead of time. Pretty fair joke — pretty fair. Here he is, Polly! Washington's come, children !—come now, don't eat him up — finish him in the house. Welcome, my boy, to a mansion that is proud to shelter the son of the best man that walks on the ground. Si Hawkins has been a good friend to me, and I believe I can say that whenever I've had a chance to put him into a good thing I've done it, and done it pretty cheerfully, too. I put him into that sugar speculation — what a grand thing that was, if we hadn't held on too long!"

True enough; but holding on too long had utterly ruined both of them; and the saddest part of it was, that they never had had so much money to lose before, for Sellers' sale of their mule crop that year in New Orleans had been a great financial success. If he had kept out of sugar and gone back home content to stick to mules it would have been a happy wisdom. As it was, he managed to kill two birds with one stone — that is to say, he killed the sugar speculation by holding for high rates till he had to sell at the bottom figure, and that calamity killed the mule that laid the golden egg — which is but a figurative expression and will be so understood. Sellers had returned home cheerful but empty-handed, and the mule business lapsed into other hands. The sale of the Hawkins property by the sheriff had followed, and the Hawkins hearts been torn to see Uncle Dan'l and his wife pass from the auction-block into the hands of a negro trader and depart for the remote South to be seen no more by the family. It had seemed like seeing their own flesh and blood sold into banishment.

Washington was greatly pleased with the Sellers mansion. It was a two-story-and-a-half brick, and much more stylish than any of its neighbors. He was borne to the family sitting-room in triumph by

the swarm of little Sellerses, the parents following with their arms about each other's waists.

The whole family were poorly and cheaply dressed; and the clothing, although neat and clean, showed many evidences of having seen long service. The Colonel's "stovepipe" hat was napless and shiny with much polishing, but nevertheless it had an almost convincing expression about it of having been just purchased new. The rest of his clothing was napless and shiny, too, but it had the air of being entirely satisfied with itself and blandly sorry for other people's clothes. It was growing rather dark in the house, and the evening air was chilly, too. Sellers said:

*' Lay off your overcoat, Washington, and draw up to the stove and make yourself at home — just consider yourself under your own shingles, my boy — I'll have a fire going, in a jiffy. Light the lamp, Polly, dear, and let's have things cheerful — just as glad to see you, Washington, as if you'd been lost a century and we'd found you again !"

By this time the Colonel was conveying a lighted match into a poor little stove. Then he propped the stove-door to its place by leaning the poker against it, for the hinges had retired from business. This door framed a small square of isinglass, which now warmed up with a faint glow. Mrs. Sellers lit a cheap, showy lamp, which dissipated a good deal of the gloom, and then everybody gathered into the light and took the stove into close companionship.

The children climbed all over Sellers, fondled him, petted him, and were lavishly petted in return. Out from this tugging, laughing, chattering disguise of legs and arms and little faces, the Colonel's voice worked its way and his tireless tongue ran blithely on without interruption; and the purring little wife, diligent with her knitting, sat near at hand and looked happy and proud and grateful; and she listened as one who listens to oracles and gospels and whose grateful soul is being refreshed with the bread of life. By and by the children quieted down to listen; clustered about their father, and resting their elbows on his legs, they hung upon his words as if he were uttering the music of the spheres.

A dreary old haircloth sofa against the wall; a few damaged chairs; the small table the lamp stood on; the crippled stove — these things constituted the furniture of the room. There was no carpet on the floor; on the wall were occasional square-shaped interruptions of the general tint of the plaster which betrayed that there used to be pictures in the house — but there were none now. There were no mantel ornaments, unless one might bring himself to regard as an ornament a clock which never came within fifteen strokes of striking the right time, and whose hands always hitched together at twenty-two minutes past anything and traveled in company the rest of the way home.

"Remarkable clock!" said Sellers, and got up and wound it. "I've been offered — well, I wouldn't expect you to believe what I've been offered for that clock. Old Gov. Hager never sees me but he says, ' Come, now, Colonel, name your price — I must have that clock!' But my goodness I'd as soon think of selling my wife. As I was saying to silence in the court, now, she's begun to

strike! You can't talk against her — you have to just be patient and hold up till she's said her say. Ah — well, as I was saying, when — she's beginning again! Nineteen, twenty, twenty-one, twenty-two,

twen ah, that's all. Yes, as I was saying to old

Judge go it, old girl, don't mind me. Now

how is that? Isn't that a good, spirited tone? She can wake the dead ! Sleep ? Why you might as well try to sleep in a thunder-factory. Now just listen at that. She'll strike a hundred and fifty, now, without stopping,— you'll see. There ain't another clock like that in Christendom."

Washington hoped that this might be true, for the din was distracting—though the family, one and all, seemed filled with joy; and the more the clock "buckled down to her work" as the Colonel expressed it, and the more insupportable the clatter became, the more enchanted they all appeared to be. When there was silence, Mrs. Sellers lifted upon Washington a face that beamed with a childlike pride, and said:

" It belonged to his grandmother."

The look and the tone were a plain call for admiring surprise, and therefore Washington said —

(it was the only thing that offered itself at the moment) :

Indeed!"

Yes, it did, didn't it, father!" exclaimed one of the twins. She was my great-grandmother—and George's too; wasn't she, father! You never saw her, but Sis has seen her, when Sis was a baby — didn't you, Sis ! Sis has seen her most a hundred times. She was awful deef—she's dead, now. Ain't she, father!"

All the children chimed in, now, with one general Babel of information about deceased — nobody offering to read the riot act or seeming to discountenance the insurrection or disapprove of it in any way — but the head twin drowned all the turmoil and held his own against the field:

" It's our clock, now — and it's got wheels inside of it, and a thing that flutters every time she strikes — don't it, father! Great-grandmother died before hardly any of us was born — she was an Old-School Baptist and had warts all over her — you ask father if she didn't. She had an uncle once that was bald-headed and used to have fits; he wasn't our uncle, I don't know what he was to us — some kin or another I reckon — father's seen him a thousand times — hain't you, father! We used to have a calf that et apples and just chawed up dishrags like nothing, and if you stay here you'll see lots of funerals—-won't he, Sis! Did you ever see a house afire? I have ! Once me and Jim Terry "

But Sellers began to speak now, and the storm ceased. He began to tell about an enormous speculation he was thinking of embarking some capital in — a speculation which some London bankers had been over to consult with him about — and soon he was building glittering pyramids of coin, and Washington was presently growing opulent under the magic of his eloquence. But at the same time Washington was not able to ignore the cold entirely. He was nearly as close to the stove as he could get, and yet he could not persuade himself that he felt the slightest heat, notwithstanding the isinglass door was still gently and serenely glowing. He tried to get a trifle closer to the stove, and the consequence was, he tripped the supporting poker and the stove-door tumbled to the floor. And then there was a revelation there was nothing in the stove but a lighted tallow-candle !

The poor youth blushed and felt as if he must die with shame. But the Colonel was only disconcerted for a moment — he straightway found his voice again:

"A little idea of my own, Washington — one of the greatest things in the world! You must write and tell your father about it — don't forget that, now. I have been reading up some European scientific reports — friend of mine, Count Fugier, sent them to me — sends me all sorts of things from Paris — he thinks the world of me, Fugier does. Well, I saw that the Academy of France had been

testing the properties of heat, and they came to the conclusion that it was a non-conductor or something like that, and of course its influence must necessarily be deadly in nervous organizations with excitable temperaments, especially where there is any tendency toward rheumatic affections. Bless you I saw in a moment what was the matter with us, and says I, out goes your fires!— no more slow torture and certain death for me, sir. What you want is the appearance of heat, not the heat itself—that's the idea. Well how to do it was the next thing. I just put my head to work, pegged away a couple of days, and here you are! Rheumatism? Why a man can't any more start a case of rheumatism in this house than he can shake an opinion out of a mummy! Stove with a candle in it and a transparent door— that's it—it has been the salvation of this family. Don't you fail to write your father about it, Washington. And tell him the idea is mine — I'm no more conceited than most people, I reckon, but you know it is human nature for a man to want credit for a thing like that."

Washington said with his blue lips that he would, but he said in his secret heart that he would promote no such iniquity. He tried to believe in the health-fulness of the invention, and succeeded tolerably well; but after all he could not feel that good health in a frozen body was any real improvement on the rheumatism.

CHAPTER VIII.

COL SELLERS ENTERTAINS WASHINGTON HAWKINS

 Whan horde is thynne, as of seruyse,

Nought replenesshed with grate diuersite Of mete & drinke, good chere may then suffise

With honest talkyng

The Book of Curtesye.

Mammon. Come on, sir. Now, you set your foot on shore In Novo Orbe ; here's the rich Peru: And there, within, sir, are the golden mines,

Great Solomon's Ophir!

Ben. Jonson. The Alchemist.

THE supper at Col. Sellers's was not sumptuous, in the beginning, but it improved on acquaintance. That is to say, that what Washington regarded at first sight as mere lowly potatoes, presently became awe-inspiring agricultural productions that had been reared in some ducal garden beyond the sea, under the sacred eye of the duke himself, who had sent them to Sellers; the bread was from corn which could be grown in only one favored locality in the earth and only a favored few could get it; the Rio coffee, which at first seemed execrable to the tas*.e, took to itself an improved flavor when

Washington was told to drink it slowly and not hurry what should be a lingering luxury in order to be fully appreciated — it was from the private stores of a Brazilian nobleman with an unrememberable name. The Colonel's tongue was a magician's wand that turned dried apples into figs and water into wine as easily as it could change a hovel into a palace and present poverty into imminent future riches.

Washington slept in a cold bed in a carpetless room and woke up in a palace in the morning; at least the palace lingered during the moment that he was rubbing his eyes and getting his bearings — and then it disappeared and he recognized that the Colonel's inspiring talk had been influencing his dreams. Fatigue had made him sleep late; when he entered the sitting-room he noticed that the old haircloth sofa was absent; when he sat down to breakfast the Colonel tossed six or seven dollars in bills on the table, counted them over, said he was a little short and must call upon his banker; then returned the bills to his wallet with the indifferent air of a man who is used to money. The breakfast was not an improvement upon the supper, but the Colonel talked it up and transformed it into an oriental feast. By and by, he said:

" I intend to look out for you, Washington, my boy. I hunted up a place for you yesterday, but I am not referring to that, now — that is a mere livelihood — mere bread and butter; but when I say I mean to look out for you I mean something very

different. I mean to put things in your way that will make a mere livelihood a trifling thing. I'll put you in a way to make more money than you'll ever know what to do with. You'll be right here where I can put my hand on you when anything turns up. I've got some prodigious operations on foot; but I'm keeping quiet; mum's the word; your old hand don't go around pow-wowing and letting everybody see his k'yards and find out his little game. But all in good time, Washington, all in good time. You'll see. Now, there's an operation in corn that looks well. Some New York men are trying to get me to go into it — buy up all the growing crops and just boss the market when they mature — ah, I tell you it's a great thing. And it only costs a trifle; two millions or two and a half will do it. I haven't exactly promised yet — there's no hurry — the more indifferent I seem, you know, the more anxious those fellows will get. And then there is the hog speculation— that's bigger still. We've got quiet men at work," [he was very impressive here,] "mousing around, to get propositions out of all the farmers in the whole West and Northwest for the hog crop, and other agents quietly getting propositions and terms out of all the manufactories — and don't you see, if we can get all the hogs and all the slaughter-houses into our hands on the dead quiet — whew! it would take three ships to carry the money. I've looked into the thing — calculated all the chances for and all the chances against, and though I shake my head

and hesitate and keep on thinking, apparently, I've got my mind made up that if the thing can be done on a capital of six millions, that's the horse to put up money on ! Why, Washington — but what's the use of talking about it — any man can see that there's whole Atlantic oceans of cash in it, gulfs and bays thrown in. But there's a bigger thing than that, yet — a bigger "

"Why, Colonel, you can't want anything bigger!" said Washington, his eyes blazing. " Oh, I wish I could go into either of those speculations — I only wish I had money — I wish I wasn't cramped and kept down and fettered with poverty, and such prodigious chances lying right here in sight! Oh, it is a fearful thing to be poor. But don't throw away those things — they are so splendid and I can see how sure they are. Don't throw them away for something still better and maybe fail in it! I wouldn't, Colonel. I would stick to these. I wish father were here and were his old self again. Oh, he never in his life had such chances as these are. Colonel, you can't improve on these — no man can improve on them!"

A sweet, compassionate smile played about the Colonel's features, and he leaned over the table with the air of a man who is " going to show you " and do it without the least trouble:

"Why Washington, my boy, these things are nothing. They look large — of course they look large to a novice, but to a man who has been all his life

accustomed to large operations — shaw ! They're well enough to while away an idle hour with, or furnish a bit of employment that will give a trifle of idle capital a chance to earn its bread while it is waiting for something to do, but—now just listen a moment — just let me give you an idea of what we old veterans of commerce call 'business.' Here's the Rothschilds' proposition — this is between you and me, you understand "

Washington nodded three or four times impatiently, and his glowing eyes said, "Yes, yes — hurry — I understand "

" for I wouldn't have it get out for a

fortune. They want me to go in with them on the sly — agent was here two weeks ago about it — go in on the sly " [voice down to an impressive whisper, now] " and buy up a hundred and thirteen wildcat banks in Ohio, Indiana, Kentucky, Illinois, and Missouri — notes of these banks are at all sorts of discount now—average discount of the hundred and thirteen is forty-four per cent.—buy them all up, you see, and then all of a sudden let the cat out of the bag! Whiz! the stock of every one of those wildcats would spin up to a tremendous premium before you could turn a handspring — profit on the speculation not a dollar less than forty millions!" [An eloquent pause, while the marvelous vision settled into W.'s focus.] "Where's your hogs now! Why, my dear innocent boy, we would just sit

down on the front doorsteps and peddle banks like lucifer matches!"

Washington finally got his breath and said:

"Oh.it is perfectly wonderful! Why couldn't these things have happened in father's day? And I — it's of no use — they simply lie before my face and mock me. There is nothing for me but to stand helpless and see other people reap the astonishing harvest."

"Never mind, Washington, don't you worry. I'll fix you. There's plenty of chances. How much money have you got?"

In the presence of so many millions, Washington could not keep from blushing when he had to confess that he had but eighteen dollars in the world.

"Well, all right — don't despair. Other people have been obliged to begin with less. I have a small idea that may develop into something for us both, all in good time. Keep your money close and add to it. I'll make it breed. I've been experimenting (to pass away the time) on a little preparation for curing sore eyes —a kind of decoction nine - tenths water and the other tenth drugs that don't cost more than a dollar a barrel; I'm still experimenting; there's one ingredient wanted yet to perfect the thing, and somehow I can't just manage to hit upon the thing that's necessary, and I don't dare talk with a chemist, of course. But I'm progressing, and before many weeks I wager the country will ring with the fame of Beriah Sellers' 7*

Infallible Imperial Oriental Optic Liniment and Salvation for Sore Eyes — the Medical Wonder of the Age! Small bottles fifty cents, large ones a dollar. Average cost, five and seven cents for the two sizes. The first year sell, say, ten thousand bottles in Missouri, seven thousand in Iowa, three thousand in Arkansas, four thousand in Kentucky, six thousand in Illinois, and say twenty-five thousand in the rest of the country. Total, fifty-five thousand bottles; profit clear of all expenses, twenty thousand dollars at the very lowest calculation. All the capital needed is to manufacture the first two thousand bottles — say a hundred and fifty dollars — then the money would begin to flow in. The second year, sales would reach 200,000 bottles — clear profit, say, $75,000 — and in the meantime the great factory would be building in St. Louis, to cost, say, $100,000. The third year we could easily sell 1,000,000 bottles in the United States and "

" O, splendid !" said Washington. " Let's commence right away — let's "

" 1,000,000 bottles in the United States —

profit at least $350,000 — and then it would begin to be time to turn our attention toward the real idea of the business."

"The real idea of it! Ain't $350,000 year a pretty real"

" Stuff! Why, what an infant you are, Washington —what a guileless, short-sighted, easily-contented

innocent you are, my poor little country-bred know-nothing ! Would I go to all that trouble and bother for the poor crumbs a body might pick up in this country? Now do I look like a man who — does my history suggest that I am a man who deals in trifles, contents himself with the narrow horizon that hems in the common herd, sees no further than the end of his nose? Now, you know that that is not me — couldn't be me. You ought to know that if I throw my time and abilities into a patent medicine, it's a patent medicine whose field of operations is the solid earth! its clients the swarming nations that inhabit it! Why what is the republic of America for an eye-water country? Lord bless you, it is nothing but a barren highway that you've got to cross to get to the true eye-water market! Why, Washington, in the Oriental countries people swarm like the sands of the desert; every square mile of ground upholds its thousands upon thousands of struggling human creatures — and every separate and individual devil of them's got the ophthalmia! It's as natural to them as noses are — and sin. It's born with them, it stays with them, it's all that some of them have left when they die. Three years of introductory trade in the Orient and what will be the result? Why, our headquarters would be in Constantinople and our hindquarters in Further India! Factories and warehouses in Cairo, Ispahan, Bagdad, Damascus, Jerusalem, Yedo, Peking, Bangkok, Delhi, Bombay, and Calcutta! Annual income —

well, God only knows how many millions and millions apiece!"

Washington was so dazed, so bewildered — his heart and his eyes had wandered so far away among the strange lands beyond the seas, and such avalanches of coin and currency had fluttered and jingled confusedly down before him, that he was now as one who has been whirling round and round for a time, and, stopping all at once, finds his surroundings still whirling and all objects a dancing chaos. However, little by little the Sellers family cooled down and crystallized into shape, and the poor room lost its glitter and resumed its poverty. Then the youth found his voice and begged Sellers to drop everything and hurry up the eye-water; and he got his eighteen dollars and tried to force it upon the Colonel — pleaded with him to take it — implored him to do it. But the Colonel would not; said he would not need the capital (in his native magnificent way he called that eighteen dollars capital) till the eye-water was an accomplished fact. He made Washington easy in his mind, though, by promising that he would call for it just as soon as the invention was finished, and he added the glad tidings that nobody but just they two should be admitted to a share in the speculation.

When Washington left the breakfast table he could have worshiped that man. Washington was one of that kind of people whose hopes are in the very clouds one day, and in the gutter the next. He

walked on air, now. The Colonel was ready to take him around and introduce him to the employment he had found for him, but Washington begged for a few moments in which to write home; with his kind of people, to ride to-day's new interest to death and put off yesterday's till another time, is nature itself. He ran upstairs and wrote glowingly, enthusiastically, to his mother about the hogs and the corn, the banks and the eye-water — and added a few inconsequential millions to each project. And he said that people little dreamed what a man Col. Sellers was, and that the world would open its eyes when it found out. And he closed his letter thus:

"So make yourself perfectly easy, mother — in a little while you .hall have everything you want, and more. I am not likely to stint you anything, I fancy. This money will not be for me, alone, but for all of us. I want all to share alike; and there is going to be far more for each than one person can spend. Break it to father cautiously — you understand the need of that — break it to him cautiously, for he has had such cruel hard fortune, and is so stricken by it that great good news might prostrate him more surely than even bad, for he is used to the bad but is grown sadly unaccustomed to the other. Tell Laura—tell all the children. And write to Gay about it if he is not with you yet. You may tell Gay that whatever I get he can freely share in — freely. He knows that that is true — there will be no need that I should sweat to that to make him believe it. Good-bye — and mind what I say: Rest perfectly easy, one and all of you, for our troubles are nearly at an end."

Poor lad, he could not know that his mother would cry some loving, compassionaate tears over his letter and put off the family with a synopsis ot its contents which conveyed a deal of love to them but not much idea of his prospects or projects.

And he never dreamed that such a joyful letter could sadden her and fill her night with sighs, and troubled thoughts, and bodings of the future, instead of filling it with peace and blessing it with restful sleep.

When the letter was done, Washington and the Colonel sallied forth, and as they walked along Washington learned what he was to be. He was to be a clerk in a real estate office. Instantly the fickle youth's dreams forsook the magic eye-water and flew back to the Tennessee Land. And the gorgeous possibilities of that great domain straightway began to occupy his imagination to such a degree that he could scarcely manage to keep even enough of his attention upon the Colonel's talk to retain the general run of what he was saying. He was glad it was a real estate office — he was a made man now, sure.

The Colonel said that General Boswell was a rich man and had a good and growing business; and that Washington's work would be light and he would get forty dollars a month and be boarded and lodged in the General's family — which was as good as ten dollars more; and even better, for he could not live as well even at the "City Hotel" as he would there, and yet the hotel charged fifteen dollars a month where a man had a good room.

General Boswell was in his office; a comfortable looking place, with plenty of outline maps hanging about the walls and in the windows, and a spectacled man was marking out another one on a long table.

The office was in the principal street. The General received Washington with a kindly but reserved politeness. Washington rather liked his looks. He was about fifty years old, dignified, well preserved, and well dressed. After the Colonel took his leave, the General talked a while with Washington — his *-alk consisting chiefly of instructions about the clerical duties of the place. He seemed satisfied as to Washington's ability to take care of the books, he was evidently a pretty fair theoretical bookkeeper, and experience would soon harden theory into practice. By and by dinner-time came, and the two walked to the General's house; and now Washington noticed an instinct in himself that moved him to keep not in the General's rear, exactly, but yet not at his side—somehow the old gentleman's dignity and reserve did not inspire familiarity.

CHAPTER IX.
SQUIRE HAWKINS DIES, LEAVING LANDS TO HIS CHILDREN

Quando ti veddi per la prima volta, Parse che mi s'aprisse il paradise, E venissano gli angioli a un per volta Tutti ad apporsi sopra al tuo bel viso, Tutti ad apporsi sopra il tuo bel volto; M'incatenasti, e non mi so'anco sciolto —

Caseilt. Chants popul. de I 1 Italic, 21.mohmi hoka, himak a yakni i immi ha chi ho

—Tajma kittornaminut inneiziungnaerame, isikkaene sinikbingmun illiej, annerningaerdlunilo siurdliminut piok.

Mas. Agl. SiurdL. 49.33.

WASHINGTON dreamed his way along the street, his fancy flitting from grain to hogs, from hogs to banks, from banks to eye-water, from eye-water to Tennessee Land, and lingering but a feverish moment upon each of these fascinations. He was conscious of but one outward thing, to wit, the General, and he was really not vividly conscious of him.

Arrived at the finest dwelling in the town, they entered it and were at home. Washington was introduced to Mrs. Boswell, and his imagination was

(104)

on the point of flitting into the vapory realms of speculation again, when a lovely girl of sixteen or seventeen came in. This vision swept Washington's mind clear of its chaos of glittering rubbish in an instant. Beauty had fascinated him before; many times he had been in love — even for weeks at a time with the same object — but his heart had never suffered so sudden and so fierce an assault as this, within his recollection.

Louise Boswell occupied his mind and drifted among his multiplication tables all the afternoon. He was constantly catching himself in a reverie — reveries made up of recalling how she looked when she first burst upon him; how her voice thrilled him when she first spoke; how charmed the very air seemed by her presence. Blissful as the afternoon was, delivered up to such a revel as this, it seemed an eternity, so impatient was he to see the girl again. Other afternoons like it followed. Washington plunged into this love affair as he plunged into everything else — upon impulse and without reflection. As the days went by it seemed plain that he was growing in favor with Louise,— not sweepingly so, but yet perceptibly, he fancied. His attentions to her troubled her father and mother a little, and they warned Louise, without stating particulars or making allusions to any special person, that a girl was sure to make a mistake who allowed herself to marry anybody but a man who could support her well.

Some instinct taught Washington that his present lack of money would be an obstruction, though possibly not a bar, to his hopes, and straightway his poverty became a torture to him which cast all his former sufferings under that head into the shade. He longed for riches now as he had never longed for them before.

He had been once or twice to dine with Col. Sellers, and had been discouraged to note that the Colonel's bill of fare was falling off both in quantity and quality — a sign, he feared, that the lacking ingredient in the eye-water still remained undiscovered— though Sellers always explained that these changes in the family diet had been ordered by the doctor, or suggested by some new scientific work the Colonel had stumbled upon. But it always turned out that the lacking ingredient was still lacking— though it always appeared, at the same time, that the Colonel was right on its heels.

Everytime the Colonel came into the real estate office Washington's heart bounded and his eyes lighted with hope, but it always turned out that the Colonel was merely on the scent of some vast, undefined landed speculation — although he was customarily able to say that he was nearer to the all-necessary ingredient than ever, and could almost name the hour when success would dawn. And then Washington's heart would sink again, and a sigh would tell when it touched bottom.

About this time a letter came, saying that Judge

Hawkins had been ailing for a fortnight, and was now considered to be seriously ill. It was thought best that Washington should come home. The news filled him with grief, for he loved and honored his father; the Boswells were touched by the youth's sorrow, and even the General unbent and said encouraging things to him. There was balm in this; but when Louise bade him good-bye, and shook his hand and said, "Don't be cast down — it will all come out right — I know it will all come out right," it seemed a blessed thing to be in misfortune, and the tears that welled up to his eyes were the messengers of an adoring and a grateful heart; and when the girl saw them and answering tears came into her own eyes, Washington could hardly contain the excess of happiness that poured into the cavities of his breast that were so lately stored to the roof with grief.

All the way home he nursed his woe and exalted it. He pictured himself as she must be picturing him: a noble, struggling young spirit persecuted by misfortune, but bravely and patiently waiting in the shadow of a dread calamity and preparing to meet the blow as became one who was all too used to hard fortune and the pitiless buffetings of fate. These thoughts made him weep, and weep more broken-heartedly than ever; and he wished that she could see his sufferings now.

There was nothing significant in the fact that Louise, dreamy and distraught, stood at her bed-

room bureau that night, scribbling "Washington" here and there over a sheet of paper. But there was something significant in the fact that she scratched the word out every time she wrote it; examined the erasure critically to see if anybody could guess at what the word had been; then buried it under a maze of obliterating lines; and, finally, as if still unsatisfied, burned the paper.

When Washington reached home, he recognized at once how serious his father's case was. The darkened room, the labored breathing and occasional meanings of the patient, the tip-toeing of the attendants and their whispered consultations, were full of sad meaning. For three or four nights Mrs. Hawkins and Laura had been watching by the bedside; Clay had arrived, preceding Washington by one day, and he was now added to the corps of watchers. Mr. Hawkins would have none but these three, though neighborly assistance was offered by old friends. From this time forth three-hour watches were instituted, and day and night the watchers kept their vigils. By degrees Laura and her mother began to show wear, but neither of them would yield a minute of their tasks to Clay. He ventured once to let the midnight hour pass without calling Laura, but he ventured no more; there was that about her rebuke when he tried to explain, that taught him that to let her sleep when she might be ministering to her father's needs, was to rob her of moments that were priceless in her eyes; he perceived that

she regarded it as a privilege to watch, not a burden. And he had noticed, also, that when midnight struck, the patient turned his eyes toward the door, with an expectancy in them which presently grew into a longing but brightened into contentment as soon as the door opened and Laura appeared. And he did not need Laura's rebuke when he heard his father say:

" Clay is good, and you are tired, poor child; but I wanted you so."

" Clay is not good, father — he did not call me. I would not have treated him so. How could you do it, Clay?"

Clay begged forgiveness and promised not to break faith again; and as he betook him to his bed, he said to himself, "It's a steadfast little soul; whoever thinks he is doing the Duchess a kindness by intimating that she is not sufficient for any undertaking she puts her hand to, makes a mistake; and if I did not know it before, I know now that there are surer ways of pleasing her than by trying to lighten her labor when that labor consists in wearing herself out for the sake of a person she loves."

A week drifted by, and all the while the patient sank lower and lower. The night drew on that was to end all suspense. It was a wintry one. The darkness gathered, the snow was falling, the wind wailed plaintively about the house or shook it with fitful gusts. The doctor had paid his last visit and gone away with that dismal remark to the nearest friend of the family that he " believed there was

nothing more that he could do "—a remark which is always overheard by some one it is not meant for and strikes a lingering half-conscious hope dead with a withering shock; the medicine phials had been removed from the bedside and put out of sight, and all things made orderly and meet for the solemn event that was impending; the patient, with closed eyes, lay scarcely breathing; the watchers sat by and wiped the gathering damps from his forehead while the silent tears flowed down their faces; the deep hush was only interrupted by sobs from the children, grouped about the bed.

After a time,— it was toward midnight now — Mr. Hawkins roused out of a doze, looked about him and was evidently trying to speak. Instantly Laura lifted his head, and in a failing voice he said, while something of the old light shone in his eyes:

*' Wife — children — come nearer — nearer. The darkness grows. Let me see you all, once more."

The group closed together at the bedside, and their tears and sobs came now without restraint.

"I am leaving you in cruel poverty. I have been — so foolish — so short-sighted. But courage ! A better day is — is coming. Never lose sight of the Tennessee Land! Be wary. There is wealth stored up for you there — wealth that is boundless! The children shall hold up their heads with the best in the land, yet. Where are the papers? Have you got the papers safe ? Show them — show them to me I"

The Gilded Age Hi

Under his strong excitement his voice had gathered power and his last sentences were spoken with scarcely a perceptible halt or hindrance. With an effort he had raised himself almost without assistance to a sitting posture. But now the fire faded out of his eyes and he fell back exhausted. The papers were brought and held before him, and the answering smile that flitted across his face showed that he was satisfied. He closed his eyes, and the signs of approaching dissolution multiplied rapidly. He lay almost motionless for a little while, then suddenly partly raised his head and looked about him as one who peers into a dim uncertain light. He muttered:

"Gone? No — I see you — still. It is — it is — over. But you are — safe. Safe. The Ten "

The voice died out in a whisper; the sentence was never finished. The emaciated fingers began to pick at the coverlet, a fatal sign. After a time there were no sounds but the cries of the mourners within and the gusty turmoil of the wind without. Laura had bent down and kissed her father's lips as the spirit left the body; but she did not sob, or utter any ejaculation; her tears flowed silently. Then she closed the dead eyes, and crossed the hands upon the breast; after a season, she kissed the forehead reverently, drew the sheet up over the face, and then walked apart and sat down with the look of one who is done with life and has no further interest in its joys and sorrows, its hopes or its ambitions. Clay buried his face in the coverlet of the bed ; when the other children and the mother realized that death was indeed come at last, they threw themselves into each others' arms and gave way to a frenzy of grief.

CHAPTER X.

LAURA'S DISCOVERY. MRS. HAWKINS'S APPEAL

- Okarbigalo: " Kia pannigatit ? Assarsara! uamnut nevsoingoarna "—

Mo. Agleg. Siurdl. 24. 23.

Nootah nuttaunes, natwontash,

Kukkeih'ish, wonk yeuyeu Wannanum kummissinninnumog

Kah Kcosh week pannuppu.

— La Giannetta rispose: Madama, voi dalla poverta di mio padre togliendomi, come figliuola cresciuta m'avete, e per questo agni vostro piacer far dovrei —

Boccacio, Decam. Giorno 2, Nov. 3.

ONLY two or three days had elapsed since the funeral, when something happened which was to change the drift of Laura's life somewhat, and influence in a greater or lesser degree the formation of her character.

Major Lackland had once been a man of note in the State — a man of extraordinary natural ability and as extraordinary learning. He had been universally trusted and honored in his day, but had finally fallen into misfortune; while serving his third term in Congress, and while upon the point of being (113)

elevated to the Senate — which was considered the summit of earthly aggrandizement in those days — he had yielded to temptation, when in distress for money wherewith to .save his estate, and sold his vote. His crime was discovered, and his fall followed instantly. Nothing could reinstate him in the confidence of the people, his ruin was irretrievable — his disgrace complete. All doors were closed against him, all men avoided him. After years of skulking retirement and dissipation, death had relieved him of his troubles at last, and his funeral followed close upon that of Mr. Hawkins. He died as he had latterly lived — wholly alone and friendless. He had no relatives — or if he had they did not acknowledge him. The coroner's jury found certain memoranda upon his body and about the premises which revealed a fact not suspected by the villagers before — viz., that Laura was not the child of Mr. and Mrs. Hawkins.

The gossips were soon at work. They were but little hampered by the fact that the memoranda referred to betrayed nothing but the bare circumstance that Laura's real parents were unknown, and stopped there. So far from being hampered by this, the gossips seemed to gain all the more freedom from it. They supplied all the missing information themselves, they filled up all the blanks. The town soon teemed with histories of Laura's origin and secret history, no two versions precisely alike, but all elaborate, exhaustive, mysterious, and interesting,and all agreeing in one vital particular — to wit, that there was a suspicious cloud about her birth, not to say a disreputable one.

Laura began to encounter cold looks, averted eyes, and peculiar nods and gestures which perplexed her beyond measure; but presently the pervading gossip found its way to her, and she understood them then. Her pride was stung. She was astonished, and at first incredulous. She was about to ask her mother if there was any truth in these reports, but upon second thought held her peace. She soon gathered that Major Lackland's memoranda seemed to refer to letters which had passed between himself and Judge Hawkins. She shaped her course without difficulty the day that that hint reached her.

That night she sat in her room till all was still, and then she stole into the garret and began a search. She rummaged long among boxes of musty papers relating to business matters of no interest to her, but at last she found several bundles of letters. One bundle was marked " private," and in that she found what she wanted. She selected six or eight letters from the package and began to devour their contents, heedless of the cold.

By the dates, these letters were from five to seven years old. They were all from Major Lackland to Mr. Hawkins. The substance of them was, that some one in the East had been inquiring of Major Lackland about a lost child and its parents, and that it was conjectured that the child might be Laura.

Evidently some of the letters were missing, fof the name of the inquirer was not mentioned; there was a casual reference to "this handsome-featured aristocratic gentleman," as if the reader and the writer were accustomed to speak of him and knew who was meant.

In one letter the Major said he agreed with Mr. Hawkins that the inquirer seemed not altogether on the wrong track; but he also agreed that it would be best to keep quiet until more convincing developments were forthcoming.

Another letter said that "the poor soul broke completely down when he saw Laura's picture, and declared it must be she."

Still another said,

" He seems entirely alone in the world, and his heart is so wrapped •op in this thing that I believe that if it proved a false hope, it would kill him; I have persuaded him to wait a little while and go west when I go."

Another letter had this paragraph in it:

" He is better one day and worse the next, and is out of his mind a good deal of the time. Lately his case has developed a something which is a wonder to the hired nurses, but which will not be much of a marvel to you if you have read medical philosophy much. It is this: his lost memory returns to him when he is delirious, and goes away again when he is himself — just as old Canada Joe used to talk the French patois of his boyhood in the delirium of typhus fever, though he could not do it when his mind was clear. Now this poor gentlemen's memory has always broken down before he reached the explosion of the steamer; he could only remember starting up the river with his wife and child, and he had an idea that there was a race, but he was not certain; he could not name the boat he was on; there was a dead blank of a month or more that supplied not an item to his recollection.

It was not for me to assist him, of course. But now in his delirium it all comes out: the names of the boats, every incident of the explosion, and likewise the details of his astonishing escape — that is, up to where, just as a yawl-boat was approaching him (he was clinging to the starboard wheel of the burning wreck at the lime), a falling timber struck him on the head. But I will write out his wonderful escape in full to-morrow or next day. Of course the physicians will not let me tell him now that our Laura is indeed his child — that must come later, when his health is thoroughly restored. His case is not considered dangerous at all; he will recover presently, the doctors say. But they insist that he must travel a little when he gets well — they recommend a short sea voyage, and they say he can be persuaded to try it if we continue to keep him in ignorance and promise to let him see L. as soon as he returns."

The letter that bore the latest date of all, contained this clause:

"It is the most unaccountable thing in the'world; the mystery remains as impenetrable as ever; I have hunted high and low for him, and inquired of everybody, but in vain; all trace of him ends at that hotel in New York; I never have seen or heard of him since, up to this day; he could hardly have sailed, for his name does not appear upon the books of any shipping office in New York or Boston or Baltimore. How fortunate it seems, now, that we kept this thing to ourselves; Laura still has a father in you, and it is better for her that we drop this subject here forever."

That was all. Random remarks here and there, being pieced together gave Laura a vague impression of a man of fine presence, about forty-three or forty-five years of age, with dark hair and eyes, and a slight limp in his walk — it was not stated which leg was defective. And this indistinct shadow represented her father. She made an exhaustive search for the missing letters, but found none. They had probably been burned; and she doubted not that the ones

she had ferreted out would have shared the same fate if Mr. Hawkins had not been a dreamer, void of method, whose mind was perhaps in a state of conflagration over some bright new speculation when he received them.

She sat long, with the letters in her lap, thinking — and unconsciously freezing. She felt like a lost person who has traveled down a long lane in good hope of escape, and, just as the night descends finds his progress barred by a bridgeless river whose further shore, if it has one, is lost in the darkness. If she could only have found these letters a month sooner! That was her thought. But now the dead had carried their secrets with them. A dreary melancholy settled down upon her. An undefined sense of injury crept into her heart. She grew very miserable.

She had just reached the romantic age — the age when there is a sad sweetness, a dismal comfort to a girl to find out that there is a mystery connected with her birth, which no other piece of good luck can afford. She had more than her rightful share of practical good sense, but still she was human; and to be human is to have one's little modicum of romance secreted away in one's composition. One never ceases to make a hero of one's self (in private), during life, but only alters the style of his heroism from time to time as the drifting years belittle certain gods of his admiration and raise up others in their stead that seem greater.

The recent wearing days and nights of watching, and the wasting grief that had possessed her, combined with the profound depression that naturally came with the reaction of idleness, made Laura peculiarly susceptible at this time to romantic impressions. She was a heroine, now, with a mysterious father somewhere. She could not really tell whether she wanted to find him and spoil it all or not; but still all the traditions of romance pointed to the making the attempt as the usual and necessary course to follow; therefore she would some day begin the search when opportunity should offer.

Now a former thought struck her — she would speak to Mrs. Hawkins. And, naturally enough, Mrs. Hawkins appeared on the stage at that moment.

She said she knew all — she knew that Laura had discovered the secret that Mr. Hawkins, the elder children, Col. Sellers, and herself had kept so long and so faithfully; and she cried and said that now that troubles had begun they would never end; her daughter's love would wean itself away from her and her heart would break. Her grief so wrought upon Laura that the girl almost forgot her own troubles for the moment in her compassion for her mother's distress. Finally Mrs. Hawkins said :

" Speak to me, child — do not forsake me. Forget all this miserable talk. Say I am your mother! — I have loved you so long, and there is no other. I am your mother, in the sight of God, and nothing shall ever take you from me!"

All barriers fell, before this appeal. Laura put her arms about her mother's neck and said:

" You are my mother, and always shall be. We will be as we have always been; and neither this foolish talk nor any other things shall part us or make us less to each other than we are this hour."

There was no longer any sense of separation or estrangement between them. Indeed, their love seemed more perfect now than it had ever been before. By and by they went downstairs and sat by the fire and talked long and earnestly about Laura's history and the letters. But it transpired that Mrs. Hawkins had never known of this correspondence between her husband and Major Lackland. With his usual consideration for his wife, Mr. Hawkins had shielded her from the worry the matter would have caused her.

Laura went to bed at last with a mind that had gained largely in tranquillity and had lost correspondingly in morbid romantic exaltation. She was pensive, the next day, and subdued; but that was not matter for remark, for she did not differ from the mournful friends about her in that respect. Clay and Washington were the same loving and admiring brothers now that they had always been. The great secret was new to some of the younger children, but their love suffered no change under the wonderful revelation.

It is barely possible that things might have presently settled down into their old rut and the mystery

have lost the bulk of its romantic sublimity in Laura's eyes, if the village gossips could have quieted down. But they could not quiet down and they did not. Day after day they called at the house, ostensibly upon visits of condolence, and they pumped away at the mother and the children without seeming to know that their questionings were in bad taste. They meant no harm — they only wanted to know. Villagers always want to know.

The family fought shy of the questionings, and of course that was high testimony—"if the Duchess was respectably born, why didn't they come out and prove it? — why did they stick to that poor thin story about picking her up out of a steamboat explosion? "

Under this ceaseless persecution, Laura's morbid self-communing was renewed. At night the day's contribution of detraction, innuendo, and malicious conjecture would be canvassed in her mind, and then she would drift into a course of thinking. As her thoughts ran on, the indignant tears would spring to her eyes, and she would spit out fierce little ejaculations at intervals. But finally she would grow calmer and say some comforting disdainful thing — something like this:

"But who are they? Animals! What are their opinions to me? Let them talk— I will not stoop

to be affected by it. I could hate Nonsense

— nobody I care for or in any way respect is changed toward me, I fancy."

She may have supposed she was thinking of many individuals, but it was not so — she was thinking of only one. And her heart warmed somewhat, too, the while. One day a friend overheard a conversation like this: and naturally came and told her all about it:

" Ned, they say you don't go there any more. How is that?"

"Well, I don't: but I tell you it's not because I don't want to and it's not because /think it is any matter who her father was or who he wasn't either; it's only on account of this talk, talk, talk. I think she is a fine girl every way, and so would you if you knew her as well as I do; but you know how it is when a girl once gets talked about — it's all up with her — the world won't ever let her alone, after that."

The only comment Laura made upon this revelation, was:

" Then it appears that if this trouble had not occurred I could have had the happiness of Mr. Ned Thurston's serious attentions. He is well favored in person, and well liked, too, I believe, and comes of one of the first families of the village. He is prosperous, too, I hear; has been a doctor a year, now, and has had two patients — no, three, I think; yes, it was three. I attended their funerals. Well, other people have hoped and been disappointed; I am not alone in that. I wish you could stay to dinner,. Maria — we are 'going to have sausages; and besides, I wanted to talk to you about Hawkeye

and make you promise to come and see us when we are settled there."

But Maria could not stay. She had come to mingle romantic tears with Laura's over the lover's defection, and had found herself dealing with a heart that could not rise to an appreciation of affliction because its interest was all centered in sausages.

But as soon as Maria was gone, Laura stamped her expressive foot and said:

The coward ! Are all books lies ? I thought he would fly to the front, and be brave and noble, and stand up for me against all the world, and defy my enemies, and wither these gossips with his scorn ! Poor crawling thing, let him go. I do begin to despise this world ! "

She lapsed into thought. Presently she said:

If the time ever comes, and I get a chance, oh, I'll "

She could not find a word that was strong enough, perhaps. By and by she said:

" Well, I am glad of it—I'm glad of it. I never cared anything for him anyway! "

And then, with small consistency, she cried a little, and patted her foot more indignantly than ever.

CHAPTER XI.

A DINNER PARTY. PLAIN FARE, BRILLIANT EXPECTATIONS

TWO months had gone by and the Hawkins ' family were domiciled in Hawkeye. Washington was at work in the real estate office again, and was alternately in paradise or the other place just as it happened that Louise was gracious to him or seemingly indifferent — because indifference or preoccupation could mean nothing else than that she was thinking of some other young person. Col. Sellers had asked him several times to dine with him, when he first returned to Hawkeye, but Washington, for no particular reason, had not accepted. No particular reason except one which he preferred to keep to himself — viz., that he could not bear to be away from Louise. It occurred to him, now, that the Colonel had not invited him lately — could he be offended ? He resolved to go that very day, and give the Colonel a pleasant surprise. It was a good idea; especially as Louise had absented her-

(124)

self from breakfast that morning, and torn his heart; he would tear hers, now, and let her see how it felt.

The Sellers family were just starting to dinner when Washington burst upon them with his surprise. For an instant the Colonel looked nonplussed, and just a bit uncomfortable; and Mrs. Sellers looked actually distressed: but the next moment the head of the house was himself again, and exclaimed:

"All right, my boy, all right — always glad to see you — always glad to hear your voice and take you by the hand. Don't wait for special invitations — that's all nonsense among friends. Just come whenever you can, and come as often as you can — the oftener the better. You can't please us any better than that, Washington ; the little woman will tell you so herself. We don't pretend to style. Plain folks, you know — plain folks. Just a plain family dinner, but such as it is, our friends are always welcome, I reckon you know that yourself, Washington. Run along, children, run along; Lafayette,* stand off the cat's tail, child, can't you

In those old days the average man called his children after his most revered literary and historical idols; consequently there was hardly a family, at least in the West, but had a Washington in it — and also a Lafayette, a Franklin, and six or eight sounding names from Byron, Scott, and the Bible, if the offspring held out. To visit such a family, was to find one's self confronted by a congress made up of representatives of the imperial myths and the majestic dead of all the ages. There was something thrilling about it, to a stranger, not to say awe-inspiring. 9*

see what you're doing? Come, come, come, Roderick Dhu, it isn't nice for little boys to hang on to young gentlemen's coat-tails — but never mind him, Washington, he's full of spirits and don't mean any harm. Children will be children, you know. Take the chair next to Mrs. Sellers, Washington — tut, tut, Marie Antoinette, let your brother have the fork if he wants it, you are bigger than he is."

Washington contemplated the banquet, and wondered if he were in his right mind. Was this the plain family dinner? And was it all present? It was soon apparent that this was indeed the dinner: it was all on the table: it consisted of abundance of clear, fresh water, and a basin of raw turnips — nothing more.

Washington stole a glance at Mrs. Sellers's face, and would have given the world, the next moment, if he could have spared her that. The poor woman's face was crimson, and the tears stood in her eyes. Washington did not know what to do. He wished he had never come there and spied out this cruel poverty and brought pain to that poor little lady's heart and shame to her cheek; but he was there, and there was no escape. Col. Sellers hitched back his coat sleeves airily from his wrists as who shoulc say " Now for solid enjoyment!" seized a fork, flourished it and began to harpoon turnips and deposit them in the plates before him:

" Let me help you, Washington — Lafayette, pass this plate to Washington — ah, well, well, my boy,

things are looking pretty bright, now, 7 tell you. Speculation — my! the whole atmosphere's full of money. I wouldn't take three fortunes for one little operation I've got on hand now — have anything from the casters? No? Well, you're right, you're right. Some people like mustard with turnips, but — now there was Baron Poniatowski — Lord, but that man did know how to live ! — true Russian you know, Russian to the backbone; I say to my wife, give me a Russian every time, for a table comrade. The Baron used to say, ' Take mustard, Sellers, try the mustard,— a man can't know what turnips are in perfection without mustard,' but I always said, ' No, Baron, I'm a plain man, and I want my food plain — none of your embellishments for Beriah Sellers—no made dishes for me! And it's the best way — high living kills more than it cures in this world, you can rest assured of that. Yes, indeed, Washington, I've got one little operation on hand that — take some more water—help yourself, won't you? help yourself, there's plenty of it. You'll find it pretty good, I guess. How does that fruit strike you ? "

Washington said he did not know that he had ever tasted better. He did not add that he detested turnips even when they were cooked — loathed them in their natural state. No, he kept this to himself, and praised the turnips to the peril of his soul.

"I thought you'd like them. Examine them — examine them — they'll bear it. See how perfectly

firm and juicy they are — they can't start any like them in this part of the country, I can tell you. These are from New Jersey —I imported them myself. They cost like sin, too; but, Lord bless me, I go in for having the best of a thing, even if it does cost a little more — its the best economy, in the long run. These are the Early Malcolm — it's a turnip that can't be produced except in just one orchard, and the supply never is up to the demand. Take some more water, Washington — you can't drink too much water with fruit — all the doctors say that. The plague can't come where this article is, my boy ! "

" Plague ? What plague ? "

"What plague, indeed? Why the Asiatic plague that nearly depopulated London a couple of centuries ago."

"But how does that concern us? There is no plague here, I reckon."

" Sh ! I've let it out! Well, never mind — just keep it to yourself. Perhaps I oughtn't said anything, but it's bound to come out sooner or later, so what is the odds? Old McDowells wouldn't like me to — to — bother it all, I'll just tell the whole thing and let it go. You see, I've been down to St. Louis, and I happened to run across old Dr. McDowells— thinks the world of me, does the doctor. He's a man that keeps himself to himself, and well he may, for he knows that he's got a reputation that covers the whole earth — he won't condescend to

open himself out to many people, but, Lord bless you, he and I are just like brothers; he won't let me go to a hotel when I'm in the city — says I'm the only man that's company to him, and I don't know but there's some truth in it, too, because although I never like to glorify myself and make a great to-do over what I am or what I can do or what I know, I don't mind saying here among friends that I am better read up in most sciences, maybe, than the general run of professional men in these days. Well, the other day he let me into a little secret, strictly on the quiet, about this matter of the plague. "You see it's booming right along in our direction— follows the Gulf Stream, you know, just as all those epidemics do,— and within three months it will be just waltzing through this land like a whirlwind ! And whoever it tOc hes can make his will and contract for the funeral. Well, you can't cure it, you know, but you can prevent it. How? Turnips! that's it! Turnips and water! Nothing like it in the world, old McDowells says, just fill yourself up two or three times a day, and you can snap your fingers at the plague. Sh! keep mum, but just you confine yourself to that diet and you're all right. I wouldn't have old McDowells know that I told about it for anything — he never would speak to me again. Take some more water, Washington — the more water you drink, the better. Here, let me give you some more of the turnips. No, no, no, now, I insist 9*

There, now. Absorb those. They're mighty sustaining— brimful of nutriment — all the medical books say so. Just eat from four to seven good-sized turnips at a meal, and drink from a pint and a half to a quart of water, and then just sit around a couple of hours and let them ferment. You'll feel like a fighting cock next day."

Fifteen or twenty minutes later the Colonel's tongue was still chattering away — he had piled up several future fortunes out of several incipient *' operations" which he had blundered into within the past week, and was now soaring along through some brilliant expectations born of late promising experiments upon the lacking ingredient of the eyewater. And at such a time Washington ought to have been a rapt and enthusiastic listener, but he was not, for two matters disturbed his mind and distracted his attention. One was, that he discovered, to his confusion and shame, that in allowing himself to be helped a second time to the turnips, he had robbed those hungry children. He had not needed the dreadful "fruit," and had not wanted it; and when he saw the pathetic sorrow in their faces when they asked for more and there was no more to give them, he hated himself for his stupidity and pitied the famishing young things with all his heart. The other matter that disturbed him was the dire inflation that had begun in his stomach. It grew and grew, it became more and more insupportable. Evidently the turnips were " fermenting." He forced himself

to sit still as long as he could, but his anguish conquered him at last.

He rose in the midst of the Colonel's talk and excused himself on the plea of a previous engagement. The Colonel followed him to the door, promising over and over again that he would use his influence to get some of the Early Malcolms for him, and insisting that he should not be such a stranger but come and take pot-luck with him every chance he got. Washington was glad enough to get away and feel free again. He immediately bent his steps toward home.

In bed he passed an hour that threatened to turn his hair gray, and then a blessed calm settled down upon him that filled his heart with gratitude. Weak and languid, he made shift to turn himself about and seek rest and sleep; and as his soul hovered upon the brink of unconsciousness, he heaved a long, deep sigh, and said to himself that in his heart he had cursed the Colonel's preventive of rheumatism, before, and now let the plague come if it must — he was done with preventives; if ever any man beguiled him with turnips and water again, let him die the death.

If he dreamed at all that night, no gossiping spirit disturbed his visions to whisper in his ear of certain matters just then in bud in the East, more than a thousand miles away, that after the lapse of a few years would develop influences which would profoundly affect the fate and fortunes of the Hawkins family.

CHAPTER XII.

HARRY AND PHILIP GO WEST TO LAY OUT A RAILROAD

Todienbuch,

, it's easy enough to make a fortune," Henry said.

"It seems to be easier than it is, I begin to think," replied Philip.

Well, why don't you go into something? You'll never dig it out of the Astor Library."

If there be any place and time in the world where and when it seems easy to "go into something" it is in Broadway on a spring morning, when one is walking cityward, and has before him the long lines of palace-shops with an occasional spire seen through the soft haze that lies over the lower town, and hears the roar and hum of its multitudinous traffic.

To the young American, here or elsewhere, the paths to fortune are innumerable and all open ; there is invitation in the air and success in all his wide

(132)

horizon. He is embarrassed which to choose, and is not unlikely to waste years in dallying with his chances, before giving himself to the serious tug and strain of a single object. He has no traditions to bind him or guide him, and his impulse is to break away from the occupation his father has followed, and make a new way for himself.

Philip Sterling used to say that if he should seriously set himself for ten years to any one of the dozen projects that were in his brain, he felt that he could be a rich man. He wanted to be rich, he had a sincere desire for a fortune, but for some unaccountable reason he hesitated about addressing himself to the narrow work of getting it. He never walked Broadway, a part of its tide of abundant shifting life, without feeling something of the flush of wealth, and unconsciously taking the elastic step of one well-to-do in this prosperous world.

Especially at night in the crowded theater — Philip was too young to remember the old Chambers street box, where the serious Burton led his hilarious and pagan crew — in the intervals of the screaming comedy, when the orchestra scraped and grunted and tooted its dissolute tunes, the world seemed full of opportunities to Philip, and his heart exulted with a conscious ability to take any of its prizes he chose to pluck.

Perhaps it was the swimming ease of the acting on the stage, where virtue had its reward in three easy acts, perhaps it was the excessive light of the house"

or the music, or the buzz of the excited talk between acts, perhaps it was youth which believed everything, but for some reason while Philip was at the theater he had the utmost confidence in life and his ready victory in it.

Delightful illusion of paint and tinsel and silk attire, of cheap sentiment and high and mighty dialogue! Will there not always be rosin enough for the squeaking fiddle-bow? Do we not all like the maudlin hero, who is sneaking round the right entrance, in wait to steal the pretty wife of his rich and tyrannical neighbor from the pasteboard cottage at the left entrance? and when he advances down to the footlights and defiantly informs the audience that, " he who lays his hand on a woman except in the way of kindness," do we not all applaud so as to drown the rest of the sentence ?

Philip never was fortunate enough to hear what would become of a man who should lay his hand on a woman with the exception named; but he learned afterward that the woman who lays her hand on a man, without any exception whatsoever, is always acquitted by the jury.

The fact was, though Philip Sterling did not know it, that he wanted several other things quite as much as he wanted wealth. The modest fellow would have liked fame thrust upon him for some worthy achievement; it might be for a book, or for the skillful management of some great newspaper, or for some daring expedition like that of Lt. Strain or

Dr. Kane. He was unable to decide exactly what it should be. Sometimes he thought he would like to stand in a conspicuous pulpit and humbly preach the gospel of repentance; and it even crossed his mind that it would be noble to give himself to a missionary life to some benighted region, where the date-palm grows, and the nightingale's voice is in tune, and the bulbul sings on the off nights. If he were good enough he would attach himself to that company of young men in the Theological Seminary, who were seeing New York life in preparation for the ministry. Philip was a New England boy and had graduated at Yale; he had not carried off with him all the learning of that venerable institution, but he knew some things that were not in the regular course of study. A very good use of the English language and considerable knowledge of its literature was one of them; he could sing a song very well, not in time to be sure, but with enthusiasm; he could make a magnetic speech at a moment's notice in the classroom, the debating society, or upon any fence or drygoods box that was convenient; he could lift himself by one arm, and do the giant swing in the gymnasium; he could strike out from his left shoulder; he could handle an oar like a professional and pull stroke in a winning race. Philip had a good appetite, a sunny temper, and a clear hearty laugh. He had brown hair, hazel eyes set wide apart, a broad but not high forehead, and a fresh winning face. He was six feet high, with broad shoulders,

long legs and a swinging gait; one of those loose-jointed, capable fellows, who saunter into the world with a free air and usually make a stir in whatever company they enter.

After he left college Philip took the advice of friends and read law. Law seemed to him well enough as a science, but he never could discover a practical case where it appeared to him worth while to go to law, and all the clients who stopped with this new clerk in the ante-room of the law office where he was writing, Philip invariably advised to settle — no matter how, but settle — greatly to the disgust of his employer, who knew that justice between man and man could only be attained by the recognized processes, with the attendant fees. Besides Philip hated the copying of pleadings, and he was certain that a life of " whereases " and " afore-saids" and whipping the devil round the stump, would be intolerable.

His pen therefore, and whereas, and not as aforesaid, strayed off into other scribbling. In an unfortunate hour, he had two or three papers accepted by first-class magazines, at three dollars the printed page, and, behold, his vocation was open to him. He would make his mark in literature. Life has no moment so sweet as that in which a young man believes himself called into the immortal ranks of the masters of literature. It is such a noble ambition, that it is a pity it has usually such a shallow foundation.

At the time of this history, Philip had gone to New York for a career. With his talent he thought he should have little difficulty in getting an editorial position upon a metropolitan newspaper; not that he knew anything about newspaper work, or had the least idea of journalism; he knew he was not fitted for the technicalities of the subordinate departments, but he could write leaders with perfect ease, he was sure. The drudgery of the newspaper office was too distasteful, and besides it would be beneath the dignity of a graduate and a successful magazine writer. He wanted to begin at the top of the ladder.

To his surprise he found that every situation in the editorial department of the journals was full, always had been full, was always likely to be full. It seemed to him that the newspaper managers didn't want genius, but mere plodding and grubbing. Philip therefore read diligently in the Astor Library, planned literary works that should compel attention, and nursed his genius. He had no friend wise enough to tell him to step into the Dorking Convention, then in session, make a sketch of the men and women on the platform, and take it to the editor of the Daily Grapevine, and see what he could get a line for it.

One day he had an offer from some country friends, who believed in him, to take charge of a provincial daily newspaper, and he went to consult Mr. Gringo — Gringo who years ago managed the Atlas — about taking the situation.

" Take it, of course," says Gringo, "take anything that offers, why not?"

"But they want me to make it an opposition paper."

" Well, make it that. That party is going to succeed, it's going to elect the next president."

"I don't believe it," said Philip, stoutly, "it's wrong in principle, and it ought not to succeed, but I don't see how I can go for a thing I don't believe in."

" Oh, very well," said Gringo, turning away with a shade of contempt, "you'll find if you are going into literature and newspaper work that you can't afford a conscience like that."

But Philip did afford it, and he wrote, thanking his friends, and declining because he said the political scheme would fail, and ought to fail. And he went back to his books and to his waiting for an opening large enough for his dignified entrance into the literary world.

It was in this time of rather impatient waiting that Philip was one morning walking down Broadway with Henry Brierly. He frequently accompanied Henry part way down town to what the latter called his office in Broad Street, to which he went, or pretended to go, with regularity every day. It was evident to the most casual acquaintance that he was a man of affairs, and that his time was engrossed in the largest sort of operations, about which there was a mysterious air. His liability to be suddenly sum-

moned to Washington, or Boston, or Montreal, or even to Liverpool, was always imminent. He never was so summoned, but none of his acquaintances would have been surprised to hear any day that he had gone to Panama or Peoria, or to hear from him that he had bought the Bank of Commerce.

The two were intimate at that time,— they had been classmates — and saw a great deal of each other. Indeed, they lived together in Ninth Street, in a boarding-house there, which had the honor of lodging and partially feeding several other young fellows of like kidney, who have since gone their several ways into fame or into obscurity.

It was during the morning walk to which reference has been made that Henry Brierly suddenly said, " Philip, how would you like to go to St. Jo.?"

"I think I should like it of all things," replied Philip, with some hesitation, " but what for?"

" Oh, it's a big operation. We are going, a lot of us, railroad men, engineers, contractors. You know my uncle is a great railroad man. I've no doubt I can get you a chance to go if you'll go."

But in what capacity would I go?"

"Well, I'm going as an engineer. You can go as one."

I don't know an engine from a coal cart."

" Field engineer, civil engineer. You can begin by carrying a rod, and putting down the figures. It's easy enough. I'll show you about that. We'll get Trautwine and some of those books."

" Yes, but what is it for, what is it all about?"

"Why, don't you see? We lay out a line, spot the good land, enter it up, know where the stations are to be, spot them, buy lots; there's heaps of money in it. We wouldn't engineer long."

11 When do you go?" was Philip s next question, after some moments of silence.

" To-morrow. Is that too soon?"

" No, it's not too soon. I've been ready to go anywhere for six months. The fact is, Henry, that I'm about tired of trying to force myself into things, and am quite willing to try floating with the stream for a while, and see where I will land. This seems like a providential call; it's sudden enough."

The two young men who were by this time full of the adventure, went down to the Wall Street office of Henry's uncle and had a talk with that wily operator. The uncle knew Philip very well, and was pleased with his frank enthusiasm, and willing enough to give him a trial in the Western venture. It was settled therefore, in the prompt way in which things are settled in New York, that they would start with the rest of the company next morning for the West.

On the way uptown these adventurers bought books on engineering, and suits of India-rubber, which they supposed they would need in a new and probably damp country, and many other things which nobody ever needed anywhere.

The night was spent in packing up and writing

letters, for Philip would not take such an important step without informing his friends. If they disapprove, thought he, I've done my duty by letting them know. Happy youth, that is ready to pack its valise, and start for Cathay on an hour's notice.

By the way," calls out Philip from his bedroom, to Henry, " where is St. Jo.?"

"Why, it's in Missouri somewhere, on the frontier, I think. We'll get a map."

" Never mind the map. We will find the place itself. I was afraid it was nearer home."

Philip wrote a long letter, first of all, to his mother, full of love and glowing anticipations of his new opening. He wouldn't bother her with business details, but he hoped that the day was not far off when she would see him return, with a moderate fortune, and something to add to the comfort of her advancing years.

To his uncle he said that he had made an arrangement with some New York capitalists to go to Missouri, in a land and railroad operation, which would at least give him a knowledge of the world and not unlikely offer him a business opening. He knew his uncle would be glad to hear that he had at last turned his thoughts to a practical matter.

It was to Ruth Bolton that Philip wrote last. He might never see her again; he went to seek his fortune. He well knew the perils of the frontier, the savage state of society, the lurking Indians, and the dangers of fever. But there was no real danger

to a person who took care of himself. Might he write to her often and tell her of his life. If he re-turned with a fortune, perhaps and perhaps. If he was unsuccessful, or if he never returned — perhaps it would be as well. No time or distance, however, would ever lessen his interest in her. He would say good-night, but not good-bye.

In the soft beginning of a spring morning, long before New York had breakfasted, while yet the air of expectation hung about the wharves of the metropolis, our young adventurers made their way to the Jersey City Railway Station of the Erie Road, to begin the long, swinging, crooked journey, over what a writer of a former day called a causeway of cracked rails and cows, to the West.

CHAPTER XIII.

COL. SELLERS WELCOMES THE YOUNG MEN TO ST. LOUIS

What ever to say he toke in his entente, his langage was so fayer & pertynante, yt semeth vnto manys herying not only the worde, but veryly the thyng. Caxton's Book of Curtesye, 1. 343-346 (ed., E. E. Text Society).

IN the party of which our travelers found themselves members, was Duff Brown, the great railroad contractor, and subsequently a well-known member of Congress; a bluff, jovial Bost'n man, thick-set, close shaven, with a heavy jaw and a low forehead — a very pleasant man if you were not in his way. He had government contracts also, custom houses, and dry-docks, from Portland to New Orleans, and managed to get out of Congress, in appropriations, about weight for weight of gold for the stone furnished.

Associated with him, and also of this party, was Rodney Schaick, a sleek New York broker, a man as prominent in the church as in the Stock Exchange, dainty in his dress, smooth of speech, the necessary complement of Duff Brown in any enterprise that needed assurance and adroitness.

(143)

It would be difficult to find a pleasanter traveling party, one that shook off more readily the artificial restraints of Puritanic strictness, and took the world with goodnatured allowance. Money was plenty for every attainable luxury, and there seemed to be no doubt that its supply would continue, and that fortunes were about to be made without a great deal of toil. Even Philip soon caught the prevailing spirit; Harry did not need any inoculation, he always talked in six figures. It was as natural for the dear boy to be rich as it is for most people to be poor.

The elders of the party were not long in discovering the fact, which almost all travelers to the West soon find out, that the water was poor. It must have been by a lucky premonition of this that they all had brandy flasks with which to qualify the water of the country; and it was no doubt from an uneasy feeling of the danger of being poisoned that they kept experimenting, mixing a little of the dangerous and changing fluid, as they passed along, with the contents of the flasks, thus saving their lives hour by hour. Philip learned afterward that temperance and the strict observance of Sunday and a certain gravity of deportment are geographical habits, which people do not usually carry with them away from home.

Our travelers stopped in Chicago long enough to see that they could make their fortunes there in two weeks' time, but it did not seem worth while; the

West was more attractive; the further one went the wider the opportunities opened. They took railroad to Alton and the steamboat from there to St. Louis, for the change and to have a glimpse of the river.

"Isn't this jolly?" cried Henry, dancing out of the barber's room, and coming down the deck with a one, two, three step, shaven, curled, and perfumed after his usual exquisite fashion.

"What's jolly?" asked Philip, looking out upon the dreary and monotonous waste through which the shaking steamboat was coughing its way.

"Why, the whole thing; it's immense, I can tell you. I wouldn't give thai to be guaranteed a hundred thousand cold cash in a year's time."

" Where's Mr. Brown?"

" He is in the saloon, playing poker with Schaick, and that long-haired party with the striped trousers, who scrambled aboard when the stage plank was half hauled in, and the big delegate to Congress from out West."

" That's a fine looking fellow, that delegate, with his glossy black whiskers; looks like a Washington man; I shouldn't think he'd be at poker."

" Oh, it's only five cent ante, just to make it interesting, the delegate said."

"But I shouldn't think a representative in Congress would play poker any way in a public steamboat."

" Nonsense, you've got to pass the time. I tried a hand myself, but those old fellows are too many

for me. The delegate knows all the points. I'd bet a hundred dollars he will ante his way right into the United States Senate when his Territory comes in. He's got the cheek for it."

*' He has the grave and thoughtful manner of expectoration of a public man, for one thing," added Philip.

" Harry," said Philip, after a pause, " what have you got on those big boots for; do you expect to wade ashore?"

" I'm breaking 'em in."

The fact was Harry had got himself up in what he thought a proper costume for a new country, and was in appearance a sort of compromise between a dandy of Broadway and a backwoodsman. Harry, with blue eyes, fresh complexion, silken whiskers, and curly chestnut hair, was as handsome as a fashion plate. He wore this morning a soft hat, a short cutaway coat, an open vest displaying immaculate linen, a leathern belt round his waist, and top-boots of soft leather, well polished, that came above his knees and required a string attached to his belt to keep them up. The light-hearted fellow gloried in these shining encasements of his well-shaped legs, and told Philip that they were a perfect protection against prairie rattlesnakes, which never strike above the knee.

The landscape still wore an almost wintry appearance when our travelers left Chicago. It was a genial spring day when they landed at St. Louis; the

birds were singing, the blossoms of peach trees in city garden plots made the air sweet, and in the roar and tumult on the long river levee they found an excitement that accorded with their own hopeful anticipations.

The party went to the Southern Hotel, where the great Duff Brown was very well known, and indeed was a man of so much importance that even the office clerk was respectful to him. He might have respected in him also a certain vulgar swagger and insolence of money, which the clerk greatly admired.

The young fellows liked the house and liked the city; it seemed to them a mighty free and hospitable town. Coming from the East they were struck with many peculiarities. Everybody smoked in the streets, for one thing, they noticed; everybody "took a drink" in an open manner whenever he wished to do so or was asked, as if the habit needed no concealment or apology. In the evening when they walked about they found people sitting on the doorsteps of their dwellings, in a manner not usual in a Northern city; in front of some of the hotels and saloons the sidewalks were filled with chairs and benches — Paris fashion, said Harry—upon which people lounged in these warm spring evenings, smoking, always smoking; and the clink of glasses and of billiard balls was in the air. It was delightful.

Harry at once found on landing that his back-•voods costume would not be needed in St. Louis, j*

and that, in fact, he had need of all the resources of his wardrobe to keep even with the young swells of the town. But this did not much matter, for Harry was always superior to his clothes. As they were likely to be detained some time in the city, Harry told Philip that he was going to improve his time. And he did. It was an encouragement to any industrious man to see this young fellow rise, carefully dress himself, eat his breakfast deliberately, smoke his cigar tranquilly, and then repair to his room, to what he called his work, with a grave and occupied manner, but with perfect cheerfulness.

Harry would take off his coat, remove his cravat, roll up his shirtsleeves, give his curly hair the right touch before the glass, get out his book on engineering, his boxes of instruments, his drawing-paper, his profile paper, open the book of logarithms, mix his India ink, sharpen his pencils, light a cigar, and sit down at the table to " lay out a line," with the most grave notion that he was mastering the details of engineering. He would spend half a day in these preparations without ever working out a problem or having the faintest conception of the use of lines or logarithms. And when he had finished, he had the most cheerful confidence that he had done a good day's work.

It made no difference, however, whether Harry was in his room in a hotel or in a tent, Philip soon found, he was just the same. In camp he would get himself up in the most elaborate toilet at his

command, polish his long boots to the top, lay out his work before him, and spend an hour or longer, if anybody was looking at him, humming airs, knitting his brows, and " working " at engineering; and if a crowd of gaping rustics were looking on all the while it was perfectly satisfactory to him.

" You see," he says to Philip one morning at the hotel when he was thus engaged, " I want to get the theory of this thing, so that I can have a check on the engineers."

" I thought you were going to be an engineer yourself," queried Philip.

" Not many times, if the court knows herself. There's better game. Brown and Schaick have, or will have, the control for the whole line of the Salt Lick Pacific Extension, forty thousand dollars a mile over the prairie, with extra for hardpan — and it'll be pretty much all hardpan, I can tell you; besides every alternate section of land on this line. There's millions in the job. I'm to have the sub-contract for the first fifty miles, and you can bet it's a soft thing."

"I'll tell you what you do, Philip," continued Harry, in a burst of generosity, " if I don't get you into my contract, you'll be with the engineers, and you just stick a stake at the first ground marked for a depot, buy the land of the farmer before he knows where the depot will be, and we'll turn a hundred or so on that. I'll advance the money for the payments, and you can sell the lots. Schaick is going

to let me have ten thousand just for a flyer in such operations."

" But that's a good deal of money."

"Wait till you are used to handling money. I didn't come out here for a bagatelle. My uncle wanted me to stay East and go in on the Mobile custom house, work up the Washington end of it; he said there was a fortune in it for a smart young fellow, but I preferred to take the chances out here. Did I tell you I had an offer from Bobbett and Fanshaw to go into their office as confidential clerk on a salary of ten thousand?"

"Why didn't you take it?" asked Philip, to whom a salary of two thousand would have seemed wealth, before he started on this journey.

" Take it? I'd rather operate on my own hook," said Harry in his most airy manner.

A few evenings after their arrival at the Southern, Philip and Harry made the acquaintance of a very agreeable gentleman, whom they had frequently seen before about the hotel corridors, and passed a casual word with. He had the air of a man of business, and was evidently a person of importance.

The precipitating of this casual intercourse into the more substantial form of an acquaintanceship was the work of the gentleman himself, and occurred in this wise. Meeting the two friends in the lobby one evening, he asked them to give him the time, and added:

" Excuse me, gentlemen — strangers in St. Louis? Ah, yes — yes. From the East, perhaps? Ah, just so, just so. Eastern born myself — Virginia. Sellers is my name — Beriah Sellers. Ah — by the way — New York, did you say? That reminds me; just met some gentlemen from your State a week or two ago — very prominent gentlemen — in public life they are; you must know them, without doubt. Let me see — let me see. Curious those names have escaped me. I know they were from your State, because I remember afterward my old friend, Governor Shackleby, said to me — fine man, is the Governor — one of the finest men our country has produced — said he, 'Colonel, how did you like those New York gentlemen? not many such men in the world, Colonel Sellers,' said the Governor — yes, it was New York he said — I remember it distinctly. I can't recall those names, somehow. But no matter. Stopping here, gentlemen — stopping at the Southern?"

In shaping their reply in their minds, the title " Mr." had a place in it; but when their turn had arrived to speak, the title "Colonel" came from their lips instead.

They said yes, they were abiding at the Southern, and thought it a very good house.

"Yes, yes, the Southern is fair. I myself go to the Planter's, old, aristocratic house. We Southern gentlemen don't change our ways, you know. I always make it my home there when I run down

from Hawkeye — my plantation is in Hawkeye, a little up in the country. You should know the Planter's."

Philip and Harry both said they should like to see a hotel that had been so famous in its day—a cheerful hostelry, Philip said it must have been when duels were fought there across the dining-room table.

" You may believe it, sir, an uncommonly pleasant lodging. Shall we walk?"

And the three strolled along the streets, the Colonel talking all the way in the most liberal and friendly manner, and with a frank open-heartedness that inspired confidence.

"Yes, born East myself, raised all along, know the West—a great country, gentlemen. The place for a young fellow of spirit to pick up a fortune, simply pick it up; it's lying round loose here. Not a day that I don't put aside an opportunity, too busy to look into it. Management of my own property takes my time. First visit? Looking for an opening?"

"Yes, looking around," replied Harry.

" Ah, here we are. You'd rather sit here in front than go to my apartments? So had I. An opening, eh?"

The Colonel's eyes twinkled. " Ah, just so. The whole country is opening up, all we want is capital to develop it. Slap down the rails and bring the land into market. The richest land on God Al-

mighty's footstool is lying right out there. If I had my capital free I could plant it for millions."

" I suppose your capital is largely in your plantation?" asked Philip.

"Well, partly, sir, partly. I'm down here now with reference to a little operation — a little side thing merely. By the way, gentlemen, excuse the liberty, but it's about my usual time—"

The Colonel paused, but as no movement of his acquaintances followed this plain remark, he added, in an explanatory manner:

"I'm rather particular about the exact time — have to be in this climate."

Even this open declaration of his hospitable intention not being understood the Colonel politely said:

" Gentlemen, will you take something?"

Col. Sellers led the way to a saloon on Fourth street under the hotel, and the young gentlemen fell into the custom of the country.

"Not that," said the Colonel to the barkeeper, who shoved along the counter a bottle of apparently corn whisky, as if he had done it before on the same order; "not that," with a wave of the hand. " That Otard, if you please. Yes. Never take an inferior liquor, gentlemen, not in the evening, in this climate. There. That's the stuff. My respects!"

The hospitable gentleman, having disposed of his liquor, remarking that it was not quite the thing — " when a man has his own cellar to go to, he is apt

to get a little fastidious about his liquors "—called for cigars. But the brand offered did not suit him; he motioned the box away, and asked for some particular Havanas, those in separate wrappers.

" I always smoke this sort, gentlemen; they are a little more expensive, but you'll learn, in this climate, that you'd better not economize on poor cigars."

Having imparted this valuable piece of information, the Colonel lighted the fragrant cigar with satisfaction, and then carelessly put his fingers into his right vest pocket. That movement being without result, with a shade of disappointment on his face, he felt in his left vest pocket. Not finding anything there, he looked up with a serious and annoyed air, anxiously slapped his right pantaloons pocket, and then his left, and exclaimed :

" By George, that's annoying. By George, that's mortifying. Never had anything of that kind happen to me before. I've left my pocketbook. Hold! Here's a bill, after all. No, thunder, it's a receipt."

Allow me," said Philip, seeing how seriously the Colonel was annoyed, and taking out his purse.

The Colonel protested he couldn't think of it, and muttered something to the barkeeper about " hanging it up," but the vender of exhilaration made no sign, and Philip had the privilege of paying the costly shot; Col. Sellers profusely apologizing and claiming the right " next time, next time."

As soon as Beriah Sellers had bade his friends good night and seen them depart, he did not retire to apartments in the Planter's, but took his way to his lodgings with a friend in a distant part of the city.

CHAPTER XIV.

AT PHILADELPHIA. RUTH BOLTON INTRODUCED

Pulchra duos inter sita stat Philadelphia rivos;
Inter quos duo sunt millia longa vise. Delawar his major, Sculkil minor ille vocatur;
Indis et Suevis notus uterque diu. Hie plateas mensor spatiis delineat aequis,
Et domui recto est ordine juncta domus.

T. Makin. Vergin era fra lor di gia matura
Verginita, d'alti pensieri e regi, D'alta belta; ma sua belta non cura,
O tanta sol, quant' onesta sen fregi.

THE letter that Philip Sterling wrote to Ruth Bolton, on the evening of setting out to seek his fortune in the West, found that young lady in her own father's house in Philadelphia. It was one of the pleasantest of the many charming suburban houses in that hospitable city, which is territorially one of the largest cities in the world, and only prevented from becoming the convenient metropolis of the country by the intrusive strip of Camden and Amboy sand which shuts it off from the Atlantic Ocean. It is a city of steady thrift, the arms of which might well be the deliberate but delicious terrapin that imparts such a royal flavor to its feasts.

(156)

It was a spring morning, and perhaps it was the influence of it that made Ruth a little restless, satisfied neither with the outdoors nor the indoors. Her sisters had gone to the city to show some country visitors Independence Hall, Girard College, and Fairmount Waterworks and Park, four objects which Americans cannot die peacefully, even in Naples, without having seen. But Ruth confessed that she was tired of them, and also of the Mint. She was tired of other things. She tried this morning an air or two upon the piano, sang a simple song in a sweet, but slightly metallic voice, and then seating herself by the open window, read Philip's letter.

Was she thinking about Philip, as she gazed across the fresh lawn over the treetops to the Chel-ton Hills, or of that world which his entrance into her tradition-bound life had been one of the means of opening to her? Whatever she thought, she was not idly musing, as one might see by the expression of her face. After a time she took up a book; it was a medical work, and to all appearance about as interesting to a girl of eighteen as the statutes at large; but her face was soon aglow over its pages, and she was so absorbed in it that she did not notice the entrance of her mother at the open door.

" Ruth?"

"Well, mother," said the young student, looking up, with a shade of impatience.

I wanted to talk with thee a little about thy plans."

Mother, thee knows I couldn't stand it at West-field; the school stifled me, it's a place to turn young people into dried fruit."

"I know," said Margaret Bolton, with a half anxious smile, " thee chafes against all the ways of Friends, but what will thee do? Why is thee so discontented?"

" If I must say it, mother, I want to go away, and get out of this dead level."

With a look half of pain and half of pity, her mother answered, " I am sure thee is little interfered with; thee dresses as thee will, and goes where thee pleases, to any church thee likes, and thee has music. I had a visit yesterday from the society's committee by way of discipline, because we have a piano in the house, which is against the rules."

" I hope thee told the elders that father and I are responsible for the piano l and that, much as thee loves music, thee is never in the room when it is played. Fortunately father is already out of meeting, so they can't discipline him. I heard father tell Cousin Abner that he was whipped so often for whistling when he was a boy that he was determined to have what compensation he could get now."

"Thy ways greatly try me, Ruth, and all thy relations. I desire thy happiness first of all, but thee is starting out on a dangerous path. Is thy father willing thee should go away to a school of the world's people?"

"I have not asked him," Ruth replied with a

THY WAYS GRKATLY TRY ME, RUTH

look that might imply that she was one of those determined little bodies who first made up her own mind and then compelled others to make up theirs in accordance with hers.

"And when thee has got the education thee wants, and lost all relish for the society of thy friends and the ways of thy ancestors, what then?"

Ruth turned square round to her mother, and with an impassive face and not the slightest change of tone, said:

Mother, I'm going to study medicine!"

Margaret Bolton almost lost for a moment her habitual placidity.

"Thee, study medicine! A slight frail girl like thee, study medicine? Does thee think thee could stand it six months? And the lectures, and the dissecting-rooms, has thee thought of the dissecting-rooms?"

" Mother," said Ruth calmly, " I have thought it all over. I know I can go through the whole, clinics, dissecting-room and all. Does thee think I lack nerve? What is there to fear in a person dead more than in a person living?"

"But thy health and strength, child; thee can never stand the severe application. And, besides, suppose thee does learn medicine?"

" I will practice it."

"Here?"

"Here."

"Where thee and thy family are known?"

 If I can get patients."

"I hope at least, Ruth, thee will let us "know when thee opens an office," said her mother, with an approach to sarcasm that she rarely indulged in, as she rose and left the room.

Ruth sat quite still for a time, with face intent and flushed. It was out now. She had begun her open battle.

The sight-seers returned in high spirits from the city. Was there any building in Greece to compare with Girard College, was there ever such a magnificent pile of stone devised for the shelter of poor orphans? Think of the stone shingles of the roof eight inches thick! Ruth asked the enthusiasts if they would like to live in such a sounding mausoleum, with its great halls and echoing rooms, and no comfortable place in it for the accommodation of anybody? If they were orphans, would they like to be brought up in a Grecian temple?

And then there was Broad street! Wasn't it the broadest and the longest street in the world? There certainly was no end to it, and even Ruth was Philadelphian enough to believe that a street ought not to have any end, or architectural point upon which the weary eye could rest.

But neither St. Girard, nor Broad street, neither wonders of the Mint nor the glories of the Hall where the ghosts of our fathers sit always signing the Declaration, impressed the visitors so much as the splendors of the Chestnut street windows, and the

bargains on Eighth street. The truth is that the country cousins had come to town to attend the Yearly Meeting, and the amount of shopping that preceded that religious event was scarcely exceeded by the preparations for the opera in more worldly circles.

"Is thee going to the Yearly Meeting, Ruth?" asked one of the girls.

" I have nothing to wear," replied that demure person. " If thee wants to see new bonnets, orthodox to a shade and conformed to the letter of the true form, thee must go to the Arch Street Meeting. Any departure from either color or shape would be instantly taken note of. It has occupied mother a long time, to find at the shops the exact shade for her new bonnet. Oh, thee must go, by all means. But thee won't see there a sweeter woman than mother."

"And thee won't go?"

" Why should I? I've been again and again. If I go to Meeting at all I like best to sit in the quiet old house in Germantown, where the windows are all open and I can see the trees, and hear the stir of the leaves. It's such a crush at the Yearly Meeting at Arch street, and then there's the row of sleek-looking young men who line the curbstone and stare at us as we come out. No, I don't feel at home there."

That evening Ruth and her father sat late by the drawing-room fire, as they were quite apt to do at night. It was always a time of confidences.

"Thee has another letter from young Sterling," said Eli Bolton. 11*

" Yes. Philip has gone to the far West."

"How far?"

He doesn't say, but it's on the frontier, and on the map everything beyond it is marked ' Indians ' and 4 desert,' and looks as desolate as a Wednesday Meeting."

" Humph. It was time for him to do something. Is he going to start a daily newspaper among the Kick-a-poos?"

" Father, thee's unjust to Philip. He's going into business."

" What sort of business can a young man go into without capital?"

" He doesn't say exactly what it is," said Ruth, a little dubiously, " but it's something about land and railroads, and thee knows, father, that fortunes are made nobody knows exactly how, in a new country."

" I should think so, you innocent puss, and in an old one too. But Philip is honest, and he has talent enough, if he will stop scribbling, to make his way. But thee may as well take care of theeself, Ruth, and not go dawdling along with a young man in his adventures, until thy own mind is a little more settled what thee wants."

This excellent advice did not seem to impress Ruth greatly, for she was looking away with that abstraction of vision which often came into her gray eyes, and at length she exclaimed, with a sort of impatience:

"I wish I could go West, or South, or some-

where. What a box women are put into, measured for it, and put in young; if we go anywhere it's in a box, veiled and pinioned and shut in by disabilities. Father, I should like to break things and get loose."

What a sweet-voiced little innocent it was, to be sure.

"Thee will no doubt break things enough when thy time comes, child; women always have; but what does thee want now that thee hasn't?"

" I want to be something, to make myself something, to do something. Why should I rust, and be stupid, and sit in inaction because I am a girl? What would happen to me if thee should lose thy property and die? What one useful thing could I do for a living, for the support of mother and the children? And if I had a fortune, would thee want me to lead a useless life?"

" Has thy mother led a useless life? "

" Somewhat that depends upon whether her children amount to anything," retorted the sharp little disputant. "What's the good, father, of a series of human beings who don't advance any?"

Friend Eli, who had long ago laid aside the Quaker dress, and was out of Meeting, and who, in fact after a youth of doubt could not yet define his belief, nevertheless looked with some wonder at this fierce young eagle of his, hatched in a Friend's dovecote. But he only said :

" Has thee consulted thy mother about a career, I suppose it is a career thee wants?"

Ruth did not reply directly; she complained that her mother didn't understand her. But that wise and placid woman understood the sweet rebel a great deal better than Ruth understood herself. She also had a history, possibly, and had sometime beaten her young wings against the cage of custom, and indulged in dreams of a new social order, and had passed through that fiery period when it seems possible for one mind, which has not yet tried its limits, to break up and rearrange the world.

Ruth replied to Philip's letter in due time and in the most cordial and unsentimental manner. Philip liked the letter, as he did everything she did; but he had a dim notion that there was more about herself in the letter than about him. He took it with him from the Southern Hotel, when he went to walk, and read it over and again in an unfrequented street as he stumbled along. The rather commonplace and unformed handwriting seemed to him peculiar and characteristic, different from that of any other woman.

Ruth was glad to hear that Philip had made a push into the world, and she was sure that his talent and courage would make a way for him. She should pray for his success, at any rate, and especially that the Indians, in St. Louis, would not take his scalp.

Philip looked rather dubious at this sentence, and wished that he had written nothing about Indians.

CHAPTER XV.

RUTH STUDIES MEDICINE. A DISSECTING ROOM

— Rationalem quidem puto medicinam esse debere: instrui vero ab evidentibus causis; obscuris omnibus non a cogitatione artificis, sed ab ipsa arte rejectis. Incidere autem vivorum corpora, et crudele, et supervacuura est: mcrtuorum corpora discentibus necessarium.

BOLTON and his wife talked over Ruth's case, as they had often done before, with no little anxiety. Alone of all their children she was impatient of the restraints and monotony of the Friends' Society, and wholly indisposed to accept the *' inner light" as a guide into a life of acceptance and inaction. When Margaret told her husband of Ruth's newest project, he did not exhibit so much surprise as she looked for. In fact, he said that he did not see why a woman should not enter the medical profession if she felt a call to it.

" But," said Margaret, " consider her total inexperience of the world, and her frail health. Can such a slight little body endure the ordeal of the preparation for, or the strain of, the practice of the profession?"

(165)

" Did thee ever think, Margaret, whether she can endure being thwarted in an object on which she has so set her heart, as she has on this? Thee has trained her thyself at home, in her enfeebled childhood, and thee knows how strong her will is, and what she has been able to accomplish in self-culture by the simple force of her determination. She never will be satisfied until she has tried her own strength."

"I wish," said Margaret, with an inconsequence that is not exclusively feminine, " that she were in the way to fall in love and marry by and by. I think that would cure her of some of her notions. I am not sure, but if she went away to some distant school, into an entirely new life, her thoughts would be diverted."

Eli Bolton almost laughed as he regarded his wife, with eyes that never looked at her except fondly, and replied —

" Perhaps thee remembers that thee had notions also, before we were married, and before thee became a member of Meeting. I think Ruth comes honestly by certain tendencies which thee has hidden under the Friend's dress."

Margaret could not say " no " to this, and while she paused, it was evident that memory was busy with suggestions to shake her present opinions.

"Why not let Ruth try the study for a time," suggested Eli; "there is a fair beginning of a Woman's Medical College in the city. Quite likely

she will soon find that she needs first a more general culture, and fall in with thy wish that she should see more of the world at some large school."

There really seemed to be nothing else to be done, and Margaret consented at length without approving. And it was agreed that Ruth, in order to spare her fatigue, should take lodgings with friends near the college and make a trial in the pursuit of that science to which we all owe our lives, and sometimes as by a miracle of escape.

That day Mr. Bolton brought home a stranger to dinner, Mr. Bigler of the great firm of Pennybacker, Bigler & Small, railroad contractors. He was always bringing home somebody, who had a scheme to build a road, or open a mine, or plant a swamp with cane to grow paper-stock, or found a hospital, or invest in a patent shad-bone separator, or start a college somewhere on the frontier, contiguous to a land speculation.

The Bolton house was a sort of hotel for this kind of people. They were always coming.

Ruth had always known them from childhood, and she used to say that her father attracted them as naturally as a sugar hogshead does flies. Ruth had an idea that a large portion of the world lived by getting the rest of the world into schemes. Mr. Bolton never could say " no " to any of them, not even, said Ruth again, to the society for stamping oyster shells with scripture texts before they were sold at retail.

Mr. Bigler's plan this time, about which he talked

loudly, with his mouth full, all dinner time, was the building of the Tunkhannock, Rattlesnake, and Youngwomans-town Railroad, which would not only be a great highway to the West, but would open to market inexhaustible coal-fields and untold millions of lumber. The plan of operations was very simple.

"We'll buy the lands," explained he, "on long time, backed by the notes of good men; and then mortgage them for money enough to get the road well on. Then get the towns on the line to issue their bonds for stock, and sell their bonds for enough to complete the road, and partly stock it, especially if we mortgage each section as we complete it. We can then sell the rest of the stock on the prospect of the business of the road through an improved country, and also sell the lands at a big advance, on the strength of the road. All we want," continued Mr. Bigler in his frank manner, " is a few thousand dollars to start the surveys, and arrange things in the legislature. There is some parties will have to be seen who might make us trouble."

" It will take a good deal of money to start the enterprise," remarked Mr. Bolton, who knew very well what "seeing" a Pennsylvania legislature meant, but was too polite to tell Mr. Bigler what he thought of him, while he was his guest; "what security would one have for it?"

Mr. Bigler smiled a hard kind of smile, and said, "You'd be inside, Mr. Bolton, and you'd have the first chance in the deal."

This was rather unintelligible to Ruth, who was nevertheless somewhat amused by the study of a type of character she had seen before. At length she interrupted the conversation by asking:

" You'd sell the stock, I suppose, Mr. Bigler, to anybody who was attracted by the prospectus?"

"Oh, certainly, serve all alike," said Mr. Bigler, now noticing Ruth for the first time, and a little puzzled by the serene, intelligent face that was turned toward him.

"Well, what would become of the poor people who had been led to put their little money into the speculation, when you got out of it and left it half way?"

It would be no more true to say of Mr. Bigler that he was or could be embarrassed, than to say that a brass counterfeit dollar-piece would change color when refused; the question annoyed him a little, in Mr. Bolton's presence.

Why, yes, Miss, of course, in a great enterprise for the benefit of the community there will little things occur, which, which — and, of course, the poor ought to be looked to; I tell my wife that the poor must be looked to; if you can tell who are poor — there's so many impostors. And, then, there's so many poor in the legislature to be looked after," said the contractor with a sort of chuckle, isn't that so, Mr. Bolton?"

Eli Bolton replied that he never had much to do with the legislature.

"Yes," continued this public benefactor, "an uncommon poor lot this year, uncommon. Consequently an expensive lot. The fact is, Mr. Bolton, that the price is raised so high on United States Senator now, that it affects the whole market; you can't get any public improvement through on reasonable terms. Simony is what I call it, Simony," repeated Mr. Bigler, as if he had said a good thing.

Mr. Bigler went on and gave some very interesting details of the intimate connection between railroads and politics, and thoroughly entertained himself all dinner time, and as much disgusted Ruth, who asked no more questions, and her father who replied in monosyllables.

" I wish," said Ruth to her father, after the guest had gone, "that you wouldn't bring home any more such horrid men. Do all men who wear big diamond breastpins flourish their knives at table, and use bad grammar, and cheat?"

" Oh, child, thee mustn't be too observing. Mr. Bigler is one of the most important men in the State; nobody has more influence at Harrisburg. I don't like him any more than thee does, but I'd better lend him a little money than to have his ill-will."

"Father, I think thee'd better have his ill-will than his company. Is it true that he gave money to help build the pretty little church of St. James the Less, and that he is one of the vestrymen?"

" Yes. He is not such a bad fellow. One of the men in Third street asked him the other day, whether his was a high church or a low church? Bigler said he didn't know; he'd been in it once, and he could touch the ceiling in the side aisle with his hand."

" I think he's just horrid," was Ruth's final summary of him, after the manner of the swift judgment of women, with no consideration of the extenuating circumstances. Mr. Bigler had no idea that he had not made a good impression on the whole family; he certainly intended to be agreeable. Margaret agreed with her daughter, and though she never said anything to such people, she was grateful to Ruth for sticking at least one pin into him.

Such was the serenity of the Bolton household that a stranger in it would never have suspected there was any opposition to Ruth's going to the medical school. And she went quietly to take her residence in town, and began her attendance of the lectures, as if it were the most natural thing in the world. She did not heed, if she heard, the busy and wondering gossip of relations and acquaintances, gossip that has no less currency among the Friends than elsewhere because it is whispered slyly and creeps about in an undertone.

Ruth was absorbed, and for the first time in her life thoroughly happy — happy in the freedom of her life, and in the keen enjoyment of the investigation that broadened its field day by day. She was in

high spirits when she came home to spend First Days; the house was full of her gayety and her merry laugh, and the children wished that Ruth would neve, go away again. But her mother noticed, with a little anxiety, the sometimes flushed face, and the sign of an eager spirit in the kindling eyes, and, as well, the serious air of determination and endurance in her face at unguarded moments.

The college was a small one, and it sustained itself not without difficulty in this city, which is so conservative, and is yet the origin of so many radical movements. There were not more than a dozen attendants on the lectures all together, so that the enterprise had the air of an experiment, and the fascinatn of pioneering for those engaged in it. There was one woman physician driving about town in her carriage, attacking the most violent diseases in all quarters with persistent courage, like a modern Beliona in her war chariot, who was popularly supposed to gather in fees to the amount of ten to twenty thousand dollars a year. Perhaps some of these students looked forward to the near day when they would support such a practice and a husband besides, but it is unknown that any of them ever went further than practice in hospitals and in their own nurseries, and it is feared that some of them were quite as ready as their sisters, in emergencies, to " call a man."

If Ruth had any exaggerated expectations of a professional life, she kept them to herself, and was

known to her fellows of the class simply as a cheerful, sincere student, eager in her investigations, and never impatient at anything, except an insinuation that women had not as much mental capacity for science as men.

" They really say," said one young Quaker sprig to another youth of his age, "that Ruth Bolton is really going to be a sawbones, attends lectures, cuts up bodies, and all that. She's cool enough for a surgeon, anyway." He spoke feelingly, for he had very likely been weighed in Ruth's calm eyes sometime, and thoroughly scared by the little laugh that accompanied a puzzling reply to one of his. conversational nothings. Such young gentlemen,, at this time, did not come very distinctly into Ruth's horizon, except as amusing circumstances.

About the details of her student life, Ruth said very little to her friends, but they had reason to know, afterwards, that it required all her nerve and the almost complete exhaustion of her physical strength, to carry her through. She began her anatomical practice upon detached portions of the human frame, which were brought into the demonstrating room — dissecting the eye, the ear, and a small tangle of muscles and nerves — an occupation which had not much more savor of death in it than the analysis of a portion of a plant out of which the life went when it was plucked up by the roots. Custom inures the most sensitive persons to that which is at first most repellent; and in the late war

we saw the most delicate women, who could not at home endure the sight of blood, become so used to scenes of carnage, that they walked the hospitals and the margins of battlefields, amid the poor remnants of torn humanity, with as perfect self-possession as if they were strolling in a flower garden.

It happened that Ruth was one evening deep in a line of investigation which she could not finish or understand without demonstration, and so eager was she in it, that it seemed as if she could not wait till the next day. She, therefore, persuaded a fellow student, who was reading that evening with her, to go down to the dissecting room of the college, and ascertain what they wanted to know by an hour's work there. Perhaps, also, Ruth wanted to test her own nerve, and to see whether the power of association was stronger in her mind than her own will.

The janitor of the shabby and comfortless old building admitted the girls, not without suspicion, and gave them lighted candles, which they would need, without other remark than "there's a new one, miss,'" as the girls went up the broad stairs.

They climbed to the third story, and paused before a door, which they unlocked, and which admitted them into a long apartment, with a row of windows on one side and one at the end. The room was without light, save from the stars and the candles the girls carried, which revealed to them dimly two long and several small tables, a few benches and chairs, a couple of skeletons hanging

on the wall, a sink, and cloth-covered heaps of something upon the tables here and there.

The windows were open, and the cool night wind came in strong enough to flutter a white covering now and then, and to shake the loose casements. But all the sweet odors of the night could not take from the room a faint suggestion of mortality.

The young ladies paused a moment. The room itself was familiar enough, but night makes almost any chamber eerie, and especially such a room of detention as this where the mortal parts of the un-buried might almost be supposed to be visited, on the sighing night winds, by the wandering spirits of their late tenants.

Opposite and at some distance across the roofs of lower buildings, the girls saw a tall edifice, the long upper story of which seemed to be a dancing hall. The windows of that were also open, and through them they heard the scream of the jiggered and tortured violin, and the pump, pump of the oboe, and saw the moving shapes of men and women in quick transition, and heard the prompter's drawl.

" I wonder," said Ruth, " what the girls dancing there would think if they saw us, or knew that there was such a room as this so near them."

She did not speak very loud, and, perhaps unconsciously, the girls drew near to each other as they approached the long table in the center of the room. A straight object lay upon it, covered with a sheet. This was doubtless "the new one" of

which the janitor spoke. Ruth advanced, and with a not very steady hand lifted the white covering from the upper part of the figure and turned it down. Both the girls started. It was a negro. The black face seemed to defy the pallor of death, and asserted an ugly life-likeness that was frightful. Ruth was as pale as the white sheet, and her comrade whispered, " Come away, Ruth, it is awful."

Perhaps it was the wavering light of the candles, perhaps it was only the agony from a death of pain, but the repulsive black face seemed to wear a scowl that said, " Haven't you yet done with the outcast, persecuted black man, but you must now haul him from his grave, and send even your women to dismember his body?"

Who is this dead man, one of thousands who died yesterday, and will be dust anon, to protest that science shall not turn his worthless carcass to some account?

Ruth could have had no such thought, for with a pity in her sweet face, that for the moment overcame fear and disgust, she reverently replaced the covering, and went away to her own table, as her companion did to hers. And there for an hour they worked at their several problems, without speaking, but not without an awe of the presence there, " the new one," and not without an awful sense of life itself, as they heard the pulsations of the music and the light laughter from the dancing hall.

When, at length, they went away, and locked the.

dreadful room behind them, and came out into the street, where people were passing, they, for the first time, realized, in the relief they felt, what a nervous strain they had been under.

CHAPTER XVI.

MODEL RAILROAD ENGINEER. SURVEY TO STONE'S LANDING

Todifnbuch, 117,

WHILE Ruth was thus absorbed in her new occupation, and the spring was wearing away, Philip and his friends were still detained at the Southern Hotel. The great contractors had concluded their business with the state and railroad officials and with the lesser contractors, and departed for the East. But the serious illness of one of the engineers kept Philip and Henry in the city and occupied in alternate watchings.

Philip wrote to Ruth of the new acquaintance they had made, Col. Sellers, an enthusiastic and hospitable gentleman, very much interested in the development of the country, and in their success. They had not had an opportunity to visit at his place " up in the country" yet, but the Colonel often dined with them, and in confidence, confided

(17!)

to them his projects, and seemed to take a great liking to them, especially to his friend Harry. It was true that he never seemed to have ready money, but he was engaged in very large operations.

The correspondence was not very brisk between these two young persons, so differently occupied; for though Philip wrote long letters, he got brief ones in reply, full of sharp little observations however, such as one concerning Col. Sellers, namely, that such men dined at their house every week.

Ruth's proposed occupation astonished Philip immensely, but while he argued it and discussed it, he did not dare hint to her his fear that it would interfere with his most cherished plans. He too sincerely respected Ruth's judgment to make any protest, however, and he would have defended her course against the world.

This enforced waiting at St. Louis was very irksome to Philip. His money was running away, for one thing, and he longed to get into the field, and see for himself what chance there was for a fortune or even an occupation. The contractors had given the young men leave to join the engineer corps as soon as they could, but otherwise had made no provision for them, and in fact had left them with only the most indefinite expectations of something large in the future.

Harry was entirely happy, in his circumstances. He very soon knew everybody, from the governor rf the State down to the waiters of the hotel. He L"

had the Wall street slang at his tongue'send; he always talked like a capitalist, and entered with enthusiasm into all the land and railway schemes with which the air was thick.

Col. Sellers and Harry talked together by the hour and by the day. Harry informed his new friend that he was going out with the engineer corps of the Salt Lick Pacific Extension, but that wasn't his real business.

"I'm to have, with another party," said Harry, "a big contract in the road, as soon as it is let; and, meantime, I'm with the engineers to spy out the best land and the depot sites."

"It's everything," suggested the Colonel, "in knowing where to invest. I've known people throw away their money because they were too consequential to take Sellers' advice. Others, again, have made their pile on taking it. I've looked over the ground, I've been studying it for twenty years. You can't put your finger on a spot in the map of Missouri that I don't know as if I'd made it. When you want to place anything," continued the Colonel, confidently, "just let Beriah Sellers know. That's all."

"Oh, I haven't got much in ready money I can lay my hands on now, but if a fellow could do anything with fifteen or twenty thousand dollars, as a beginning, I shall draw for that when I see the right opening."

"Well, that's something, that's something, fifteeo

or twenty thousand dollars, say twenty — as an advance," said the Colonel reflectively, as if turning over in his mind for a project that could be entered on with such a trifling sum.

"I'll tell you what it is — but only to you, Mr. Brierly, only to you, mind; I've got a little project that I've been keeping. 'It looks small, looks small on paper, but it's got a big future. What should you say, sir, to a city, built up like the rod of Aladdin had touched it, built up in two years, where now you wouldn't expect it anymore than you'd expect a lighthouse on the top of Pilot Knob? and you could own the land ! It can be done, sir. It can be done!"

The Colonel hitched up his chair close to Harry, laid his hand on his knee, and, first looking about him, said in a low voice, "The Salt Lick Pacific Extension is going to run through Stone's Landing! The Almighty never laid out a cleaner.piece of level prairie for a city; and it's the natural center of all that region of hemp and tobacco."

"What makes you think the road will go there? It's twenty miles, on the map, off the straight line of the road?"

" You can't tell what is the straight line till the engineers have been over it. Between us, I have talked with Jeff Thompson, the division engineer. He understands the wants of Stone's Landing, and the claims of the inhabitants — who are to be there. Jeff says that a railroad is for the accommodation of

the people and not for the benefit of gophers; and if he don't run this to Stone's Landing he'll be damned ! You ought to know Jeff; he's one of the most enthusiastic engineers in this Western country, and one of the best fellows that ever looked through the bottom of a glass."

The recommendation was not undeserved. There was nothing that Jeff wouldn't do, to accommodate a friend, from sharing his last dollar with him, to winging him in a duel. When he understood from Col. Sellers how the land lay at Stone's Landing, he cordially shook hands with that gentleman, asked him to drink, and fairly roared out, "Why, God bless my soul, Colonel, a word from one Virginia gentleman to another is ' nuff ced.' There's Stone's Landing been waiting for a railroad more than four thousand years, and damme if she shan't have it."

Philip had not so much faith as Harry in Stone's Landing when the latter opened the project to him, but Harry talked about it as if he already owned that incipient city.

Harry thoroughly believed in all his projects and inventions, and lived day by day in their golden atmosphere. Everybody liked the young fellow, for how could they help liking one of such engaging manners and large fortune ? The waiters at the hotel would do more for him than for any other guest, and he made a great many acquaintances among the people of St. Louis, who liked his sensible and liberal views about the development of the Western

country, and about St. Louis. He said it ought to be the national capital. Harry made partial arrangements with several of the merchants for furnishing supplies for his contract on the Salt Lick Pacific Extension; consulted the maps with the engineers, and went over the profiles with the contractors, figuring out estimates for bids. He was exceedingly busy with those things when he was not at the bedside of his sick acquaintance, or arranging the details of his speculation with Col. Sellers.

Meantime the days went along and the weeks, and the money in Harry's pocket got lower and lower. He was just as liberal with what he had as before; indeed, it was his nature to be free with his money or with that of others, and he could lend or spend a dollar with an air that made it seem like ten. At length, at the end of one week, when his hotel bill was presented, Harry found not a cent in his pocket to meet it. He carelessly remarked to the landlord that he was not that day in funds, but he would draw on New York, and he sat down and wrote to the contractors in that city a glowing letter about the prospects of the road, and asked them to advance a hundred or two, until he got at work. No reply came. He wrote again, in an unoffended business-like tone, suggesting that he had better draw at three days. A short answer came to this, simply saying that money was very tight in Wall street just then, and that he had better join the engineer corps as soon as he could.

But the bill had to be paid, and Harry took it to Philip, and asked him if he thought he hadn't better draw on his uncle. Philip had not much faith in Harry's power of " drawing," and told him that he would pay the bill himself. Whereupon Harry dismissed the matter then and thereafter from his thoughts, and, like a light-hearted good fellow as he was, gave himself no more trouble about his board-bills. Philip paid them, swollen as they were with a monstrous list of extras; but he seriously counted the diminishing bulk of his own hoard, which was all the money he had in the world. Had he not tacitly agreed to share with Harry to the last in this adventure, and would not the generous fellowdivide with him if he, Philip, were in want and Harry had anything?

The fever at length got tired of tormenting the stout young engineer, who lay sick at the hotel, and left him, very thin, a little sallow but an "acclimated " man. Everybody said he was " acclimated " now, and said it cheerfully. What it is to be acclimated to Western fevers no two persons exactly agree. Some day it is a sort of vaccination that renders death by some malignant type of fever less probable. Some regard it as a sort of initiation, like that into the Odd Fellows, which renders one liable to his regular dues thereafter. Others consider it merely the acquisition of a habit of taking every morning before breakfast a dose of bitters, composed of whisky and asafoetida, out of the acclimation jug.

Jeff Thompson afterwards told Philip that he once asked Senator Atchison, then acting vice-president of the United States, about the possibility of acclimation ; he thought the opinion of the second officer of our great government would be valuable on this point. They were sitting together on a bench before a country tavern, in the free converse permitted by our democratic habits. suppose, Senator, that you have become acclimated to this country?"

" Well," said the vice-president, crossing his legs, pulling his wideawake down over his forehead, causing a passing chicken to hop quickly one side by the accuracy of his aim, and speaking with senatorial deliberation,think I have. I've been here twenty-five years, and dash dash my dash to dash, if I haven't entertained twenty-five separate and distinct earthquakes, one a year. The niggro is the only person who can stand the fever and ague of this region."

The convalescence of the engineer was the signal for breaking up quarters at St. Louis, and the young fortune-hunters started up the river in good spirits. It was only the second time either of them had been upon a Mississippi steamboat, and nearly everything they saw had the charm of novelty. Col. Sellers was at the landing to bid them good-bye.

' ' I shall send you up that basket of champagne by the next boat; no, no; no thanks; you'll find it not bad in camp," he cried out as the plank was

hauled in. " My respects to Thompson. Tell him to sight for Stone's. Let me know, Mr. Brierly, when you are ready to locate; I'll come over from Hawkeye. Good-bye."

And the last the young fellows saw of the Colonel, he was waving his hat, and beaming prosperity and good luck.

The voyage was delightful, and was not long enough to become monotonous. The travelers scarcely had time indeed to get accustomed to the splendors of the great saloon where the tables were spread for meals, a marvel of paint and gilding, its ceiling hung with fancifully cut tissue-paper of many colors, festooned and arranged in endless patterns. The whole was more beautiful than a barber's shop. The printed bill of fare at dinner was longer and more varied, the proprietors justly boasted, than that of any hotel in New York. It must have been the work of an author of talent and imagination, and it surely was not his fault if the dinner itself was to a certain extent a delusion, and if the guests got something that tasted pretty much the same whatever dish they ordered; nor was it his fault if a general flavor of rose in all the dessert dishes suggested that they had passed through the barber's saloon on their way from the kitchen.

The travelers landed at a little settlement on the left bank, and at once took horses for the camp in the interior, carrying their clothes and blankets strapped behind the saddles. Harry was dressed as

•vre have seen him once before, and his long and shining boots attracted not a little the attention of the few persons they met on the road, and especially of the bright-faced wenches who lightly stepped along the highway, picturesque in their colored kerchiefs, carrying light baskets, or riding upon mules and balancing before them a heavier load.

Harry sang fragments of operas and talked about their fortune. Philip even was excited by the sense of freedom and adventure, and the beauty of the landscape. The prairie, with its new grass and unending acres of brilliant flowers — chiefly the innumerable varieties of phlox — bore the look of years of cultivation, and the occasional open groves of white oaks gave it a park-like appearance. It was hardly unreasonable to expect to see at any moment the gables and square windows of an Elizabethan mansion in one of the well-kept groves.

Toward sunset of the third day, when the young gentlemen thought they ought to be near the town of Magnolia, near which they had been directed to find the engineers' camp, they descried a log-house and drew up before it to enquire the way. Half the building was store, and half was dwelling-house. At the door of the latter stood a negress with a bright turban on her head, to whom Philip called:

"Can you tell me, auntie, how far it is to the town of Magnolia?"

"Why, bress you chile," laughed the woman. you's dere now."

It was true. This log-house was the compactly built town, and all creation was its suburbs. The engineers' camp was only two or three miles distant.

"You's boun' to find it," directed auntie, "if you don't keah numn 'bout de road, and go fo' de sundown."

A brisk gallop brought the riders in sight of the twinkling light of the camp, just as the stars came out. It lay in a little hollow, where a small stre m ran through a sparse grove of young white oaks. A half-dozen tents were pitched under the trees, horses and oxen were corraled at a little distance, and a group of men sat on camp stools or lay on blankets about a bright fire. The twang of a banjo became audible as they drew nearer, and they saw a couple of negroes, from some neighboring plantation, "breaking down" a juba in approved style, amid the " hi, hi's " of the spectators.

Mr. Jeff Thompson, for it was the camp of this redoubtable engineer, gave the travelers a hearty welcome, offered them ground room in his own tent, ordered supper, and set out a small jug, a drop from which he declared necessary on account of the chill of the evening.

" I never saw an Eastern man," said Jeff, " who knew how to drink from a jug with one hand. It's as easy as lying. So." He grasped the handle with the right hand, threw the jug back upon his arm, and applied his lips to the nozzle. It was an act as graceful as it was simple. "Besides," said

Mr. Thompson, setting it down, " it puts every man on his honor as to quantity."

Early to turn in was the rule of the camp, and by nine o'clock everybody was under his blanket, except Jeff himself, who worked awhile at his table over his fieldbook, and then arose, stepped outside the tent door and sang, in a strong and not unmelo-dious tenor, the " Star Spangled Banner" from beginning to end. It proved to be his nightly practice to let off the unexpended steam of his conversational powers, in the words of this stirring song.

It was a long time before Philip got to sleep. He saw the fire light, he saw the clear stars through the tree-tops, he heard the gurgle of the stream, the stamp of the horses, the occasional barking of the dog which followed the cook's wagon, the hooting of an owl; and when these failed he saw Jeff, standing on a battlement, mid the rocket's red glare, and heard him sing, "Oh, say, can you see?" It wa< the first time he had ever slept on the ground. 13*

CHAPTER XVII.

STONE'S LANDING BECOMES CITY OF NAPOLEON —ON PAPER

— " We have view'd it, And measur'd it within all by the scale: The richest tract of land, love, in the kingdom! There will be made seventeen or eighteen millions, Or more, as't may be handled!

Ben. Jonson. The Devil is an Ass.

NOBODY dressed more like an engineer than Mr. Henry Brierly. The completeness of his appointments was the envy of the corps, and the gay fellow himself was the admiration of the camp servants, axemen, teamsters, and cooks.

" I reckon you didn't git them boots no wher's this side o' Sent Louis?" queried the tall Missouri youth who acted as commissary's assistant.

"No, New York."

" Yas, I've heern o' New York," continued the butternut lad, attentively studying each item of Harry's dress, and endeavoring to cover his design with interesting conversation. " 'N there's Massachusetts."

" It' snot far off."

"I've heern Massachusetts was a of a place.

Les' see, what state's Massachusetts in?"

(190)

"Massachusetts," kindly replied Harry, "is in the state of Boston."

" Abolish'n wan't it? They must a cost right smart," referring to the boots.

Harry shouldered his rod and went to the field, tramped over the prairie by day, and figured up results at night, with the utmost cheerfulness and industry, and plotted the line on the profile paper, without, however, the least idea of engineering, practical or theoretical. Perhaps there was not a great deal of scientific knowledge in the entire corps, nor was very much needed. They were making what is called a preliminary survey, and the chief object of a preliminary survey was to get up an excitement about the road, to interest every town in that part of the state in it, under the belief that the road would run through it, and to get the aid of every planter upon the prospect that a station would be on his land.

Mr. Jeff Thompson was the most popular engineer who could be found for this work. He did not bother himself much about details or practicabilities of location, but ran merrily along, sighting from the top of one divide to the top of another, and striking " plumb " every town site and big plantation within twenty or thirty miles of his route. In his own language he "just went booming."

This course gave Harry an opportunity, as he said, to learn the practical details of engineering, and it gave Philip a chance to see the country, and

to judge for himself what prospect of a fortune it offered. Both he and Harry got the "refusal" of more than one plantation as they went along, and wrote urgent letters to their Eastern correspondents, upon the beauty of the land and the certainty that it would quadruple in value as soon as the road was finally located. It seemed strange to them that capitalists did not flock out there and secure this land.

They had not been in the field over two weeks when Harry wrote to his friend, Col. Sellers, that he'd better be on the move, for the line was certain to go to Stone's Landing. Any one who looked at the line on the map, as it was laid down from day to day, would have been uncertain which way it was going; but Jeff had declared that in his judgment the only practicable route from the point they then stood on was to follow the divide to Stone's Landing, and it was generally understood that that town would be the next one hit.

"We'll make it, boys," said the chief, "if we have to go in a balloon."

And make it they did. In less than a week, this indomitable engineer had carried his moving caravan over slues and branches, across bottoms and along divides, and pitched his tents in the very heart of the city of Stone's Landing.

"Well, I'll be dashed," was heard the cheery voice of Mr. Thompson, as he stepped outside the tent door at sunrise next morning. "If this don't

get me. I say, you, Grayson, get out your sighting iron and see if you can find old

Sellers's town. Blame me if we wouldn't have run plumb by it if twilight had held on a little longer. Oh! Sterling, Brierly, get up and see the city. There's a steamboat just coming round the bend." And Jeff roared with laughter. "The mayor'll be round here to breakfast."

The fellows turned out of the tents, rubbing their eyes, and stared about them. They were camped on the second bench of the narrow bottom of a crooked, sluggish stream, that was some five rods wide in the present good stage of water. Before them were a dozen log cabins, with stick and mud chimneys, irregularly disposed on either side of a not very well defined road, which did not seem to know its own mind exactly, and, after straggling through the town, wandered off over the rolling prairie in an uncertain way, as if it had started for nowhere and was quite likely to reach its destination. Just as it left the town, however, it was cheered and assisted by a guideboard, upon which was the legend " 10 Mils to Hawkeye."

The road had never been made except by the travel over it, and at this season — the rainy June — it was a way of ruts cut in the black soil, and of fathomless mud-holes. In the principal street of the city it had received more attention; for hogs, great and small, rooted about in it and wallowed in it, turning the street into a liquid quagmire which could 13*

only be crossed on pieces of plank thrown here and there.

About the chief cabin, which was the store and grocery of this mart of trade, the mud was more liquid than elsewhere, and the rude platform in front of it and the dry-goods boxes mounted thereon were places of refuge for all the loafers of the place. Down by the stream was a dilapidated building which served for a hemp warehouse, and a shaky wharf extended out from it into the water. In fact, a flat-boat was there moored by it, its setting poles lying across the gunwales. Above the town the stream was crossed by a crazy wooden bridge, the supports of which leaned all ways in the soggy soil; the absence of a plank here and there in the flooring made the crossing of the bridge faster than a walk an offense not necessary to be prohibited by law.

"This, gentlemen," said Jeff, "is Columbus River, alias Goose Run. If it was widened, and deepened, and straightened, and made long enough, it would be one of the finest rivers in the Western country."

As the sun rose and sent his level beams along the stream, the thin stratum of mist, or malaria, rose also and dispersed, but the light was not able to snliven the dull water nor give any hint of its apparently fathomless depth. Venerable mud-turtles crawled up and roosted upon the old logs in the stream, their backs glistening in the sun, the first

inhabitants of the metropolis to begin the active business of the day.

It was not long, however, before smoke began to issue from the city chimneys; and before the engineers had finished breakfast they were the object of the curious inspection of six or eight boys and men, who lounged into the camp and gazed about them with languid interest, their hands in their pockets, every one.

" Good morning, gentlemen," called out the chief engineer, from the table.

" Good mawning," drawled out the spokesman of the party. "I allow thish-yers the railroad, I heern it was a-comin'."

"Yes, this is the railroad, all but the rails and the iron-horse."

" I reckon you kin git all the rails you want outen my white oak timber over thar," replied the first speaker, who appeared to be a man of property and willing to strike up a trade.

"You'll have to negotiate with the contractors about the rails, sir," said Jeff; " here's Mr. Brierly, I've no doubt would like to buy your rails when the time comes."

"Oh," said the man, " I thought maybe you'd fetch the whole bilin along with you. But if you want rails, I've got em, haint I Eph."

" Heaps," said Eph, without taking his eyes off the group at the table.

" Well," said Mr. Thompson, rising from his seat

and moving towards his tent, " the railroad has come to Stone's Landing, sure; I move we take a drink on it all round."

The proposal met with universal favor. Jeff gave prosperity to Stone's Landing and navigation to Goose Run, and the toast was washed down with gusto, in the simple fluid of corn, and with the return compliment that a railroad was a good thing, and that Jeff Thompson was no slouch.

About ten o'clock a horse and wagon was descried making a slow approach to the camp over the prairie. As it drew near, the wagon was seen to contain a portly gentleman, who hitched impatiently forward on his seat, shook the reins and gently touched up his horse, in the vain attempt to communicate his own energy to that dull beast, and looked eagerly at the tents. When the conveyance at length drew up to Mr. Thompson's door, the gentleman descended with great deliberation, straightened himself up, rubbed his hands, and, beaming satisfaction from every part of his radiant frame, advanced to the group that was gathered to welcome him, and which had saluted him by name as soon as he came within hearing.

" Welcome to Napoleon, gentlemen, welcome. I am proud to see you here' Mr. Thompson. You are looking well Mr. Sterling. This is the country, sir. Right glad to see you Mr. Brierly. You got that basket of champagne? No? Those blasted river thieves! I'll never send anything more by

'em. The best brand, Roederer. The last I had in my cellar, from a lot sent me by Sir George Gore — took him out on a buffalo hunt, when he visited our country. Is always sending me some trifle. You haven't looked about any yet, gentlemen? It's in the rough yet, in the rough. Those buildings will all have to come down. That's the place for the public square, court-house, hotels, churches, jail — all that sort of thing. About where we stand, the deepo. How does that strike your engineering eye, Mr. Thompson? Down yonder the business streets, running to the wharves. The University up there, on rising ground, sightly place, see the river for miles. That's Columbus River, only forty-nine miles to the Missouri. You see what it is, placid, steady, no current to interfere with navigation, wants widening in places and dredging, dredge out the harbor and raise a levee in front of the town; made by nature on purpose for a mart. Look at all this country, not another building within ten miles, no other navigable stream, lay of the land points right here; hemp, tobacco, corn, must come here. The railroad will do it, Napoleon won't know itself in a year."

"Don't now, evidently," said Philip aside to Harry. " Have you breakfasted, Colonel?"

"Hastily. Cup of coffee. Can't trust any coffee I don't import myself. But I put up a basket of provisions; wife would put in a few delicacies, women always will, and a half-dozen .of that

Burgundy, I was telling you of, Mr. Brierly. By the way, you never got to dine with me." And the Colonel strode away to the wagon and looked under the seat for the basket.

Apparently it was not there. For the Colonel raised up the flap, looked in front and behind, and then exclaimed:

" Confound it! That comes of not doing a thing yourself. I trusted to the women folks to set that basket in the wagon, and it ain't there."

The camp cook speedily prepared a savory breakfast for the Colonel, broiled chicken, eggs, corn-bread, and coffee, to which he did ample justice, and topped off with a drop of Old Bourbon, from Mr. Thompson's private store, a brand which he said he knew well, he should think it came from his own sideboard.

While the engineer corps went to the field, to run back a couple of miles and ascertain, approximately, if a road could ever get down to the Landing, and to sight ahead across the Run, and see if it could ever get out again, Col. Sellers and Harry sat down and began to roughly map out the city of Napoleon on a large piece of drawing paper.

" I've got the refusal of a mile square here," said the Colonel, " in our names, for a year, with a quarter interest reserved for the four owners."

They laid out the town liberally, not lacking room, leaving space for the railroad to come in, and for the river as it was to be when improved.

The engineers reported that the railroad could come in, by taking a little sweep and crossing the stream on a high bridge, but the grades would be steep. Col. Sellers said he didn't care so much about the grades, if the road could only be made to reach the elevators on the river. The next day Mr. Thompson made a hasty survey of the stream for a mile or two, so that the Colonel and Harry were enabled to show on their map how nobly that would accommodate the city. Jeff took a little writing from the Colonel and Harry for a prospective share, but Philip declined to join in, saying that he had no money, and didn't want to make engagements he couldn't fulfill.

The next morning the camp moved on, followed till it was out of sight by the listless eyes of the group in front of the store, one of whom remarked that, " he'd be doggoned if he ever expected to see that railroad any mo'."

Harry went with the Colonel to Hawkeye to complete their arrangements, a part of which was the preparation of a petition to Congress for the improvement of the navigation of Columbus River.

CHAPTER XVIII.
LAURA DECEIVED BY A MOCK MARRIAGE
Bedda ag Id da.
— " E ve us lo covinentz qals er, Que voill que m prendatz a tnoiler.
— Qu'en aissi 1'a Dieus establida,
Per que not pot esser partida." Roman de Jaufre. Raynouard. Lexique Roman, i. 139.

FLIGHT years have passed since the death of Mr. L- Hawkins. Eight years are not many in the life of a nation or the history of a state, but they may be years of destiny that shall fix the current of the century following. Such years were those that followed the little scrimmage on Lexington Common. Such years were those that followed the double-shotted demand for the surrender of Fort Sumter. History is never done with inquiring of these years, and summoning witnesses about them, and trying to understand their significance.

The eight years in America from 1860 to 1868 uprooted institutions that were centuries old,

(200)

changed the politics of a people, transformed the social life of half the country, and wrought so profoundly upon the entire national character that the influence cannot be measured short of two or three generations.

As we are accustomed to interpret the economy of providence, the life of the individual is as nothing to that of the nation or the race; but who can say, in the broader view and the more intelligent weight of values, that the life of one man is not more than that of a nationality, and that there is not a tribunal where the tragedy of one human soul shall not seem more significant than the overturning of any human institution whatever?

When one thinks of the tremendous forces of the upper and the nether world which play for the mastery of the soul of a woman during the few years in which she passes from plastic girlhood to the ripe maturity of womanhood, he may well stand in awe before the momentous drama.

What capacities she has of purity, tenderness, goodness; what capacities of vileness, bitterness, and evil. Nature must needs be lavish with the mother and creator of men, and center in her all the possibilities of life. And a few critical years can decide whether her life is to be full of sweetness and light, whether she is to be the vestal of a holy temple, or whether she will be the fallen priestess of a desecrated shrine. There are women, it is true, who seem to be capable neither of rising much nor of

falling much, and whom a conventional life saves from any special development of character.

But Laura was not one of them. She had the fatal gift of beauty, and that more fatal gift which does not always accompany mere beauty, the power of fascination, a power that may, indeed, exist without beauty. She had will, and pride, and courage, and ambition, and she was left to be very much her own guide at the age when romance comes to the aid of passion, and when the awakening powers of her vigorous mind had little object on which to discipline themselves.

The tremendous conflict that was fought in this girl's soul none of those about her knew, and very few knew that her life had in it anything unusual or romantic or strange.

Those were troublous days in Hawkeye as well as in most other Missouri towns, days of confusion, when between Unionist and Confederate occupations^ sudden maraudings and bushwhackings and raids, individuals escaped observation or comment in actions that would have filled the town with scandal in quiet times.

Fortunately, we only need to deal with Laura's life at this period historically, and look back upon such portions of it as will serve to reveal the woman as she was at the time of the arrival of Mr. Harry Brierly in Hawkeye.

The Hawkins family were settled there, and had a hard enough struggle with poverty and the neces-

sity of keeping up appearances in accord with their own family pride and the large expectations they secretly cherished of a fortune in the Knobs of East Tennessee. How pinched they were perhaps no one knew but Clay, to whom they looked for almost their whole support. Washington had been in Hawkeye off and on, attracted away occasionally by some tremendous speculation, from which he invariably returned to Gen. Boswell's office as poor as he went. He was the inventor of no one knew how many useless contrivances, which were not worth patenting, and his years had been passed in dreaming and planning to no purpose; until he was now a man of about thirty, without a profession or a permanent occupation, a tall, brown-haired, dreamy person of the best intentions and the frailest resolution. Probably, however, the eight years had been happier to him than to any others in his circle, for the time had been mostly spent in a blissful dream of the coming of enormous wealth.

He went out with a company from Hawkeye to the war, and was not wanting in courage, but he would have been a better soldier if he had been less engaged in contrivances for circumventing the enemy by strategy unknown to the books.

It happened to him to be captured in one of his self-appointed expeditions, but the Federal colonel released him, after a short examination, satisfied that he could most injure the Confederate forces opposed to the Unionists by returning him to his regiment.

Col. Sellers was of course a prominent man during the war. He was captain of the home guards in Hawkeye, and he never left home except upon one occasion, when, on the strength of a rumor, he executed a flank movement and fortified Stone's Landing, a place which no one unacquainted with the country would be likely to find.

"Gad," said the Colonel afterwards, "the Landing is the key to upper Missouri, and it is the only place the enemy never captured. If other places had been defended as well as that was, the result would have been different, sir."

The Colonel had his own theories about war, as he had in other things. If everybody had stayed at home as he did, he said, the South never would have been conquered. For what would there have been to conquer? Mr. Jeff Davis was constantly writing him to take command of a corps in the Confederate army, but Col. Sellers said, no, his duty was at home. And he was by no means idle. He was the inventor of the famous air torpedo, which came very near destroying the Union armies in Missouri, and the city of St. Louis itself.

His plan was to fill a torpedo with Greek fire and poisonous and deadly missiles, attach it to a balloon, and then let it sail away over the hostile camp and explode at the right moment, when the time-fuse burned out. He intended to use this invention in

the capture of St. Louis, exploding his torpedoes over the city, and raining destruction upon it until the army of occupation would gladly capitulate. He was unable to procure the Greek fire, but he constructed a vicious torpedo which would have answered the purpose, but the first one prematurely exploded in his woodhouse, blowing it clean away, and setting fire to his house. The neighbors helped him put out the conflagration, but they discouraged any more experiments of that sort.

The patriotic old gentleman, however, planted so much powder and so many explosive contrivances in the roads leading into Hawkeye, and then forgot the exact spots of danger, that people were afraid to travel the highways, and used to come to town across the fields. The Colonel's motto was: " Millions for defense, but not one cent for tribute."

When Laura came to Hawkeye she might have forgotten the annoyances of the gossips of Mur-pheysburg and have outlived the bitterness that was growing in her heart, if she had been thrown less upon herself, or if the surroundings of her life had been more congenial and helpful. But she had little society, less and less as she grew older that was congenial to her, and her mind preyed upon itself, and the mystery of her birth at once chagrined her and raised in her the most extravagant expectations.

She was proud and she felt the sting of poverty. She could not but be conscious of her beauty also, and she was vain of that, and came to take a sort of

delight in the exercise of her fascinations upon the rather loutish young men who came in her way and whom she despised.

There was another world opened to her — a world of books. But it was not the best world of that sort, for the small libraries she had access to in Hawkeye were decidedly miscellaneous, and largely made up of romances and fictions which fed her imagination with the most exaggerated notions of life, and showed her men and women in a very false sort of heroism. From these stories she learned what a woman of keen intellect and some culture, Joined to beauty and fascination of manner, might expect to accomplish in society as she read of it; and along with these ideas she imbibed other very crude ones in regard to the emancipation of woman.

There were also other books — histories, biographies of distinguished people, travels in far lands, poems, especially those of Byron, Scott and Shelley and Moore, which she eagerly absorbed, and appropriated therefrom what was to her liking. Nobody in Hawkeye had read so much or, after a fashion, studied so diligently as Laura. She passed for an accomplished girl, and no doubt thought herself one, as she was, judged by any standard near her.

During the war there came to Hawkeye a Confederate officer, Col. Selby, who was stationed there for a time, in command of that district. He was a

handsome, soldierly man of thirty years, a graduate of the University of Virginia, and of distinguished family, if his story might be believed, and, it was evident, a man of the world and of extensive travel and adventure.

To find in such an out-of-the-way country place a woman like Laura was a piece of good luck upon which Col. Selby congratulated himself. He was studiously polite to her and treated her with a consideration to which she was unaccustomed. She had read of such men, but she had never seen one before, one so high-bred, so noble in sentiment, so entertaining in conversation, so engaging in manner.

It is a long story; unfortunately it is an old story, and it need not be dwelt on. Laura loved him, and believed that his love for her was as pure and deep as her own. She worshiped him, and would have counted her life a little thing to give him, if he would only love her and let her feed the hunger of her heart upon him.

The passion possessed her whole being, and lifted her up, till she seemed to walk on air. It was all true, then, the romances she had read, the bliss of love she had dreamed of. Why had she never noticed before how blithesome the world was, how jocund with love; the birds sang it, the trees whispered it to her as she passed, the very flowers beneath her feet strewed the way as for a bridal march.

When the Colonel went away they were- engaged to be married, as soon as he could make certain

arrangements which he represented to be necessary, and quit the army.

He wrote to her from Harding, a small town in the southwest corner of the State, saying that he should be held in the service longer than he had expected, but that it would not be more than a few months, then he should be at liberty to take her to Chicago where he had property, and should have business, either now or as soon as the war was over, which he thought could not last long. Meantime why should they be separated ? He was established in comfortable quarters, and if she could find company and join him, they would be married, and gain so many more months of happiness.

Was woman ever prudent when she loved? Laura went to Harding, the neighbors supposed to nurse Washington who had fallen ill there.

Her engagement was, of course, known in Hawk-eye, and was indeed a matter of pride to her family. Mrs. Hawkins would have told the first inquirer that Laura had gone to be married; but Laura had cautioned her; she did not want to be thought of, she said, as going in search of a husband; let the news come back after she was married.

So she traveled to Harding on the pretence we have mentioned, and was married. She was married, but something must have happened on that very day or the next that alarmed her. Washington did not know then or after what it was, but Laura bound him not to send news of her marriage to

Hawkeye yet, and to enjoin her mother not to speak of it. Whatever cruel suspicion or nameless dread this was, Laura tried bravely to put it away, and not let it cloud her happiness.

Communication that summer, as maybe imagined, was neither regular nor frequent between the remote Confederate camp at Harding and Hawkeye, and Laura was in a measure lost sight of — indeed, every one had troubles enough of his own without borrowing from his neighbors.

Laura had given herself utterly to her husband, and if he had faults, if he was selfish, if he was sometimes coarse, if he was dissipated, she did not or would not see it. It was the passion of her life, the time when her whole nature went to flood tide and swept away all barriers. Was her husband ever cold or indifferent? She shut her eyes to everything but her sense of possession of her idol.

Three months passed. One morning her husband informed her that he had been ordered South, and must go within two hours.

" I can be ready," said Laura, cheerfully.

"But I can't take you. You must go back to Hawkeye."

" Can't — take — me?" Laura asked, with wonder in her eyes. " I can't live without you. You said — "

" O bother what I said "—and the Colonel took up his sword to buckle it on, and then continued coolly, ** the fact is, Laura, our romance is played out."

14*

Laura heard, but she did not comprehend. She caught his arm and cried, "George, how can you joke so cruelly? I will go anywhere with you. I will wait anywhere. I can't go back to Hawkeye."

"Well, go where you like. Perhaps," continued he with a sneer, " you would do as well to wait here, for another colonel."

Laura's brain whirled. She did not yet comprehend. "What does this mean? Where are you going?"

" It means," said the officer, in measured words, " that you haven't anything to show for a legal marriage, and that I am going to New Orleans."

" It's a lie, George, it's a lie. I am your w?fe. I shall go. I shall follow you to New Orleans."

*' Perhaps my wife might not like it!"

Laura raised her head, her eyes flamed with fire, she tried to utter a cry, and fell senseless on the floor.

When she came to herself the Colonel was gone. Washington Hawkins stood at her bedside. Did she come to herself? Was there anything left in her heart but hate and bitterness, a sense of an infamous wrong at the hands of the only man she had ever loved?

She returned to Hawkeye. With the exception of Washington and his mother, no one knew what had happened. The neighbors supposed that the engagement with Col. Selby had fallen through. Laura was ill for a long time, but she recovered; she

had that resolution in her that could conquer death almost. And with her health came back her beauty, and an added fascination, a something that might be mistaken for sadness. Is there a beauty in the knowledge of evil, a beauty that shines out in the face of a person whose inward life is transformed by some terrible experience? Is the pathos in the eyes of the Beatrice Cenci from her guilt or her innocence?

Laura was not much changed. The lovely woman had a devil in her heart. That was all.

CHAPTER XIX.

BRIKRLY FLIRTS WITH LAURA, AND IS FASCINATED

MR. HARRY BRIERLY drew his pay as an engineer while he was living at the City

Hotel in Hawkeye. Mr. Thompson had been kind enough to say that it didn't make any difference whether he was with the corps or not ; and although Harry protested to the Colonel daily and to Washington Hawkins that he must go back at once to the line and superintend the layout with reference to his contract, yet he did not go, but wrote instead long letters to Philip, instructing him to keep his eye out, and to let him know when any difficulty occurred that required his presence.

Meantime Harry blossomed out in the society of Hawkeye, as he did in any society where fortune cast him and he had the slightest opportunity to(an,

expand, indeed, the talents of a rich and accomplished young fellow like Harry were not likely to go unappreciated in such a place. A land operator, engaged in vast speculations, a favorite in the select circles of New York, in correspondence with brokers and bankers, intimate with public men at Washington, one who could play the guitar and touch the banjo lightly, and who had an eye for a pretty girl, and knew the language of flattery, was welcome everywhere in Hawkeye. Even Miss Laura Hawkins thought it worth while to use her fascinations upon him, and to endeavor to entangle the volatile fellow in the meshes of her attractions.

"Gad," says Harry to the Colonel, "she's a superb creature, she'd make a stir in New York, money or no money. There are men I know would give her a railroad or an opera house, or whatever she wanted — at least they'd promise."

Harry had a way of looking at women as he looked at anything else in the world he wanted, and he half resolved to appropriate Miss Laura, during his stay in Hawkeye. Perhaps the Colonel divined his thoughts, or was offended at Harry's talk, for he replied:

" No nonsense, Mr. Brierly. Nonsense won't do in Hawkeye, not with my friends. The Hawkins blood is good blood, all the way from Tennessee. The Hawkinses are under the weather now, but their Tennessee property is millions when it comes into market."

" Of course, Colonel. Not the least offense intended. But you can see she is a fascinating woman. I was only thinking, as to this appropriation, now, what such a woman could do in Washington. All correct, too, all correct. Common thing, I assure you, in Washington; the wives of senators, representatives, cabinet officers, all sorts of wives, and some who are not wives, use their influence. You want an appointment? Do you go to Senator X? Not much. You get on the right side of his wife. Is it an appropriation? You'd go straight to the committee, or to the Interior Office, I suppose? You'd learn better than that. It takes a woman to get anything through the Land Office. I tell you, Miss Laura would fascinate an appropriation right through the Senate and the House of Representatives in one session, if she was in Washington, as your friend, Colonel, of course as your friend."

" Would you have her sign our petition?" asked the Colonel, innocently.

Harry laughed. " Women don't get anything by petitioning Congress; nobody does, that's for form. Petitions are referred somewhere, and that's the last of them; you can't refer a handsome woman so easily, when she is present. They prefer 'em mostly."

The petition, however, was elaborately drawn up, with a glowing description of Napoleon and the adjacent country, and a statement of the absolute necessity to the prosperity of that region and of one

of the stations on the great through route to the Pacific, of the immediate improvement of Columbus River; to this was appended a map of the city and a survey of the river. It was signed by all the people at Stone's Landing who could write their names, by Col. Beriah Sellers, and the Colonel agreed to have the names headed by all the senators and representatives from the State and by a sprinkling of ex-governors and ex-members of Congress. When completed it was a formidable document. Its preparation and that of more minute plots of the new city consumed the valuable time of Sellers and Harry for many weeks, and served to keep them both in the highest spirits.

In the eyes of Washington Hawkins, Harry was a superior being, a man who was able to bring things to pass in a way that excited his enthusiasm. He never tired of listening to his stories of what he had done and of what he was going to do. As for Washington, Harry thought he was a man of ability and comprehension, but "too visionary," he told the Colonel. The Colonel said he might be right, but he had never noticed anything visionary about him.

" He's got his plans, sir. God bless my soul, at his age I was full of plans. But experience sobers a man. I never touch anything now that hasn't been weighed in my judgment; and when Beriah Sellers puts his judgment on a thing, there it is."

Whatever might have been Harry's intentions

with regard to Laura, he saw more and more of her every day, until he got to be restless and nervous when he was not with her. That consummate artist in passion allowed him to believe that the fascination was mainly on his side, and so worked upon his vanity, while inflaming his ardor, that he scarcely knew what he was about. Her coolness and coyness were even 1 made to appear the simple precautions of a modest timidity, and attracted him even more than the little tendernesses into which she was occasionally surprised. He could never be away from her long, day or evening; and in a short time their intimacy was the town talk. She played with him so adroitly that Harry thought she was absorbed in love for him, and yet he was amazed that he did not get on faster in his conquest.

And when he thought of it, he was piqued as well. A country girl, poor enough, that was evident ; living with her family in a cheap and most unattractive frame house, such as carpenters build in America, scantily furnished and unadorned ; without the adventitious aids of dress or jewels or the fine manners of society — Harry couldn't understand it. But she fascinated him, and held him just beyond the line of absolute familiarity at the same time. While he was with her she made him forget that the Hawkins house was nothing but a wooden tenement, with four small square rooms on the ground floor and a half story; it might have been a palace for aught he knew.

Perhaps Laura was older than Harry. She was, at any rate, at that ripe age when beauty in woman seems more solid than in the budding period of girlhood, and she had come to understand her powers perfectly, and to know exactly how much of the susceptibility and archness of the girl it was profitable to retain. She saw that many women, with the best intentions, make the mistake of carrying too much girlishness into womanhood. Such a woman would have attracted Harry at any time, but only a woman with a cool brain and exquisite art could have made him lose his head in this way; for Harry thought himself a man of the world. The young fellow never dreamed that he was merely being experimented on; he was to her a man of another society and another culture, different from that she had any knowledge of except in books, and she was not unwilling to try on him the fascinations of her mind and person.

For Laura had her dreams. She detested the narrow limits in which her lot was cast, she hated poverty. Much of her reading had been of modern works of fiction, written by her own sex, which had revealed to her something of her own powers and given her, indeed, an exaggerated notion of the influence, the wealth, the position a woman may attain who has beauty and talent and ambition and a little culture, and is not too scrupulous in the use of them. She wanted to be rich, she wanted luxury, she wanted men at her feet, her slaves, and she had

not — thanks to some of the novels she had read — the nicest discrimination between notoriety and reputation ; perhaps she did not know how fatal notoriety usually is to the bloom of womanhood.

With the other Hawkins children Laura had been brought up in the belief that they had inherited a fortune in the Tennessee Lands. She did not by any means share all the delusion of the family; but her brain was not seldom busy with schemes about it. Washington seemed to her only to dream of it and to be willing to wait for its riches to fall upon him in a golden shower; but she was impatient, and wished she were a man to take hold of the business.

" You men must enjoy your schemes and your activity and liberty to go about the world," she said to Harry one day, when he had been talking of New York and Washington and his incessant engagements.

Oh, yes," replied that martyr to business, "it's all well enough, if you don't have too much of it, but it only has one object."

"What is that?"

" If a woman doesn't know, it's useless to tell her. What do you suppose I am staying in Hawk-eye for week after week, when I ought to be with my corps?"

" I suppose it's your business with Col. Sellers about Napoleon; you've always told me so," answered Laura, with a look intended to contradict her words.

"And now I tell you that is all arranged, I suppose you'll tell me I ought to go?"

"Harry!" exclaimed Laura, touching his arm and letting her pretty hand rest there a moment. "Why should I want you to go away? The only person in Havvkeye who understands me."

"But you refuse to understand me," replied Harry, flattered but still petulant. "You are like an iceberg, when we are alone."

Laura looked up with wonder in her great eyes, and something like a blush suffusing her face, followed by a look of languor that penetrated Harry's heart as if it had been longing. " Did I ever show any want of confidence in you, Harry?" And she gave him her hand, which Harry pressed with effusion— something in her manner told him that he must be content with that favor.

It was always so. She excited his hopes and denied him, inflamed his passion and restrained it, and wound him in her toils day by day. To what purpose? It was keen delight to Laura to prove that she had power over men.

Laura liked to hear about life at the East, and especially about the luxurious society in which Mr. Brierly moved when he was at home. It pleased her imagination to fancy herself a queen in it.

" You should be a winter in Washington," Harry said.

" But I have no acquaintances there."

" Don't know any of the families of the Congressmen? They like to have a pretty woman staying with them."

"Not one."

" Suppose Col. Sellers should have business there; say, about this Columbus River appropriation?"

" Sellers !" and Laura laughed.

"You needn't laugh. Queerer things have happened. Sellers knows everybody from Missouri, and from the West, too, for that matter. He'd introduce you to Washington life quick enough. It doesn't need a crowbar to break your way into society there as it does in Philadelphia. It's democratic, Washington is. Money or beauty will open any door. If I were a handsome woman, J shouldn't want any better place than the capital to pick up a prince or a fortune."

" Thank you," replied Laura. " But I prefer the quiet of home, and the love of those I know;" and her face wore a look of sweet contentment and un-worldliness that finished Mr. Harry Brierly for the day.

Nevertheless, the hint that Harry had dropped fell upon good ground, and bore fruit an hundred fold; it worked in her mind until she had built up a plan on it, and almost a career for herself. Why not, she said, why s'louldn't I do as other women have done? She toe'c the first opportunity to see Col. Sellers, and to sound him about the Washington visit. How was he getting on with his navigation scheme, would it be likely to take him from home to Jefferson City, or to Washington, perhaps?

Well, maybe. If the people of Napoleon want me to go to Washington, and look after that matter, I might tear myself from my home. It's been suggested to me, but—not a word of it to Mrs. Sellers and the children. Maybe they wouldn't like to think of their father in Washington. But Dilworthy, Senator Dilworthy, says to me, ' Colonel, you are the man, you could influence more votes than any one else on such a measure, an old settler, a man of the people, you know the wants of Missouri; you've a respect for religion too, says he, and know how the cause of the gospel goes with improvements.' Which is true enough, Miss Laura, and hasn't been enough thought of in connection with Napoleon. He's an able man, Dilworthy, and a good man. A man has got to be good to succeed as he has. He's only been in Congress a few years, and he must be worth a million. First thing in the morning when he stayed with me he asked about family prayers, whether we had 'em before or after breakfast. I hated to disappoint the Senator, but I had to out with it, tell him we didn't have 'em, not steady. He said he understood, business interruptions and all that, some men were well enough without, but as for him he never neglected the ordinances of religion. He doubted if the Columbus River appropriation would succeed if we did not invoke the Divine Blessing on it."

Perhaps it is unnecessary to say to the reader that
Senator Dilworthy had not stayed with Col. Sellers '5*
while he was in Hawkeye; this visit to his house being only one of the Colonel's
hallucinations — one of those instant creations of his fertile fancy, which were always flashing
into his brain and out of his mouth in the course of any conversation and without interrupting the
flow of it.

During the summer Philip rode across the country and made a short visit in Hawkeye,
giving Harry an opportunity to show him the progress that he and the Colonel had made in their
operation at Stone's Landing, to introduce him also to Laura, and to borrow a little money when
he departed. Harry bragged about his conquest, as was his habit, and took Philip round to see his
Western prize.

Laura received Mr. Philip with a courtesy and a slight hauteur that rather surprised and
not a little interested him. He saw at once that she was older than Harry, and soon made up his
mind that she was leading his friend a country dance to which he was unaccustomed. At least he
thought he saw that, and half hinted as much to Harry, who flared up at once; but on a second
visit Philip was not so sure — the young lady was certainly kind and friendly and almost
confiding with Harry, and treated Philip with the greatest consideration. She deferred to his
opinions, and listened attentively when he talked, and in time met his frank manner with an equal
frankness, so that he was quite convinced that whatever she might feel toward Harry, she was
sincere with him. Perhaps

his manly way did win her liking. Perhaps in her mind, she compared him with Harry,
and recognized in him a man to whom a woman might give her whole soul, recklessly and with
little care if she lost it. Philip was not invincible to her beauty nor to the intellectual charm of her
presence.

The week seemed very short that he passed in Hawkeye, and when he bade Laura good-
bye, he seemed to have known her a year.

" We shall see you again, Mr. Sterling," she said as she gave him her hand, with just a
shade of sadness in her handsome eyes.

And when he turned away she followed him with a look that might have disturbed his
serenity, if he had not at the moment had a little square letter in his breast pocket, dated at
Philadelphia, and signed "Ruth."

CHAPTER XX.

DILWORTHY, THE GOLDEN-TONGUED STATESMAN

-4hMk&ttt bjoijDSlOTwd 3° ti)btt*itS eeitle,n cotiwle, 50 ec*ibb|n * SAC *ei) *e «T
cfo*-

"TTHE visit of Senator Abner Dilworthy was an • event in Hawkeye. When a Senator,
whose place is in Washington moving among the Great and guiding the destinies of the nation,
condescends to mingle among the people and accept the hospitalities of such a place as
Hawkeye, the honor is not considered a light one. All parties are flattered by it, and politics are
forgotten in the presence of one so distinguished among his fellows.

Senator Dilworthy, who was from a neighboring State, had been a Unionist in the darkest
days of his country, and had thriven by it, but was that any reason why Col. Sellers, who had
been a Confederate and had not thriven by it, should give him the cold shoulder?

The Senator was the guest of his old friend, Gen. Boswell, but it almost appeared that he
was indebted

(224)

to Col. Sellers for the unreserved hospitalities of the town. It was the large-hearted Colonel who, in a manner, gave him the freedom of the city.

"You are known here, sir," said the Colonel, " and Hawkeye is proud of you. You will find every door open, and a welcome at every hearthstone. I should insist upon your going to my house, if you were not claimed by your older friend, Gen.Boswell. But you will mingle with our people,and you will see here developments that will surprise you."

The Colonel was so profuse in his hospitality that he must have made the impression upon himself that he had entertained the Senator at his own mansion during his stay; at any rate, he afterwards always spoke of him as his guest, and not seldom referred to the Senator's relish of certain viands on his table. He did, in fact, press him to dine upon the morning of the day the Senator was going away.

Senator Dilworthy was large and portly, though not tall — a pleasant spoken man, a popular man with the people.

He took a lively interest in the town and all the surrounding country, and made many inquiries as to the progress of agriculture, of education, and of religion, and especially as to the condition of the emancipated race.

" Providence," he said, " has placed them in our hands, and although you and I, General, might have chosen a different destiny for them, under the Constitution, yet Providence knows best." 15"

" You can't do much with 'em," interrupted Col. Sellers. "They are a speculating race, sir, disinclined to work for white folks without security, planning how to live by only working for themselves. Idle, sir, there's my garden just a ruin of weeds. Nothing practical in 'em."

"There is some truth in your observation, Colonel, but you must educate them."

" You educate the niggro and you make him more speculating than he was before. If he won't stick to any industry except for himself now, what will he do then?"

"But, Colonel, the negro when educated will be more able to make his speculations fruitful."

" Never, sir, never. He would only have a wider scope to injure himself. A niggro has no grasp, sir. Now, a white man can conceive great operations, and carry them out; a niggro can't."

"Still," replied the Senator, "granting that he might injure himself in a worldly point of view, his elevation through education would multiply his chances for the hereafter — which is the important thing after all, Colonel. And no matter what the result is, we must fulfil our duty by this being."

"I'd elevate his soul," promptly responded the Colonel; "that's just it; you can't make his soul too immortal, but I wouldn't touch him, himself. Yes, sir! make his soul immortal, but don't disturb the niggro as he is."

Of course one of the entertainments offered the

Senator was a public reception, held in the court house, at which he made a speech to his fellow citizens. Col. Sellers was master of ceremonies. He escorted the band from the city hotel to Gen. Boswell's; he marshaled the procession of Masons, of Odd Fellows, and of Firemen, the Good Templars, the Sons of Temperance, the Cadets of Temperance, the Daughters of Rebecca, the Sunday-school children, and citizens generally, which followed the Senator to the court-house; he bustled about the room long after everyone else was seated, and loudly cried "Order!" in the dead silence which preceded the introduction of the Senator by Gen. Boswell. The occasion was one to call out his finest powers of personal appearance, and one he long dwelt on with pleasure.

This not being an edition of the Congressional Globe it is impossible to give Senator Dilworthy's speech in full. He began somewhat as follows:

" Fellow citizens: It gives me great pleasure to thus meet and mingle with you, to lay aside for a moment the heavy duties of an official and burdensome station, and confer in familiar converse with my friends in your great State. The good opinion of my fellow citizens of all sections is the sweetest solace in all my anxieties. I look forward with longing to the time when I can lay aside the cares of office—" [" Dam sight," shouted a tipsy fellow near the door. Cries of " Put him out."]

" My friends, do not remove him. Let the mis-

guided man stay. I see that he is a victim of that evil which is swallowing up public virtue and sapping the foundation of society. As I was saying, when I can lay down the cares of office and retire to the sweets of private life in some such sweet, peaceful, intelligent, wide-awake, and patriotic place as Hawkeye [applause]. I have traveled much, I have seen all parts of our glorious Union, but I have never seen a lovelier village than yours, or one that has more signs of commercial and industrial and religious prosperity — " [more applause].

The Senator then launched into a sketch of our great country, and dwelt for an hour or more upon its prosperity and the dangers which threatened it.

He then touched reverently upon the institutions of religion, and upon the necessity of private purity, if we were to have any public morality. " I trust," he said, "that there are children within the sound of my voice," and after some remarks to them, the Senator closed with an apostrophe to " the genius of American Liberty, walking with the Sunday-school in one hand and Temperance in the other up the glorified steps of the National Capitol."

Col. Sellers did not, of course, lose the opportunity to impress upon so influential a person as the Senator the desirability of improving the navigation of Columbus River. He and Mr. Brierly took the Senator over to Napoleon and opened to him their plan. It was a plan that the Senator could understand without a great deal of explanation, for he

seemed to be familiar with the like improvements elsewhere. When, however, they reached Stone's Landing the Senator looked about him and inquired :

" Is this Napoleon?"

*' This is the nucleus, the nucleus," said the Colonel, unrolling his map. " Here is the deepo, the church, the City Hall, and so on."

"Ah, I see. How far from here is Columbus River? Does that stream empty—"

"That, why, that's Goose Run. Thar ain't no Columbus, thout'n it's over to Hawkeye," interrupted one of the citizens, who had come out to stare at the strangers. "A railroad come here last summer, but it haint been here no mo'."

" Yes, sir," the Colonel hastened to explain, " in the old records Columbus River is called Goose Run. You see how it sweeps round the town — forty-nine miles to the Missouri; sloop navigation all the way, pretty much, drains this whole country; when it's improved steamboats will run right up here. It's got to be enlarged, deepened. You see by the map, Columbus River. This country must have water communication!"

" You'll want a considerable appropriation, Col. Sellers."

" I should say a million; is that your figure, Mr. Briefly?"

"According to our surveys," said Harry, "a million would do it; a million spent on the river would make Napoleon worth two millions at least."

" I see," nodded the Senator. " But you'd better begin by asking only for two or three hundred thousand, the usual way. You can begin to sell town lots on that appropriation, you know."

The Senator, himself, to do him justice, was not very much interested in the country or the stream, but he favored the appropriation, and he gave the Colonel and Mr. Brierly to understand that he would endeavor to get it through. Harry, who thought he was shrewd and understood Washington, suggested an interest.

But he saw that the Senator was wounded by the suggestion.

" You will offend me by repeating such an observation," he said. " Whatever I do will be for the public interest. It will require a portion of the appropriation for necessary expenses, and I am sorry to say that there are members who will have to be seen. But you can reckon upon my humble services."

This aspect of the subject was not again alluded to. The Senator possessed himself of the facts, not from his observation of the ground, but from the lips of Col. Sellers, and laid the appropriation scheme away among his other plans for benefiting the public.

It was on this visit also that the Senator made the acquaintance of Mr. Washington Hawkins, and was greatly taken with his innocence, his guileless manner, and perhaps with his ready adaptability to enter upon any plan proposed.

Col. Sellers was pleased to see this interest that Washington had awakened, especially since it was likely to further his expectations with regard to the Tennessee Lands; the Senator having remarked to the Colonel, that he delighted to help any deserving young man, when the promotion of a private advantage could at the same time be made to contribute to the general good. And he did not doubt that this was an opportunity of that kind.

The result of several conferences with Washington was that the Senator proposed that he should go to Washington with him and become his private secretary and the secretary of his committee; a proposal which was eagerly accepted.

The Senator spent Sunday in Hawkeye and attended church. He cheered the heart of the worthy and zealous minister by an expression of his sympathy in his labors, and by many inquiries in regard to the religious state of the region. It was not a very promising state, and the good man felt how much lighter his task would be, if he had the aid of such a man as Senator Dilworthy.

" I am glad to see, my dear sir," said the Senator, " that you give them the doctrines. It is owing to a neglect of the doctrines, that there is such a fearful falling away in the country. I wish that we might have you in Washington — as chaplain, now, in the Senate."

The good man could not but be a little flattered, and if sometimes, thereafter, in his discouraging

work, he allowed the thought that he might perhaps be called to Washington as chaplain of the Senate, to cheer him, who can wonder. The Senator's commendation at least did one service for him, it elevated him in the opinion of Hawkeye.

Laura was at church alone that day, and Mr. Brierly walked home with her. A part of their way lay with that of General Boswell and Senator Dil-worthy, and introductions were made. Laura had her own reasons for wishing to know the Senator, and the Senator was not a man who could be called indifferent to charms such as hers. That meek young lady so commended herself to him in the short walk, that he announced his intentions of paying his respects to her the next day, an intention which Harry received glumly; and when the Senator was out of hearing he called him " an old fool."

"Fie," said Laura, " I do believe you are jealous, Harry. He is a very pleasant man. He said you were a young man of great promise."

The Senator did call next day, and the result of his visit was that he was confirmed in his impression that there was something about him very attractive to ladies. He saw Laura again and again during his stay, and felt more and more the subtle influence of her feminine beauty, which every man felt who came near her.

Harry was beside himself with rage while the Senator remained in town; he declared that women were always ready to drop any man for higher game;

and he attributed his own ill-luck to the Senator's appearance. The fellow was in fact crazy about her beauty and ready to beat his brains out in chagrin. Perhaps Laura enjoyed his torment, but she soothed him with blandishments that increased his ardor, and she smiled to herself to think that he had, with all his protestations of love, never spoken of marriage. Probably the vivacious fellow never had thought of it. At any rate, when he at length went away from Hawkeye he was no nearer it. But there was no telling to what desperate lengths his passion might not carry him.

Laura bade him good-bye with tender regret, which, however, did not disturb her peace or interfere with her plans. The visit of Senator Dilworthy had become of more importance to her, and it by and by bore the fruit she longed for, in an invitation to visit his family in the National Capital during the winter session of Congress.

CHAPTER XXI.

RUTH AT A SEMINARY. NEW FRIENDSHIP AND PLEASURES

Unusquisque sua noverit ire via.— Propert. Eleg. ii. 25.

O lift your natures up:

Embrace our aims: work out your freedom. Girls, Knowledge is now no more a fountain sealed; Drink deep until .the habits of the slave. The sins of emptiness, gossip and spite And slander, die.

Tke Pnttctss.

WHETHER medicine is a science, or only an empirical method of getting a living out of the ignorance of the human race, Ruth found before her first term was over at the medical school that there were other things she needed to know quite as much as that which is taught in medical books, and that she could never satisfy her aspirations without more general culture.

"Does your doctor know anything —I don't mean about medicine, but about things in general, is he a man of information and good sense?" once asked an old practitioner. "If he doesn't know anything but medicine the chance is he doesn't know that."

(234)

The close application to her special study waa beginning to tell upon Ruth's delicate health also, and the summer brought with it only weariness and indisposition for any mental effort.

In this condition of mind and body the quiet of her home and the unexciting companionship of those about her were more than ever tiresome.

She followed with more interest Philip's sparkling account of his life in the West, and longed for his experiences, and to know some of those people of a world so different from hers, who alternately amused and displeased him. He at least was learning the world, the good and the bad of it, as must happen to every one who accomplishes anything in it.

But what, Ruth wrote, could a woman do, tied up by custom, and cast into particular circumstances out of which it was almost impossible to extricate herself? Philip thought that he would go some day and extricate Ruth, but he did not write that, for he had the instinct to know that this was not the extrication she dreamed of, and that she must find out by her own experience what her heart really wanted.

Philip was not a philosopher, to be sure, but he had the old-fashioned notion, that whatever a woman's theories of life might be, she would come round to matrimony, only give her time. He could indeed recall to mind one woman — and he never knew a nobler — whose whole soul was devoted and who believed that her life was consecrated to a certain benevolent project in singleness of life, who

yielded to the touch of matrimony, as an icicle yields to a sunbeam.

Neither at home nor elsewhere did Ruth utter any complaint, or admit any weariness or doubt of her ability to pursue the path she had marked out for herself. But her mother saw clearly enough her struggle with infirmity, and was not deceived by either her gaiety or by the cheerful composure which she carried into all the ordinary duties that fell to her. She saw plainly enough that Ruth needed an entire change of scene and of occupation, and perhaps she believed that such a change, with the knowledge of the world it would bring, would divert Ruth from a course for which she felt she was physically entirely unfitted.

It therefore suited the wishes of all concerned, when autumn came, that Ruth should go away to school. She selected a large New England seminary, of which she had often heard Philip speak, which was attended by both sexes and offered almost collegiate advantages of education. Thither she went in September, and began for the second time in the year a life new to her.

The Seminary was the chief feature of FallkiH, a village of two to three thousand inhabitants. It was a prosperous school, with three hundred students, a large corps of teachers, men and women, and with a venerable rusty row of academic buildings on the shaded square of the town. The students lodged and boarded in private families in the

place, and so it came about that while the school did a great deal to support the town, the town gave the students society and the sweet influences of home life. It is at least respectful to say that the influences of home life are sweet.

Ruth's home, by the intervention of Philip, was in a family — one of the rare exceptions in life or in fiction — that had never known better days. The Montagues, it is perhaps well to say, had intended to come over in the Mayflower, but were detained at Delft Haven by the illness of a child. They came over to Massachusetts Bay in another vessel, and thus escaped the onus of that brevet nobility under which the successors of the Mayflower Pilgrims have descended. Having no factitious weight of dignity to carry, the Montagues steadily improved their condition from the day they landed, and they were never more vigorous or prosperous than at the date of this narrative. With character compacted by the rigid Puritan discipline of more than two centuries, they had retained its strength and purity and thrown off its narrowness, and were now blossoming under the generous modern influences. Squire Oliver Montague, a lawyer, who had retired from the practice of his profession except in rare cases, dwelt in a square old-fashioned New England mansion a quarter of a mile away from the green. It was called a mansion because it stood alone with ample fields about it, and had an avenue of trees leading to

it from the road, and on the west commanded a 16*

view of a pretty little lake with gentle slopes and nodding groves. But it was just a plain, roomy house, capable of extending to many guests an unpretending hospitality.

The family consisted of the Squire and his wife, a son and a daughter married and not at home, a son in college at Cambridge, another son at the Seminary, and a daughter Alice, who was a year or more older than Ruth. Having only riches enough to be able to gratify reasonable desires, and yet make their gratifications always a novelty and a pleasure, the family occupied that just mean in life which is so rarely attained, and still more rarely enjoyed without discontent.

If Ruth did not find so much luxury in the house as in her own home, there were evidences of culture, of intellectual activity and of a zest in the affairs of all the world, which greatly impressed her. Every room had its book-cases or book-shelves, and was more or less a library; upon every table was liable to be a litter of new books, fresh periodicals, and daily newspapers. There were plants in the sunny windows and some choice engravings on the walls, with bits of color in oil or water-colors; the piano was sure to be open and strewn with music; and there were photographs and little souvenirs here and there of foreign travel. An absence of any " whatnots " in the corners with rows of cheerful shells, and Hindoo gods, and Chinese idols, and nests of useless boxes of lacquered wood, might be taken as

denoting a languidness in the family concerning foreign missions, but perhaps unjustly.

At any rate the life of the world flowed freely into this hospitable house, and there was always so much talk there of the news of the day, of the new books and of authors, of Boston radicalism and New York civilization, and the virtue of Congress, that small gossip stood a very poor chance.

All this was in many ways so new to Ruth that she seemed to have passed into another world, in which she experienced a freedom and a mental exhilaration unknown to her before. Under this influence she entered upon her studies with keen enjoyment, finding for a time all the relaxation she needed, in the charming social life at the Montague house.

It is strange, she wrote to Philip, in one of her occasional letters, that you never told me more about this delightful family, and scarcely mentioned Alice, who is the life of it, just the noblest girl, unselfish, knows how to do so many things, with lots of talent, with a dry humor, and an odd way of looking at things, and yet quiet and even serious often — one of your " capable " New England girls. We shall be great friends. It had never occurred to Philip that there was anything extraordinary about the family that needed mention. He knew dozens of girls like Alice, he thought to himself, but only one like Ruth.

Good friends the two girls were from the begin-

ning. Ruth was a study to Alice, the product of a culture entirely foreign to her experience, so much a child in some things, so much a woman in others; and Ruth in turn, it must be confessed, probing Alice sometimes with her serious gray eyes, wondered what her object in life was, and whether she had any purpose beyond living as she now saw her. For she could scarcely conceive of a life that should not be devoted to the accomplishment of some definite work, and she had no doubt that in her own case everything else would yield to the professional career she had marked out.

" So you know Philip Sterling," said Ruth one day as the girls sat at their sewing. Ruth never embroidered, and never sewed when she could avoid it. Bless her!

"Oh yes, we are old friends. Philip used to come to Fallkill often while he was in college. He was once rusticated here for a term."

" Rusticated?"

" Suspended for some college scrape. He was a great favorite here. Father and he were famous friends. Father said that Philip had no end of nonsense in him and was always blundering into something, but he was a royal good fellow and would come out all right."

" Did you think he was fickle?"

" Why, I never thought whether he was or not," replied Alice, looking up. "I suppose he was always in love with some girl or another, as college

boys are. He used to make me his confidant now and then, and be terribly in the dumps."

"Why did he come to you?" pursued Ruth; "you were younger than he."

"I'm sure I don't know. He was at our house a good deal. Once at a picnic by the lake, at the risk of his own life, he saved sister Millie from drowning, and we all liked to have him here. Perhaps he thought as he had saved one sister, the other ought to help him when he was in trouble. I don't know."

The fact was that Alice was a person who invited confidences, because she never betrayed them, and gave abundant sympathy in return. There are persons, whom we all know, to whom human confidences, troubles, and heartache flow as naturally as streams to a placid lake.

This is not a history of Fallkill, nor of the Montague family, worthy as both are of that honor, and this narrative cannot be diverted into long loitering with them. If the reader visits the village to-day, he will doubtless be pointed out the Montague dwelling, where Ruth lived, the cross-lots path she traversed to the Seminary, and the venerable chapel with its cracked bell.

In the little society of the place, the Quaker girl was a favorite, and no considerable social gathering or pleasure party was thought complete without her. There was something in this seemingly transparent and yet deep character, in her childlike gayety and 16-enjoyment of the society about her, and in her not seldom absorption in herself, that would have made her long remembered there if no events had subsequently occurred to recall her to mind.

To the surprise of Alice, Ruth took to the small gayeties of the village with a zest of enjoyment that seemed foreign to one who had devoted her life to a serious profession from the highest motives. Alice liked society well enough, she thought, but there was nothing exciting in that of Fallkill, nor anything novel in the attentions of the well-bred young gentlemen one met in it. It must have worn a different aspect to Ruth, for she entered into its pleasures at first with curiosity, and then with interest, and finally with a kind of staid abandon that no one would have deemed possible for her. Parties, picnics, rowing-matches, moonlight strolls, nutting-expeditions in the October woods,— Alice declared that it was a whirl of dissipation. The fondness of Ruth, which was scarcely disguised, for the company of agreeable young fellows, who talked nothings, gave Alice opportunity for no end of banter.

" Do you look upon them as ' subjects,' dear?" she would ask.

And Ruth laughed her merriest laugh, and then looked sober again. Perhaps she was thinking, after all, whether she knew herself.

If you should rear a duck in the heart of the Sahara, no doubt it would swim if you brought it to the Nile.

Surely no one would have predicted when Ruth left Philadelphia that she would become absorbed to this extent, and so happy, in a life so unlike that she thought she desired. But no one can tell how a woman will act under any circumstances. The reason novelists nearly always fail in depicting women when they make them act, is that they let them do what they have observed some woman has done at some time or another. And that is where they make a mistake; for a woman will never do again what has been done before. It is this uncertainty that causes women, considered as materials for fiction, to be so interesting to themselves and to others.

As the fall went on and the winter, Ruth did not distinguish herself greatly at the Fallkill Seminary as a student, a fact that apparently gave her no anxiety, and did not diminish her enjoyment of a new sort of power which had awakened within her.

CHAPTER XXII.

PHILIP AT FALLKILL, IN LOVE. HARRY SPREADS HIMSELF

Wohl giebt es im Leben kein sUsseres GlUck,

Als der Liebe Gestandniss im Liebchen's Blick;

Wohl giebt es im Leben nicht haher Lust,
Als Freuden der Liebe an liebender Brast.
Dem hat nie das Leben freundlich begegnet,
Den nicht die Weihe der Liebe gesegnet.
Doch der Liebe Gltlck, so himmlisch, so schon Kann nie ohne Glauben an Tugend bestehn.

Korner.

O ke aloha ka mea i oi aku ka maikai mamua o ka umeki poi a me ka ipukaia.

IN midwinter, an event occurred of unusual interest to the inhabitants of the Montague house, and to the friends of the young ladies who sought their society.

This was the arrival at the Sassacus Hotel of two young gentlemen from the West.

It is the fashion in New England to give Indian names to the public houses, not that the late lamented savage knew how to keep a hotel, but that his warlike name may impress the traveler who humbly craves shelter there, and make him grateful

(244)

to the noble and gentlemanly clerk if he is allowed to depart with his scalp safe.

The two young gentlemen were neither students for the Fallkill Seminary, nor lecturers on physiology, nor yet life assurance solicitors, three suppositions that almost exhausted the guessing power of the people at the hotel in respect to the names of " Philip Sterling and Henry Brierly, Missouri," on the register. They were handsome enough fellows, that was evident, browned by outdoor exposure, and with a free and lordly way about them that almost awed the hotel clerk himself. Indeed, he very soon set down Mr. Brierly as a gentleman of large fortune, with enormous interests on his shoulders. Harry had a way of casually mentioning Western investments, through lines, the freighting business, and the route through the Indian territory to Lower California, which was calculated to give an importance to his lightest word.

" You've a pleasant town here, sir, and the most comfortable looking hotel I've seen out of New York," said Harry to the clerk; "we shall stay here a few days if you can give us a roomy suite of apartments."

Harry usually had the best of everything, where-ever he went, as such fellows always do have in this accommodating world. Philip would have been quite content with less expensive quarters, but there was no resisting Harry's generosity in such matters.

Railroad surveying and real-estate operations were at a standstill during the winter in Missouri, and the young men had taken advantage of the lull to come East, Philip to see if there was any disposition in his friends, the railway contractors, to give him a share in the Salt Lick Union Pacific Extension, and Harry to open out to his uncle the prospects of the new city at Stone's Landing, and to procure congressional appropriations for the harbor and for making Goose Run navigable. Harry had with him a map of that noble stream and of the harbor, with a perfect network of railroads centering in it, pictures of wharves, crowded with steamboats, and of huge grain-elevators on the bank, all of which grew out of the combined imaginations of Colonel Sellers and Mr. Brierly. The Colonel had entire confidence in Harry's influence with Wall street, and with congressmen, to bring about the consummation of their scheme, and he waited his return in the empty house at Hawkeye, feeding his pinched family upon the most gorgeous expectations with a reckless prodigality.

44 Don't let 'em into the thing more than is necessary," says the Colonel to Harry; "give 'em a small interest; a lot apiece in the suburbs of the Landing ought to do a congressman, but I reckon you'll have to mortgage a part of the city itself to the brokers."

Harry did not find that eagerness to lend money on Stone's Landing in Wall street which Colonel

Sellers had expected (it had seen too many such maps as he exhibited), although his uncle and some of the brokers looked with more favor on the appropriation for improving the navigation of Columbus River, and were not disinclined to form a company for that purpose. An appropriation was a tangible thing, if you could get hold of it, and it made little difference what it was appropriated for, so long as you got hold of it.

Pending these weighty negotiations, Philip has persuaded Harry to take a little run up to Fallkill, a not difficult task, for that young man would at any time have turned his back upon all the land in the West at sight of a new and pretty face, and he had, it must be confessed, a facility in love-making which made it not at all an interference with the more serious business of life. He could not, to be sure, conceive how Philip could be interested in a young lady who was studying medicine, but he had no objection to going, for he did not doubt that there were other girls in Fallkill who were worth a week's attention.

The young men were received at the house of the Montagues with the hospitality which never failed there.

" We are glad to see you again," exclaimed the Squire heartily; "you are welcome, Mr. Brierly. any friend of Phil's is welcome at our house."

"It's more like home to me, than any place except my own home," cried Philip, as he looked

about the cheerful house and went through a general hand-shaking.

"It's a long time, though, since you have been here to say so," Alice said, with her father's frankness of manner; " and I suspect we owe the visit now to your sudden interest in the Fallkill Seminary."

Philip's color came, as it had an awkward way of doing in his tell-tale face; but before he could stammer a reply, Harry came in with —

"That accounts for Phil's wish to build a seminary at Stone's Landing, our place in Missouri, when Colonel Sellers insisted it should be a university. Phil appears to have a weakness for seminaries."

" It would have been better for your friend Sellers," retorted Philip, "if he had had a weakness for district schools. Colonel Sellers, Miss Alice, is a great friend of Harry's who is always trying to build a house by beginning at the top."

" I suppose it's as easy to build a university on paper as a seminary, and it looks better," was Harry's reflection; at which the Squire laughed, and said he quite agreed with him. The old gentleman understood Stone's Landing a good deal better than he would have done after an hour's talk with either of its expectant proprietors.

At this moment, and while Philip was trying to frame a question that he found it exceedingly difficult to put into words, the door opened quietly, and Ruth entered. Taking in the group with a quick

glance, her eye lighted up, and with a merry smile she advanced and shook hands with Philip. She was so unconstrained and sincerely cordial, that it made that hero of the West feel somehow young, and very ill at ease.

For months and months he had thought of this meeting and pictured it to himself a hundred times, but he had never imagined it would be like this. He should meet Ruth unexpectedly, as she was walking alone from the school, perhaps, or entering the room where he was waiting for her, and she would cry "Oh! Phil," and then check herself, and perhaps blush, and Philip, calm but eager and enthusiastic, would reassure her by his warm manner, and he would take her hand impressively, and she would look up timidly, and, after his long absence, perhaps he would be permitted to . Good

heavens ! how many times he had come to this point, and wondered if it could happen so. Well, well; he had never supposed that he should be the one embarrassed, and above all by a sincere and cordial welcome.

"We heard you were at the Sassacus House," were Ruth's first words; "and this, I suppose, is your friend?"

" I beg your pardon," Philip at length blundered out, " this is Mr. Brierly of whom I have written you."

And Ruth welcomed Harry with a friendliness that Philip thought was due to his friend, to be sure,

but which seemed to him too level with her reception of himself, but which Harry received as his due from the other sex.

Questions were asked about the journey and about the West, and the conversation became a general one, until Philip at length found himself talking with the Squire in relation to land and railroads and things he couldn't keep his mind on; especially as he heard Ruth and Harry in an animated discourse, and caught the words " New York," and " opera," and "reception," and knew that Harry was giving his imagination full range in the world of fashion.

Harry knew all about the opera, green-room and all (at least he said so), and knew a good many of the operas, and could make very entertaining stories of their plots, telling how the soprano came in here, and the basso here, humming the beginning of their airs — tum-ti-tum-ti-ti — suggesting the profound dissatisfaction of the basso recitative — down-among-the-dead-men — and touching off the whole with an airy grace quite captivating; though he couldn't have sung a single air through to save himself, and he hadn't an ear to know whether it was sung correctly. All the same he doted on the opera, and kept a box there, into which he lounged occasionally to hear a favorite scene and meet his society friends. If Ruth was ever in the city he should be happy to place his box at the disposal of Ruth and her friends. Needless to say that she was delighted with the offer.

When she told Philip of it, that discreet young fellow only smiled, and said that he hoped she would be fortunate enough to be in New York some evening when Harry had not already given the use of his private box to some other friend.

The Squire pressed the visitors to let him send for their trunks, and urged them to stay at his house, and Alice joined in the invitation, but Philip had reasons for declining. They stayed to supper, however, and in the evening Philip had a long talk apart with Ruth, a delightful hour to him, in which she spoke freely of herself as of old, of her studies at Philadelphia and of her plans, and she entered into his adventures and prospects in the West with a genuine and almost sisterly interest; an interest, however, which did not exactly satisfy Philip — it was too general and not personal enough to suit him. And with all her freedom in speaking of her own hopes, Philip could not detect any reference to himself in them; whereas, he never undertook anything that he did not think of Ruth in connection with it, he never made a plan that had not reference to her, and he never thought of anything as complete if she could not share it. Fortune, reputation — these had no value to him except in Ruth's eyes, and there were times when it seemed to him that if Ruth was not on this earth, he should plunge off into some remote wilderness and live in a purposeless seclusion.

" I hoped," said Philip, " to get a little start in

connection with this new railroad, and make a little money, so that I could come East and engage in something more suited to my tastes. I shouldn't like to live in the West. Would you?"

" It never occurred to me whether I would or not," was the unembarrassed reply. " One of our graduates went to Chicago, and has a nice practice there. I don't know where I shall go. It would mortify mother dreadfully to have me driving about Philadelphia in a doctor's gig."

Philip laughed at the idea of it. "And does it seem as necessary to you to do it as it did before you came to Fallkill?"

It was a home question, and went deeper than Philip knew, for Ruth at once thought of practicing her profession among the young gentlemen and ladies of her acquaintance in the village; but she was reluctant to admit to herself that her notions of a career had undergone any change.

" Oh, I don't think I should come to Fallkill to practice, but I must do something when I am through school; and why not medicine?"

Philip would have liked to explain why not, but the explanation would be of no use if it were not already obvious to Ruth.

Harry was equally in his element whether instructing Squire Montague about the investment of capital in Missouri, the improvement of Columbus River, the project he and some gentlemen in New York had for making a shorter Pacific connection with the

Mississippi than the present one; or diverting Mrs. Montague with his experience in cooking in camp; or drawing for Miss Alice an amusing picture of the social contrasts of New England and the border where he had been.

Harry was a very entertaining fellow, having his imagination to help his memory, and telling his stories as if he believed them — as perhaps he did. Alice was greatly amused with Harry, and listened so seriously to his romancing that he exceeded his usual limits. Chance allusions to his bachelor establishment in town and the place of his family on the Hudson, could not have been made by a millionaire more naturally.

"I should think," queried Alice, "you would rather stay in New York than to try the rough life at the West you have been speaking of."

" Oh, adventure," says Harry, " I get tired of New York. And besides I got involved in some operations that I had to see through. Parties in New York only last week wanted me to go down into Arizona in a big diamond interest. I told them, no, no speculation for me. I've got my interests in Missouri; and I wouldn't leave Philip, as long as he stays there."

When the young gentlemen were on their way back to the hotel, Mr. Philip, who was not in very good humor, broke out:

"What the deuce, Harry, did you go on in that
style to the Montagues for?" 17*

"Go on?" cried Harry. " Why shouldn't I try to make a pleasant evening? And besides, ain't I going to do those things? What difference does it make about the mood and tense of a mere verb? Didn't uncle tell me only last Saturday, that I might as well go down to Arizona and hunt for diamonds? A fellow might as well make a good impression as a poor one."

"Nonsense. You'll get to believing your own romancing by and by."

"Well, you'll see. When Sellers and I get that appropriation, I'll show you an establishment in town and another on the Hudson and a box at the opera."

" Yes, it will be like Colonel Sellers' plantation at Hawkeye. Did you ever see that?"

"Now, don't be cross, Phil. She's just superb, that little woman. You never told me."

"Who's just superb?" growled Philip, fancying this turn of the conversation less than the other.

"Well, Mrs. Montague, if you must know." And Harry stopped to light a cigar, and then puffed on in silence.

The little quarrel didn't last over night, for Harry never appeared to cherish any ill-will half a second, and Philip was too sensible to continue a row about nothing; and he had invited Harry to come with him.

The young gentlemen stayed in Fallkill a week, and were every day at the Montagues, and took part in the winter gayeties of the village. There were

parties here and there to which the friends of Ruth and the Montagues were, of course, invited, and Harry, in the generosity of his nature, gave in return a little supper at the hotel, very simple indeed, with dancing in the hall, and some refreshments passed round. And Philip found the whole thing in the bill when he came to pay it.

Before the week was over Philip thought he had a new light on the character of Ruth. Her absorption in the small gayeties of the society there surprised him. He had few opportunities for serious conversation with her. There was always some butterfly or another flitting about, and when Philip showed by his manner that he was not pleased, Ruth laughed merrily enough and rallied him on his soberness — she declared he was getting to be grim and unsocial. He talked, indeed, more with Alice than with Ruth, and scarcely concealed from her the trouble that was in his mind. It needed, in fact, no word from him, for she saw clearly enough what was going forward, and knew her sex well enough to know there was no remedy for it but time.

"Ruth is a dear girl, Philip, and has 'as much firmness of purpose as ever, but don't you see she has just discovered that she is fond of society? Don't you let her see you are selfish about it, is my advice."

The last evening they were to spend in Fallkill, they were at the Montagues, and Philip hoped that ^he would find Ruth in a different mood. But she

was never more gay, and there was a spice of mischief in her eye and in her laugh. " Confound it," said Philip to himself, " she's in a perfect twitter." He would have liked to quarrel with her, and fling himself out of the housc in tragedy style r going perhaps so far as to blindly wander off miles into the country and bathe his throbbing brow in the chilling rain of the stars, as people do in novels; but he had no opportunity. For Ruth was as serenely unconscious of mischief as women can be at times, and fascinated him more than ever with her little demure-nesses and half-confidences. She even said " thee " to him once in reproach for a cutting speech he began. And the sweet little word made his heart beat like a trip-hammer, for never in all her life had she said " thee " to him before.

Was she fascinated with Harry's careless bonhomie and gay assurance? Both chatted away in high spirits, and made the evening whirl along in the most mirthful manner. Ruth sang for Harry, and that young gentleman turned the leaves for her at the piano, and put in a bass note now and then where he thought it would tell.

Yes, it was a merry evening, and Philip was heartily glad when it was over, and the long leave-taking with the family was through with.

"Farewell, Philip. Good night, Mr. Brierly," Ruth's clear voice sounded after them as they went down the walk.

And she spoke Harry's name last, thought Philip.

CHAPTER XXIII.

PHJLIP AND HARRY GO TO WORK

"O see ye not yon narrow road

So thick beset wi' thorns and briers? That is the Path of Righteousness, Though after it but few inquires.

"And see ye not yon braid, braid road,

That lies across the lily leven? That is the Path of Wickedness,

Though some call it the road to Heaven."

Thomas the Rhymer.

PHILIP and Harry reached New York in very different states of mind. Harry was buoyant. He found a letter from Colonel Sellers urging him to go to Washington and confer with Senator Dil-worthy. The petition was in his hands. It had been signed by everybody of any importance in Missouri, and would be presented immediately.

" I should go on myself," wrote the Colonel, " but I am engaged in the invention of a process for lighting such a city as St. Louis by means of water; just attach my machine to the water-pipes anywhere and the decomposition of the fluid begins, and you will have floods of light for the mere cost 17* (257)

of the machine. I've nearly got the lighting part, but I want to attach to it a heating, cooking, washing, and ironing apparatus. It's going to be the great thing, but we'd better keep this appropriation going while I am perfecting it."

Harry took letters to several congressmen from his uncle and from Mr. Duff Brown, each of whom had an extensive acquaintance in both houses where they were well known as men engaged in large private operations for the public good, and men, besides, who, in the slang of the day, understood the virtues of " addition, division, and silence."

Senator Dilworthy introduced the petition into the Senate with the remark that he knew, personally, the signers of it, that they were men interested, it was true, in the improvement of the country, but he believed without any selfish motive, and that so far as he knew the signers were loyal. It pleased him to see upon the roll the names of many colored citizens, and it must rejoice every friend of humanity to know that this lately emancipated race were intelligently taking part in the development of the resources of their native land. He moved the reference of the petition to the proper committee.

Senator Dilworthy introduced his young friend to influential members, as a person who was very well informed about the Salt Lick Extension of the Pacific, and was one of the engineers who had made a careful survey of Columbus River; and left him to exhibit his maps and plans and to show the con-

nection between the public treasury, the city of Napoleon, and legislation for the benefit of the whole country.

Harry was the guest of Senator Dilworthy. There was scarcely any good movement in which the Senator was not interested. His house was open to all the laborers in the field of total abstinence, and much of his time was taken up in attending the meetings of this cause. He had a Bible class in the Sunday-school of the church which he attended, and he suggested to Harry that he might take a class during the time he remained in Washington; Mr. Washington Hawkins had a class. Harry asked the Senator if there was a class of young ladies for him to teach, and after that the Senator did not press the subject.

Philip, if the truth must be told, was not well satisfied with his western prospects, nor altogether with the people he had fallen in with. The railroad contractors held out large but rather indefinite promises. Opportunities for a fortune he did not doubt existed in Missouri, but for himself he saw no better means for livelihood than the mastery of the profession he had rather thoughtlessly entered upon. During the summer he had made considerable practical advance in the science of engineering; he had been diligent, and made himself to a certain extent necessary to the work he was engaged on. The contractors called him into their consultations frequently, as to the character of the country he had

been over, and the cost of constructing the road, the nature of the work, etc.

Still Philip felt that if he was going to make either reputation or money as an engineer, he had a great deal of hard study before him, and it is to his credit that he did not shrink from it. While Harry was in Washington dancing attendance upon the national legislature and making the acquaintance of the vast lobby that encircled it, Philip devoted himself day and night, with an energy and a concentration he was capable of, to the learning and theory of his profession, and to the science of railroad building. He wrote some papers at this time for '' The Plow, the Loom, and the Anvil," upon the strength of materials, and especially upon bridge-building, which attracted considerable attention, and were copied into the English " Practical Magazine." They served, at any rate, to raise Philip in the opinion of his friends, the contractors, for .practical men have a certain superstitious estimation of ability with the pen, and though they may a little despise the talent, they are quite ready to make use of it.

Philip sent copies of his performances to Ruth's father and to other gentlemen whose good opinion he coveted, but he did not rest upon his laurels. Indeed, so diligently had he applied himself, that when it came time for him to return to the West, he felt himself, at least in theory, competent to take charge of a division in the field.

CHAPTER XXIV.

THE CITY OF WASHINGTON

Cante-teca. lapi-Waxte otonwe kin he cajeyatapi nawahon; otonwe wijice hinca keyapt se wacanmi.

Toketu-kaxta. Han, hecetu; takuwicawaye wijicapi ota hen dpi.

Mahp. Ekta Oicim. ya.

THE capital of the Great Republic was a new world to country-bred Washington Hawkins. St. Louis was a greater city, but its floating population did not hail from great distances, and so it had the general family aspect of the permanent population; but Washington gathered its people from the four winds of heaven, and so the manners, the faces and the fashions there, presented a variety that was infinite. Washington had never been in "society" in St. Louis, and he knew nothing of the ways of its wealthier citizens, and had never inspected one of their dwellings. Consequently, everything in the nature of modern fashion and grandeur was a new and wonderful revelation to him. Washington is an interesting city to any of us. It seems to become more and more interesting the oftener we visit it. Perhaps the reader has never

(261)

been there? Very well. You arrive either at night, rather too late to do anything or see anything until morning, or you arrive so early in the morning that you consider it best to go to your hotel and sleep an hour or two while the sun bothers along over the Atlantic. You cannot well arrive at a pleasant intermediate hour because the railway corporation that keeps the keys of the only door that leads into the town or out of it take care of that. You arrive in tolerably good spirits, because it is only thirty-eight miles from Baltimore to the capital, and so you have only been insulted three times (provided you are not in a sleeping car — the average is higher, there) : once when you renewed your ticket after stopping over in Baltimore, once when you were about to enter the " ladies' car " without knowing it was a lady's car, and once when you asked the conductor at what hour you would reach Washington.

You are assailed by a long rank of hackmen who shake their whips in your face as you step out upon the sidewalk; you enter what they regard as a "carriage," in the capital, and you wonder why they do not take it out of service and put it in the museum: we have few enough antiquities, and it is little to our credit that we make scarcely any effort to preserve the few we have. You reach your hotel, presently — and here let us draw the curtain of charity — because of course you have gone to the wrong one. You being a stranger, how could you do otherwise? There are a hundred and eigh-

teen bad hotels, and only one good one. The most renowned and popular hotel of them all is perhaps the worst one known to history.

It is winter, and night. When you arrived, it was snowing. When you reached the hotel, it was sleeting. When you went to bed, it was raining. During the night it froze hard, and the wind blew some chimneys down. When you got up in the morning, it was foggy. When you finished your breakfast at ten o'clock and went out, the sunshine was brilliant, the weather balmy and delicious, and the mud and slush deep and all-pervading. You will like the climate — when you get used to it.

You naturally wish to view the city; so you take an umbrella, an overcoat, and a fan, and go forth. The prominent features you soon locate and get familiar with; first you glimpse the ornamental upper works of a long, snowy palace projecting above a grove of trees, and a tall, graceful white dome with a statue on it surmounting the palace and pleasantly contrasting with the background of blue sky. That building is the Capitol; gossips will tell you that by the original estimates it was to cost $12,000,000, and that the government did come within $27,200,000 of building it for that sum.

You stand at the back of the Capitol to treat yourself to a view, and it is a very noble one. You understand, the Capitol stands upon the verge of a high piece of table land, a fine commanding position, and its front looks out over this noble situation for a

city — but it don't see it, for the reason that when the Capitol extension was decided upon, the property owners at once advanced their prices to such inhuman figures that the people went down and built the city in the muddy low marsh behind the temple of liberty; so now the lordly front of the building, with its imposing colonnades, its projecting, graceful wings, its picturesque groups of statuary, and its long terraced ranges of steps, flowing down in white marble waves to the ground, merely looks out upon a sorrowful little desert of cheap boarding houses.

So you observe, that you take your view from the back of the Capitol. And yet not from the airy outlooks of the dome, by the way, because to get there you must pass through the great rotunda: and to do that, you would have to see the marvelous Historical Paintings that hang there, and the bas-reliefs — and what have you done that you should suffer thus? And besides, you might have to pass through the old part of the building, and you could not help seeing Mr. Lincoln, as petrified by a young lady artist for $10,000 — and you might take his marble emancipation proclamation, which he holds out in his hand and contemplates, for a folded napkin; and you might conceive from his expression and his attitude, that he is finding fault with the washing. Which is not the case. Nobody knows what is the matter with him; but everybody feels for him. Well, you ought not to go into the dome anyhow, because it would be utterly impossible to go up

there without seeing the frescoes in it — and why should you be interested in the delirium tremens of art?

The Capitol is a very noble and a very beautiful building, both within and without, but you need not examine it now. Still, if you greatly prefer going into the dome, go. Now your general glance gives you picturesque stretches of gleaming water, on your left, with a sail here and there and a lunatic asylum on shore; over beyond the water, on a distant elevation, you see a squat yellow temple which your eye dwells upon lovingly through a blur of unmanly moisture, for it recalls your lost boyhood and the Parthenons done in molasses candy which made it blest and beautiful. Still in the distance, but on this side of the water and close to its edge, the Monument to the Father of his Country towers out of the mud — sacred soil is the customary term. It has the aspect of a factory chimney with the top broken off. The skeleton of a decaying scaffolding lingers about its summit, and tradition says that the spirit of Washington often comes down and sits on those rafters to enjoy this tribute of respect which the nation has reared as the symbol of its unappeasable gratitude. The Monument is to be finished, some day, and at that time our Washington will have risen still higher in the nation's veneration, and will be known as the Great-Great-Grandfather of his Country. The memorial Chimney stands in a quiet pastoral locality that is full of reposeful ex-

pression. With a glass you can see the cow-sheds about its base, and the contented sheep nibbling pebbles in the desert solitudes that surround it, and the tired pigs dozing in the holy calm of its protecting shadow.

Now you wrench your gaze loose and you look down in front of you and see the broad Pennsylvania Avenue stretching straight ahead for a mile or more till it brings up against the iron fence in front of a pillared granite pile, the Treasury building — an edifice that would command respect in any capital. The stores and hotels that wall in this broad avenue are mean, and cheap, and dingy, and are better left without comment. Beyond the Treasury is a fine large white barn, with wide unhandsome grounds about it. The President lives there. It is ugly enough outside, but that is nothing to what it is inside. Dreariness, flimsiness, bad taste reduced to mathematical completeness is what the inside offers to the eye, if it remains yet what it always has been.

The front and right hand views give you the city at large. It is a wide stretch of cheap little brick houses, with here and there a noble architectural pile lifting itself out of the midst— government buildings, these. If the thaw is still going on when you come down and go about .town, you will wonder at the short-sightedness of the city fathers, when you come to inspect the streets, in that they do not dilute the mud a little more and use them for canals.

If you inquire around a little, you will find that

there are more boarding houses to the square acre in Washington than there are in any other city in the land, perhaps. If you apply for a home in one of them, it will seem odd to you to have the landlady inspect you with a severe eye and then ask you if you are a member of Congress. Perhaps, just as a pleasantry, you will say yes. And then she will tell you that she is "full." Then you show her her advertisement in the morning paper, and there she stands, convicted and ashamed. She will try to blush, and it will be only polite in you to take the effort for the deed. She shows you her rooms, now, and lets you take one — but she makes you pay in advance for it. That is what you will get for pretending to be a member of Congress. If you had been content to be merely a private citizen, your trunk would have been sufficient security for your board. If you are curious and inquire into this thing, the chances are that your landlady will be ill-natured enough to say that the person and property of a Congressman are exempt from arrest or detention, and that with the tears in her eyes she has seen several of the people's representatives walk off to their several States and Territories carrying her unreceipted board bills in their pockets for keepsakes. And before you have been in Washington many weeks you will be mean enough to believe her, too. Of course you contrive to see everything and find out everything. And one of the first and most startling things you find out is, that every individual you encounter in the city of Washington almost — and certainly every separate and distinct individual in the public employment, from the highest bureau chief, clear down to the maid who scrubs Department halls, the night watchmen of the public buildings, and the darkey boy who purifies the Department spittoons — represents Political Influence. Unless you can get the ear of a Senator, or a Congressman, or a Chief of a Bureau or Department, and persuade him to use his " influence " in your behalf, you cannot get an employment of the most trivial nature in Washington. Mere merit, fitness, and capability, are useless baggage to you without "influence." The population of Washington consists pretty much entirely of government employe's and the people who board them. There are thousands of these employe's, and they have gathered there from every corner of the Union and got their berths through the intercession (command is nearer the word) of the Senators and Representatives of their respective States. It would be an odd circumstance to see a girl get employment at three or four dollars a week in one of the great public cribs without any political grandee to back her, but merely because she was worthy, and competent, and a good citizen of a free country that " treats all persons alike." Washington would be mildly thunderstruck at such a thing as that. If you are a member of Congress (no offense), and one of your constituents who doesn't know anything, and does not want to go into the

bother of learning something, and has no money, and no employment, and can't earn a living, comes besieging you for help, do you say, "Come, my friend, if your services were valuable you could get employment elsewhere — don't want you here"? Oh, no. You take him to a Department and say, 14 Here, give this person something to pass away the time at — and a salary " — and the thing is done. You throw him on his country. He is his country's child, let his country support him. There is something good and motherly about Washington, the grand old benevolent National Asylum for the Helpless.

The wages received by this great hive of employes are placed at the liberal figure meet and just for skilled and competent labor. Such of them as are immediately employed about the two Houses of Congress are not only liberally paid also, but are remembered in the customary Extra Compensation bill which slides neatly through, annually, with the general grab that signalizes the last night of a session, and thus twenty per cent, is added to their wages, tor — for fun, no doubt.

Washington Hawkins' new life was an unceasing delight to him. Senator Dilworthy lived sumptuously, and Washington's quarters were charming — gas; running water, hot and cold; bathroom, coal fires, rich carpets, beautiful pictures on the walls; books on religion, temperance, public charities, and

financial schemes; trim colored servants, dainty 18*

food — everything a body could wish for. And as for stationery, there was no end to it; the government furnished it; postage stamps were not needed — the Senator's frank could convey a horse through the mails, if necessary.

And then he saw such dazzling company. Renowned generals and admirals, who had seemed but colossal myths when he was in the far West, went in and out before him or sat at the Senator's table, solidified into palpable flesh and blood; famous statesmen crossed his path daily; that once rare and awe-inspiring being, a Congressman, was become a common spectacle — a spectacle so common, indeed, that he could contemplate it without excitement, even without embarrassment; foreign ministers were visible to the naked eye at happy intervals ; he had looked upon the President himself, and lived. And more, this world of enchantment teemed with speculation — the whole atmosphere was thick with it — and that, indeed, was Washington Hawkins' native air; none other refreshed his lungs so gratefully. He had found paradise at last.

The more he saw of his chief the Senator, the more he honored him, and the more conspicuously the moral grandeur of his character appeared to stand out. To possess the friendship and the kindly interest of such a man, Washington said Ln a letter to Louise, was a happy fortune for a young man whose career had been so impeded and so clouded as his.

The weeks drifted by; Harry Brierly flirted, danced, added lustre to the brilliant Senatorial receptions, and diligently "buzzed" and "buttonholed " Congressmen in the interest of the Columbus River scheme; meantime Senator Dilworthy labored hard in the ?ame interest — and in others of equal national importance. Harry wrote frequently to Sellers, and always encouragingly; and from these letters it was easy to see that Harry was a pet with all Washington, and was likely to carry the thing through; that the assistance rendered him by "old Dilworthy" was pretty fair — pretty fair; "and every little helps, you know," said Harry.

Washington wrote Sellers officially, now and then. In one of his letters it appeared that whereas no member of the House committee favored the scheme at first, there was now needed but one more vote to compass a majority report. Closing sentence :

" Providence seems to farther our efforts. (Signed) " ABNER DILWORTHY, U. S. S., per WASHINGTON HAWKINS, P. S."

At the end of a week, Washington was able to send the happy news,— officially, as usual,— that the needed vote had been added and the bill favorably reported from the committee. Other letters recorded its perils in committee of the whole, and by and by its victory, by just the skin of its teeth, on third reading and final passage. Then came letters telling of Mr. Dilworthy's struggles with a

stubborn majority in his own committee in the Sen ate; of how these gentlemen succumbed, one by one, till a majority was secured.

Then there was a hiatus Washington watched every move on the board, and he was in a good position to do this, for he was clerk of this committee, and also one other. He received no salary as private secretary, but these two clerkships, procured by his benefactor, paid him an aggregate of twelve dollars a day, without counting the twenty per cent, extra compensation which would, of course, be voted to him on the last night of the session.

He saw the bill go into committee of the whole and struggle for its life again, and finally worry through. In the fullness of time he noted its second reading, and by and by the day arrived when the grand ordeal came, and it was put upon its final passage. Washington listened with bated breath to the "Aye!" "No!" "No!" "Aye!" of the voters, for a few dread minutes, and then could bear the suspense no longer. He ran down from the gallery and hurried home to wait.

At the end of two or three hours the Senator arrived in the bosom of his family, and dinner was waiting. Washington sprang forward, with the eager question on his lips, and the Senator said :

"We may rejoice freely, now, my son — Providence has crowned our efforts with success."

WORK AT NAPOLEON (STONE'S LANDING)

WASHINGTON sent grand good news to Colonel Sellers that night. To Louise he wrote:

It is beautiful to hear him talk when his heart is full of thankfulness for some manifestation of the Divine favor. You shall know him, some day, my Louise, and knowing him you will honor him, as I do."

Harry wrote:

I pulled it through, Colonel, but it was a tough job, there rs no question about that. There was not a friend to the measure in the House Committee when I began, and not a friend in the

Senate committee except old Dil himself, but they were all fixed for a majority report when I hauled off my forces. Everybody here says you can't get a thing like this through Congress without buying committees for straight-out cash on delivery, but I think I've taught them a thing or two — if I could only nake them believe it. When I tell the old resident-18- (273)

ers that this thing went through without buying a vote or making a promise, they say, * That's rather too thin.' And when I say, thin or not thin, it's a fact, anyway, they say ' Come, now, but do you really believe that?' and when I say I don't believe anything about it, I know it, they smile and say, 4 Well, you are pretty innocent, or pretty blind, one or the other—there's no getting around that.' Why they really do believe that votes have been bought — they do, indeed. But let them keep on thinking so. I have found out that if a man knows how to talk to women, and has a little gift in the way of argument with men, he can afford to play for an appropriation against a money bag and give the money bag odds in the game. We've raked in $200,000 of Uncle Sam's money, say what they will — and there is more where this came from, when we want it, and I rather fancy I am the person that can go in and occupy it, too, if I do say it myself, that shouldn't, perhaps. I'll be with you within a week. Scare up all the men you can, and put them to work at once. When I get there I propose to make things hum."

The great news lifted Sellers into the clouds. He went to work on the instant. He flew hither and thither making contracts, engaging men, and steeping his soul in the ecstasies of business. He was the happiest man in Missouri. And Louise was the happiest woman; for presently came a letter from Washington which said:

"Rejoice with me, for the long agony is over! We have waited patiently and faithfully, all these years, and now at last the reward is at hand. A man is to pay our family $40,000 for the Tennessee Land! It is but a little sum compared to what we could get by waiting, but I do so long to see the day when I can call you my own, that I have said to myself, better take this and enjoy life in a humble way than wear out our best days in this miserable separation. Besides, I can put this money into operations here that will increase it a hundred fold, yes, a thousand fold, in a few months. The air is full of such chances, and I know our family would consent in a moment that I should put in their shares with mine. Without a doubt we shall be worth half a million dollars in a year from this time — I put it at the very lowest figure, because it is always best to be on the safe side — half a million at the very lowest calculation, and then your father will give his consent and we can marry at last. Oh, that will be a glorious day. Tell our friends the good news — I want all to share it."

And she did tell her father and mother, but they said, let it be kept still for the present. The careful father also told her to write Washington and warn him not to speculate with the money, but to wait a little and advise with one or two wise old heads. She did this. And she managed to keep the good news to herself, though it would seem that the most careless observer might have seen by her springing

step and her radiant countenance that some fine piece of good fortune had descended upon her.

Harry joined the Colonel at Stone's Landing, and that dead place sprang into sudden life. A swarm of men were hard at work, and the dull air was filled with the cheery music of labor. Harry had been constituted engineer-in-general, and he threw the full strength of his powers into his work. He moved among his hirelings like a king. Authority seemed to invest him with a new splendor. Colonel Sellers, as general superintendent of a great public enterprise, was all that a mere human being could be — and more. These two grandees went at their imposing "improvement" with the air of men who had been charged with the work of altering the foundations of the globe.

They turned their first attention to straightening the river just above the Landing, where it made a deep bend, and where the maps and plans showed that the process of straightening would not only shorten distance but increase the * 4 fall." They started a cut-off canal across the peninsula formed by the bend, and such another tearing up of the earth and slopping around in the mud as followed the order to the men had never been seen in that region before. There was such a panic among the turtles that at the end of six hours there was not one to be found within three miles of Stone's Landing. They took the young and the aged, the decrepit and the sick upon their backs and left for tide-water in

disorderly procession, the tadpoles following and the bull-frogs bringing up the rear.

Saturday night came, but the men were obliged to wait, because the appropriation had not come. Harry said he had written to hurry up the money, and it would be along presently. So the work continued, on Monday. Stone's Landing was making quite a stir in the vicinity, by this time. Sellers threw a lot or two on the market, " as a feeler," and they sold well. He re-clothed his family, laid in a good stock of provisions, and still had money left. He started a bank account, in a small way — and mentioned the deposit casually to friends; and to strangers, too; to everybody, in fact; but not as a new thing — on the contrary, as a matter of lifelong standing. He could not keep from buying trifles every day that were not wholly necessary, it was such a gaudy thing to get out his bank book and draw a check, instead of using his old customary formula, " Charge it." Harry sold a lot or two, also — and had a dinner party or two at Hawkeye and a general good time with the money. Both men held on pretty strenuously for the coming big prices, however.

At the end of a month things were looking bad. Harry had besieged the New York headquarters of the Columbus River Slackwater Navigation Company with demands, then commands, and finally appeals, but to no purpose; the appropriation did not come; the letters were not even answered. The

workmen were clamorous, now. The Colonel and Harry retired to consult.

" What's to be done?" said the Colonel.

"Hang'dif I know."

 Company say anything?"

" Not a word."

" You telegraphed yesterday?"

" Yes, and the day before, too."

" No answer?"

" None — confound them !"

Then there was a long pause. Finally both spoke at once:

"I've got it!"

"'vegotit!"

"What's yours?" said Harry.

" Give the boys thirty-day orders on the company for the backpay."

" That's it — that's my own idea to a dot. But then — but then "

"Yes, I know," said the Colonel; " I know they can't wait for the orders to go to New York and be cashed, but what's the reason they can't get them discounted in Hawkeye?"

" Of course they can. That solves the difficulty. Everybody knows the appropriation's been made and the company's perfectly good."

So the orders were given and the men appeased, though they grumbled a little at first. The orders went Well enough for groceries and such things at a fair discount, and the work danced along gaily for a

time. Two or three purchasers put up frame houses at the Landing and moved in, and of course a far-sighted but easy-going journeyman printer wandered along and started the " Napoleon Weekly Telegraph and Literary Repository"—a paper with a Latin motto from the Unabridged Dictionary, and plenty of "fat" conversational tales and double-leaded poetry — all for two dollars a year, strictly in advance. Of course the merchants forwarded the orders at once to New York — and never heard of them again.

At the end of some weeks Harry's orders were a drug in the market — nobody would take them at any discount whatever. The second month closed with a riot. Sellers was absent at the time, and Harry began an active absence himself with the mob at his heels. But being on horseback, he had the advantage. He did not tarry in Hawkeye, but went on, thus missing several appointments with creditors. He was far on his flight eastward, and well out of danger when the next morning dawned. He telegraphed the Colonel to go down and quiet the laborers— he was bound East for money — everything would be right in a week — tell the men so — tell them to rely on him and not be afraid.

Sellers found the mob quiet enough when he reached the Landing. They had gutted the Navigation office, then piled the beautiful engraved stock books and things in the middle of the floor and enjoyed the bonfire while it lasted. They had a liking

for the Colonel, but still they had some idea of hanging him, as a sort of makeshift that might answer, after a fashion, in place of more satisfactory game.

But they made the mistake of waiting to hear what he had to say first. Within fifteen minutes his tongue had done its work and they were all rich men. He gave every one of them a lot in the suburbs of the city of Stone's Landing, within a mile and a half of the future post-office and railway station, and they promised to resume work as soon as Harry got East and started the money along. Now things were blooming and pleasant again, but the men had no money, and nothing to live on. The Colonel divided with them the money he still had in bank — an act which had nothing surprising about it because he was generally ready to divide whatever he had with anybody that wanted it, and it was owing to this very trait that his family spent their days in poverty and at times were pinched with famine.

When the men's minds had cooled and Sellers was gone, they hated themselves for letting him beguile them with fine speeches, but it was too late, now — they agreed to hang him another time — such time as Providence should appoint.

CHAPTER XXVI.

MR. BOLTON MAKES ANOTHER VENTURE uearu> erupp

PjUMORS of Ruth's frivolity and worldliness at *£ Fallkill traveled to Philadelphia in due time, and occasioned no little undertalk among the Bolton relatives.

Hannah Shoecraft told another cousin that, for her part, she never believed that Ruth had so much more "mind" than other people; and Cousin Hulda added that she always thought Ruth was fond of admiration, and that was the reason she was unwilling to wear plain clothes and attend Meeting. The story that Ruth was "engaged" to a young gentleman of fortune in Fallkill came with the other news, and helped to give point to the little satirical remarks that went round about Ruth's desire to be a doctor !

Margaret Bolton was too wise to be either surprised or alarmed by these rumors. They might be true; she knew a woman's nature too well to think them improbable, but she also knew how steadfast

Ruth was in her purposes, and that, as a brook breaks into ripples and eddies and dances and sports by the way, and yet keeps on to the sea, it was in Ruth's nature to give back cheerful answer to the solicitations of friendliness and pleasure, to appear idly delaying even, and sporting in the sunshine, while the current of her resolution flowed steadily on.

That Ruth had this delight in the mere surface play of life — that she could, for instance, be interested in that somewhat serious by-play called " flirtation," or take any delight in the exercise of those little arts of pleasing and winning which are none the less genuine and charming because they are not intellectual, Ruth, herself, had never suspected until she went to Fallkill. She had believed it her duty to subdue her gayety of temperament, and let nothing divert her from what are called serious pursuits. In her limited experience she brought everything to the judgment of her own conscience, and settled the affairs of all the world in her own serene judgment hall. Perhaps her mother saw this, and saw also that there was nothing in the Friends' society to prevent her from growing more and more opinionated.

When Ruth returned to Philadelphia, it must be confessed — though it would not have been by her — that a medical career did seem a little less necessary for her than formerly; and coming back in a glow of triumph, as it were, and in the consciousness

of the freedom and life in a lively society and in new and sympathetic friendship, she anticipated pleasure in an attempt to break up the stiffness and levelness of the society at home, and infusing into it something of the motion and sparkle which were so agreeable at Fallkill. She expected visits from her new friends, she would have company, the new books and the periodicals about which all the world was talking, and, in short, she would have life.

For a little while she lived in this atmosphere which she had brought with her. Her mother was delighted with this change in her, with the improvement in her health and the interest she exhibited in home affairs. Her father enjoyed the society of his favorite daughter as he did few things besides; he liked her mirthful and teasing ways, and not less a keen battle over something she had read. He had been a great reader all his life, and a remarkable memory had stored his mind with encyclopacdic information. It was one of Ruth's delights to cram herself with some out-of-the-way subject and endeavor to catch her father; but she almost always failed. Mr. Bolton liked company, a house full of it, and the mirth of young people, and he would have willingly entered into any revolutionary plans Ruth might have suggested in relation to Friends' society.

But custom and the fixed order are stronger than the most enthusiastic and rebellious young lady, as Ruth very soon found. In spite of all her brave

efforts, her frequent correspondence, and her determined animation, her books and her music, she found herself settling into the clutches of the old monotony, and as she realized the hopelessness of her endeavors, the medical scheme took new hold of her, and seemed to her the only method of escape.

" Mother, thee does not know how different it is in Fallkill, how much more interesting the people are one meets, how much more life there is."

" But thee will find the world, child, pretty much all the same, when thee knows it better. I thought once as thee does now, and had as little thought of being a Friend as thee has. Perhaps when thee has seen more, thee will better appreciate a quiet life."

" Thee married young. I shall not marry young, and perhaps not at all," said Ruth, with a look of vast experience.

"Perhaps thee doesn't know thee own mind; I have known persons of thy age who did not.

Did thee see anybody whom thee would like to live with always in Fallkill?"

"Not always," replied Ruth with a little laugh. "Mother, I think I wouldn't say 'always' to any one until I have a profession and am as independent as he is: Then my love would be a free act, and not in any way a necessity."

Margaret Bolton smiled at this new-fangled philosophy. " Thee will find that love, Ruth, is a thing thee won't reason about, when it comes, nor make

any bargains about. Thee wrote that Philip Sterling was at Fallkill."

" Yes, and Henry Brierly, a friend of his; a very amusing young fellow and not so serious-minded as Philip, but a bit of a fop, maybe."

" And thee preferred the fop to the serious-minded?"

" I didn't prefer anybody, but Henry Brierly was good company, which Philip wasn't always."

"Did thee know thee father had been in correspondence with Philip?"

Ruth looked up surprised and with a plain question in her eyes.

"Oh, it's not about thee."

" What then?" and if there was any shade of disappointment in her tone, probably Ruth herself did not know it.

"It's about some land up in the country. That man Bigler has got father into another speculation."

"That odious man! Why will father have anything to do with him? Is it that railroad?"

" Yes. Father advanced money and took land as security, and whatever has gone with the money and the bonds, he has on his hands a large tract of wild land."

" And what has Philip to do with that?"

" It has good timber, if it could ever be got out, and father says that there must be coal in it; it's in a coal region. He wants Philip to survey it, and

examine it for indications of coal." :

"It's another of father's fortunes, I suppose said Ruth. " He has put away so many fortunes for us that I'm afraid we never shall find them."

Ruth was interested in it, nevertheless, and perhaps mainly because Philip was to be connected with the enterprise. Mr. Bigler came to dinner with her father next day, and talked a great deal about Mr. Bolton's magnificent tract of land, extolled the sagacity that led him to secure such a property, and led the talk along to another railroad which would open a northern communication to this very land.

" Pennybacker says it's full of coal, he's no doubt of it, and a railroad to strike the Erie would make it a fortune."

" Suppose you take the land and work the thing up, Mr. Bigler; you may have the tract for three dollars an acre."

"You'd throw it away, then," replied Mr. Bigler, " and I'm not the man to take advantage of a friend. But if you'll put a mortgage on it for the northern road, I wouldn't mind taking an interest, if Pennybacker is willing; but Pennybacker, you know, don't go much on land, he sticks to the legislature." And Mr. Bigler laughed.

When Mr. Bigler had gone, Ruth asked her father about Philip's connection with the land scheme.

"There's nothing definite," said Mr. Bolton. "Philip is showing aptitude for his profession. I hear the best reports of him in New York, though

those sharpers don't intend to do anything but use him. I've written and offered him employment ia surveying and examining the land. We want to know what it is. And if there is anything in it that his enterprise can dig out, he shall have an interest. I should be glad to give the young fellow a lift."

All his life Eli Bolton had been giving young fellows a lift, and shouldering the losses when things turned out unfortunately. His ledger, take it altogether, would not show a balance on the right side; but perhaps the losses on his books will turn out to be credits in a world where accounts are kept on a different basis. The left hand of the ledger will appear the right, looked at from the other side.

Philip wrote to Ruth rather a comical account of the bursting up of the city of Napoleon and the navigation improvement scheme, of Harry's flight and the Colonel's discomfiture. Harry left in such a hurry that he hadn't even time to bid Miss Laura Hawkins good-bye, but he had no doubt that Harry would console himself with the next pretty face he saw — a remark which was thrown in for Ruth's benefit. Colonel Sellers had in all probability, by this time, some other equally brilliant speculation in his brain.

As to the railroad, Philip had made up his n* .d that it was merely kept on foot for speculative purposes in Wall street, and he was about to quit it. Would Ruth be glad to hear, he wondered, that he was coming East? For he was coming, in spite of

a letter from Harry in New York, advising him to hold on until he had made some arrangements in regard to contracts, he to be a little careful about Sellers, who was somewhat visionary, Harry said.

The summer went on without much excitement for Ruth. She kept up a correspondence with Alice, who promised a visit in the fall, she read, she earnestly tried to interest herself in home affairs and such people as came to the house; but she found herself falling more and more into reveries, and growing weary of things as they were. She felt that everybody might become in time like two relatives from a Shaker establishment in Ohio, who visited the Boltons about this time, a father and son, clad exactly alike, and alike in manners. The son, however, who was not of age, was more unworldly and sanctimonious than his father; he always addressed his parent as "Brother Plum," and bore himself altogether in such a superior manner that Ruth longed to put bent pins in his chair. Both father and son wore the long single-breasted collarless coats of their society, without buttons, before or behind, but with a row of hooks and eyes on either side in front. It was Ruth's suggestion that the coats would be improved by a single hook and eye sewed on in the small of the back where the buttons usually are.

Amusing as this Shaker caricature of the Friends was, it oppressed Ruth beyond measure, and increased her feeling of being stifled.

It was a most unreasonable feeling. No home could be pleasanter than Ruth's. The house, a little out of the city, was one of those elegant country residences which so much charm visitors to the suburbs of Philadelphia. A modern dwelling, and luxurious in everything that wealth could suggest for comfort, it stood in the midst of exquisitely kept lawns, with groups of trees, parterres of flowers massed in colors, with greenhouse, grapery, and garden; and on one side, the garden sloped away in undulations to a shallow brook that ran over a pebbly bottom and sang under forest trees. The country about was the perfection of cultivated landscape, dotted with cottages, and stately mansions of Revolutionary date, and sweet as an English countryside, whether seen in the soft bloom of May or in the mellow ripeness of late October.

It needed only the peace of the mind within, to make it a paradise. One riding by on the Old Germantown road, and seeing a young girl swinging in the hammock on the piazza, and intent upon some volume of old poetry or the latest novel, would no doubt have envied a life so idyllic. He could not have imagined that the young girl was reading a volume of reports of clinics and longing to be elsewhere.

Ruth could not have been more discontented if all the wealth about her had been as unsubstantial as a dream. Perhaps she so thought it.

" I feel," she once said to her father, " as if I were living in a house of cards." 19*

" And thee would like to turn it into a hospital?"

" No. But tell me, father," continued Ruth, not to be put off, *' is thee still going on with thatBigler and those other men who come here and entice thee?"

Mr. Bolton smiled, as men do when they talk with women about "business." " Such men have their uses, Ruth. They keep the world active, and I owe a great many of my best operations to such men. Who knows, Ruth, but this new land purchase, which I confess I yielded a little too much to Bigler in, may not turn out a fortune for thee and the rest of the children?"

" Ah, father, thee sees everything in a rose-colored light. I do believe thee wouldn't have so readily allowed me to begin the study of medicine, if it hadn't had the novelty of an experiment to thee."

" And is thee satisfied with it?"

" If thee means, if I have had enough of it, no. I just begin to see what I can do in it, and what a noble profession it is for a woman. Would thee have me sit here like a bird on a bough and wait for somebody to come and put me in a cage?"

Mr. Bolton was not sorry to divert the talk from his own affairs, and he did not think it worth while to tell his family of a performance that very day which was entirely characteristic of him.

Ruth might well say that she felt as if she were living in a house of cards, although the Bolton

household had no idea of the number of perils that hovered over them, any more than thousands of families in America have of the business risks and contingencies upon which their prosperity and luxury hang.

A sudden call upon Mr. Bolton for a large sum of money, which must be forthcoming at once, had found him in the midst of a dozen ventures, from no one of which a dollar could be realized. It was in vain that he applied to his business acquaintances and friends; it was a period of sudden panic and no money. "A hundred thousand! Mr. Bolton," said Plumly. " Good God, if you should ask me for ten, I shouldn't know where to get it."

And yet that day Mr. Small (Pennybacker, Big-ler, and Small) came to Mr. Bolton with a piteous story of ruin in a coal operation, if he could not raise ten thousand dollars. Only ten, and he was sure of a fortune. Without it he was a beggar. Mr. Bolton had already Small's notes for a large amount in his safe, labeled "doubtful"; he had helped him again and again, and always with the same result. But Mr. Small spoke with a faltering voice of his family, his daughter in school, his wife ignorant of his calamity, and drew such a picture of their agony, that Mr. Bolton put by his own more pressing necessity, and devoted the day to scraping together, here and there, ten thousand dollars for this brazen beggar, who had never kept a promise to him nor paid a debt.

Beautiful credit! The foundation of modern society. Who shall say that this is not the golden age of mutual trust, of unlimited reliance upon human promises? That is a peculiar condition of society which enables a whole nation to instantly recognize point and meaning in the familiar newspaper anecdote, which puts into the mouth of a distinguished speculator in lands and mines this remark : " I wasn't worth a cent two years ago, and now I owe two millions of dollars."

CHAPTER XXVIL

COL. SELLERS IN DIFFICULTIES; BUT SEES A WAV

Bishop Butter. In Arundines Cami.

IT was a hard blow to poor Sellers to see the work on his darling enterprise stop, and the noise and bustle and confusion that had been such refreshment to his soul, sicken and die out. It was hard to come down to humdrum ordinary life again after being a General Superintendent and the most conspicuous man in the community. It was sad to see his name disappear from the newspapers; sadder still to see it resurrected at intervals, shorn of its aforetime gaudy gear of compliments and clothed on with rhetorical tar and feathers.

But his friends suffered more on his account than he did. He was a cork that could not be kept under the water many moments at a time.

(293)

He had to bolster up his wife's spirits every now and then. On one of these occasions he said:

" It's all right, my dear, all right; it will all come right in a little while. There's $200,000 coming, and that will set things booming again. Harry seems to be having some difficulty, but that's to be expected—you can't move these big operations to the tune of Fisher's Hornpipe, you know. But Harry will get it started along presently, and then you'll see! I expect the news every day now."

" But Beriah, you've been expecting it every day, all along, haven't you?"

"Well, yes; yes — I don't know but I have. But anyway, the longer it's delayed, the nearer it grows to the time when it will start — same as every day you live brings you nearer to — nearer — "

" The grave?"

"Well, no — not that exactly; but you can't understand these things, Polly dear — women haven't much head for business, you know. You make yourself perfectly comfortable, old lady, and you'll see how we'll trot this right along. Why, bless you, let the appropriation lag, if it wants to — that's no great matter — there's a bigger thing than that."

" Bigger than $200,000, Beriah?"

" Bigger, child? — why, what's $200,000? Pocket money! Mere pocket money ! Look at the railroad ! Did you forget the railroad? It ain't many months till spring; it will be coming right along, and the railroad swimming right along behind it.

Where'll it be by the middle of summer? Just stop and fancy a moment — just think a little — don't anything suggest, itself? Bless your heart, you dear women live right in the present all the time — but a man, why a man lives "

" In the future, Beriah? But don't we live in the future most too much, Beriah? We do somehow seem to manage to live on next year's crop of corn and potatoes as a general thing while this year is still dragging along, but sometimes it's not a robust diet,— Beriah. But don't look that way, dear — don't mind what I say. I don't mean to fret, I don't mean to worry; and I dorit, once a month, do I, dear? But when I get a little low and feel bad, I get a bit troubled and worrisome, but it don't mean anything in the world. It passes right away. I know you're doing all you can, and I don't want to seem repining and ungrateful — for I'm not, Beriah — you know I'm not, don't you?"

" Lord bless you, child, I know you are the very best little woman that ever lived — that ever lived on the whole face of the earth! And I know that I would be a dog not to work for you and think for you and scheme for you with all my might. And I'll bring things all right yet, honey — cheer up and don't you fear. The railroad "

" Oh, I had forgotten the railroad, dear, but when a body gets blue, a body forgets everything. Yes, the railroad — tell me about the railroad."

"Aha, my girl, don't you see? Things ain't so

dark, are they? Now 7 didn't forget the railroad. Now just think for a moment — just figure up a little on the future dead moral certainties. For instance, call this waiter St. Louis.

"And we'll lay this fork (representing the railroad) from St. Louis to this potato, which is Slouchburg:

"Then with this carving-knife we'll continue the railroad from Slouchburg to Doodleville, shown by the black pepper:

" Then we run along the — yes — the comb — to the tumbler — that's Brimstone:

" Thence by the pipe to Belshazzar, which is the salt-cellar:

"Thence to, to — that quill — Catfish — hand me the pincushion, Marie Antoinette:

"Thence right along these shears to this horse, Babylon:

" Then by the spoon to Bloody Run — thank you, the ink:

"Thence to Hail Columbia — snuffers, Polly, please — move that cup and saucer close up, that's Hail Columbia:

"Then — let me open my knife — to Hark-from-the-Tomb, where we'll put the candle-stick — only a little distance from Hail Columbia to Hark-from-the-Tomb — down grade all the way.

"And there we strike Columbus River — pass me two or three skeins of thread to stand for the river; the sugar-bowl will do for Hawkeye, and the rat-trap

for Stone's Landing — Napoleon, I mean — and you can see how much better Napoleon is located than Hawkeye. Now here you are with your railroad complete, and showing its continuation to Hallelujah, and thence to Corruptionville.

"Now, then — there you are! It's a beautiful road, beautiful. Jeff Thompson can out-engineer any civil engineer that ever sighted through an aneroid, or a theodolite, or whatever they call it — he calls it sometimes one and sometimes the other — just whichever levels off his sentence neatest, I reckon. But ain't it a ripping road, though? I tell you, it'll make a stir when it gets along. Just see what a country it goes through. There's your onions at Slouchburg — noblest onion country that graces God's footstool; and there's your turnip country all around Doodleville — bless my life, what fortunes are going to be made there when they get that contrivance perfected for extracting olive oil out of turnips — if there's any in them; and I reckon there is, because Congress has made an appropriation of money to test the thing, and they wouldn't have done that just on conjecture, of course. And now we come to the Brimstone region — cattle raised there till you can't rest — and corn, and all that sort of thing. Then you've got a little stretch along through Belshazzar that don't produce anything now — at least nothing but rocks — but irrigation will fetch it. Then from Catfish to Babylon it's a little swampy, but there's dead loads of

peat down under there somewhere. Next is the Bloody Run and Hail Columbia country — tobacco enough can be raised there to support two such railroads. Next is the sassparilla region. I reckon there's enough of that truck along in there on the line of the pocket-knife, from Hail Columbia to Hark-from-the-Tomb to fat up all the consumptives in all the hospitals from Halifax to the Holy Land. It ju-t grows like weeds! I've got a little belt of sassparilla land in there just tucked away unob-strusively waiting for my little Universal Expectorant to get into shape in my head. And I'll fix that, you know. One of these days I'll have all the nations of the earth expecto "

"But Beriah, dear "

"Don't interrupt me, Polly —I don't want you to lose the run of the map — well, take your toy-horse, James Fitz-James, if you must have it — and run along with you. Here, now — the soap will do for Babylon. Let me see — where was I? Oh yes — now we run down to Stone's Lan — Napoleon — now we run down to Napoleon. Beautiful road. Look at that, now. Perfectly straight line — straight as the way to the grave. And see where it leaves Hawkeye — clear out in the cold, my dear, clear out in the cold. That town's as bound to die as — well if I owned it I'd get its obituary ready, now, and notify the mourners. Polly, mark my words — in three years from this, Hawkeye'll be a howling wilderness. You'll see. And just look at that river

— noblest stream that meanders over the thirsty earth! — calmest, gentlest artery that refreshes her weary bosom! Railroad goes all over it and all through it—wades right along on stilts. Seventeen bridges in three miles and a half — forty-nine bridges from Hark-from-the-Tomb to Stone's Landing altogether— forty-nine bridges, and culverts enough to culvert creation itself! Hadn't skeins of thread enough to represent them all — but you get an idea

— perfect trestle-work of bridges for seventy-two miles. Jeff Thompson and I fixed all that, you know; he's to get the contracts and I'm to put them through on the divide. Just oceans of money in those bridges. It's the only part of the railroad I'm interested in, — down along the line — and it's all I want, too. It's enough, I should judge. Now here we are at Napoleon. Good enough country — plenty good enough — all it wants is population. That's all right — that will come. And it's no bad country now for calmness and solitude, I can tell you — though there's no money in that, of course. No money, but a man wants rest, a man wants peace — a man don't want to rip and tear around all the time. And here we go, now, just as straight as a string for Hallelujah — it's a beautiful angle — handsome up-grade all the way — and then away you go to Corruptionville, the gaudiest country for early carrots and cauliflowers that ever — good missionary field, too. There ain't such another missionary field outside the jungles of Central

Africa. And patriotic? — why, they named it after Congress itself. Oh, I warn you, my dear, there's a good time coming, and it'll be right along before you know what you're about, too. That railroad's fetching it. You see what it is as far as I've got, and if I had enough bottles and soap and bootjacks and such things to carry it along to where it joins onto the Union Pacific, fourteen hundred miles from here, I should exhibit to you in that little internal improvement a spectacle of inconceivable sublimity. So, don't you see? We've got the railroad to fall back on; and in the meantime, what are we worrying about that $200,000 appropriation for? That's all right. I'd be willing to bet anything that the very next letter that comes from Harry will "

The eldest boy entered just in the nick of time and brought a letter, warm from the post-office.

"Things do look bright, after all, Beriah. I'm sorry I was blue, but it did seem as if everything had been going against us for whole ages. Open the letter — open it quick, and let's know all about it before we stir out of our places. I am all in a fidget to know what it says."

The letter was opened, without any unnecessary delay.

CHAPTER XXVIII.

HOW APPROPRIATION BILLS ARE CARRIED Hvo der vil kjobe Poise af Hunden maa give ham Flesk igjen.

— Mil seinem eignen Verstande wurde Thrasyllus schwerlich durch-gekommen seyn. Aber in solchen Fallen finden seinesgleichen fur ihr Geld immer einen Spitzbuben, der ihnen seinen Kopf leiht ; und dann ist es so viel als ob sie selbst einen batten.

H'teland. Die Abderiten.

WHATEVER may have been the language of Harry's letter to the Colonel, the information it conveyed was condensed or expanded, one or the other, from the following episode of his visit to New York:

He called, with official importance in his mien, at No. — Wall street, where a great gilt sign betokened the presence of the headquarters of the " Columbus River Slackwater Navigation Company." He entered and gave a dressy porter his card, and was requested to wait a moment in a sort of anteroom. The porter returned in a minute, and asked whom he would like to see?

"The president of the company, of course." "He is busy with some gentlemen, sir; says he will be done with them directly."

(301)

That a copper-plate card with u Engineer-in-Chief" on it should be received with such tranquillity as this, annoyed Mr. Brierly not a little. But he had to submit. Indeed, his annoyance had time to augment a good deal; for he was allowed to cool his heels a full half hour in the ante-room before those gentlemen emerged and he was ushered into the presence. He found a stately dignitary occupying a very official chair behind a long green morocco-covered table, in a room sumptuously carpeted and furnished, and well garnished with pictures.

" Good-morning, sir; take a seat — take a seat."

"Thank you, sir," said Harry, throwing as much chill into his manner as his ruffled dignity prompted.

" We perceive by your reports and the reports of the chief superintendent, that you have been making gratifying progress with the work. We are all very much pleased."

" Indeed? We did not discover it from your letters — which we have not received; nor by the treatment our drafts have met with — which were not honored; nor by the reception of any part of the appropriation, no part of it having come to hand."

"Why, my dear Mr. Brierly, there must be some mistake. I am sure we wrote you and also Mr. Sellers, recently — when my clerk comes he will show copies — letters informing you of the ten per cent, assessment."

" Oh, certainly, we got those letters. But what we wanted was money to carry on the work — money to pay the men."

" Certainly, certainly—true enough — but we credited you both for a large part of your assessments— I am sure that was in our letters."

" Of course that was in — I remember that."

"Ah, very well, then. Now we begin to understand each other."

" Well, I don't see that we do. There's two months' wages due the men, and "

" How? Haven't you paid the men?"

" Paid them! How are we going to pay them when you don't honor our drafts?"

"Why, my dear sir, I cannot see how you can find any fault with us^ I am sure we have acted in a perfectly straightforward business way. Now let us look at the thing a moment. You subscribed for 100 shares of the capital stock, at $1,000 a share, I believe?"

"Yes, sir, I did."

" And Mr. Sellers took a like amount?"

"Yes, sir."

" Very well. No concern can get along without money. We levied a ten per cent, assessment. It was the original understanding that you and Mr. Sellers were to have the positions you now hold, with salaries of $600 a month each, while in active service. You were duly elected to these places, and you accepted them. Am I right?"

" Certainly."

"Very well. You were given your instructions and put to work. By your reports it appears that you have expended the sum of $9,640 upon the said work. Two months' salary to you two officers amounts altogether to $2,400 — about one-eighth of your ten per cent, assessment, you see; which leaves you in debt to the company for the other seven-eighths of the assessment — viz., something over $8,000 apiece. Now, instead of requiring you to forward this aggregate of $16,000 or $17,000 to New York, the company voted unanimously to let you pay it over to the contractors, laborers from time to time, and give you credit on the books for it. And they did it without a murmur, too, for they were pleased with the progress you had made, and were glad to pay you that little compliment — and a very neat one it was, too, I am sure. The work you did fell short of $10,000, a trifle. Let me see — $9,640 from $20,000 — salary $2,400 added — ah, yes, the balance due the company from yourself and Mr. Sellers is $7,960, which I will take the responsibility of allowing to stand for the present, unless you prefer to draw a check now, and thus "

*' Confound it, do you mean to say that instead of the company owing us $2,400, we owe the company $7,960?"

"Well, yes."

*' And that we owe the men and the contractors nearly ten thousand dollars besides?"

" Owe them ! Oh bless my soul, you can't mean that you have not paid these people?"

" But I do mean it!"

The president rose and walked the floor like a man in bodily pain. His brows contracted, he put his hand up and clasped his forehead, and kept saying, " Oh, it is too bad, too bad, too bad ! Oh, it is bound to be found out — nothing can prevent it—nothing!"

Then he threw himself into his chair and said:

"My dear Mr. Bryerson, this is dreadful — perfectly dreadful. It will be found out. It is bound to tarnish the good name of the company; our credit will be seriously, most seriously impaired. How could you be so thoughtless — the men ought to have been paid though it beggared us all!"

" They ought, ought they? Then why the devil — my name is not Bryerson, by the way — why the mischief didn't the compa — why what in the nation ever became of the appropriation? Where is that appropriation? — if a stockholder may make so bold as to ask."

"The appropriation? — that paltry $200,000, do you mean?"

"Of course — but I didn't know that $200,000 was so very paltry. Though I grant, of course, that it is not a large sum, strictly speaking. But where is it? "

" My dear sir, you surprise me. You surely cannot have had a large acquaintance with this sort of 20*

thing. Otherwise you would not have expected much of a result from a mere initial appropriation like that. It was never intended for anything but a mere nest egg for the future and real appropriations to cluster around."

"Indeed? Well, was it a myth, or was it a reality? Whatever become of it? "

" Why the matter is simple enough. A Congressional appropriation costs money. Just reflect, for instance. A majority of the House committee, say $10,000 apiece — $40,000; a majority of the Senate committee, the same each — say $40,000; a little extra to one or two chairmen of one or two such committees, say $10,000 each — $20,000; and there's $100,000 of the money gone, to begin with. Then, seven male lobbyists, at $3,000 each — $21,000; one female lobbyist, $10,000; a high moral Congressman or Senator here and there — the high moral ones cost more, because they give tone to a measure — say ten of these at $3,000 each, is $30,000; then a lot of small-fry country members who won't vote for anything whatever without pay

— say twenty at $500 apiece, is $10,000; a lot of dinners to members — say $10,000 altogether; lot of jimcracks for Congressmen's wives and children

— those go a long way — you can't spend too much money in that line — well, those things cost in a lump, say $10,000 — along there somewhere; — and then comes your printed documents — your maps, your tinted engravings, your pamphlets, you?

illuminated show cards, your advertisements in a hundred and fifty papers at ever so much a line — because you've got to keep the papers all right or you are gone up, you know. Oh, my dear sir, printing bills are destruction itself. Ours, so far amount to — let me see—10; 52; 22; 13;—and then there's 11 ; 14; 33—well, never mind the details, the total in clean numbers foots up $118,254.-42 thus far!"

"What!"

" Oh, yes indeed. Printing's no bagatelle, I can tell you. And then there's your contributions, as a company, to Chicago fires and Boston fires, and orphan asylums and all that sort of thing — head the list, you see, with the company's full name and a thousand dollars set opposite — great card, sir — one of the finest advertisements in the world — the preachers mention it in the pulpit when it's a religious charity— one of the happiest advertisements in the world is your benevolent donation. Ours have amounted to sixteen thousand dollars and some cents up to this time."

Good heavens!"

" Oh, yes. Perhaps the biggest thing we've done in the advertising line was to get an officer of the U. S. government, of perfectly Himalayan official altitude, to write up our little internal improvement for a religious paper of enormous circulation — I tell you, that makes our bonds go handsomely among the pious poor. Your religious paper is by far the

best vehicle for a thing of this kind, because they'll ' lead ' your article and put it right in the midst of the reading matter; and if it's got a few Scripture quotations in it, and some temperance platitudes, and a bit of gush here and there about Sunday-schools, and a sentimental snuffle now and then about ' God's precious ones, the honest hard-handed poor,' it works the nation like a charm, my dear sir, and never a man suspects that it is an advertisement; but your secular paper sticks you right into the advertising columns and of course you don't take a trick. Give me a religious paper to advertise in, every time; and if you'll just look at their advertising pages, you'll observe that other people think a good deal as I do—-especially people who have got little financial schemes to make everybody rich with. Of course, I mean your great big metropolitan religious papers that know how to serve God and make money at the same time — that's your sort, sir, that's your sort — a religious paper that isn't run to make money is no use to us, sir, as an advertising medium — no use to anybody in our line of business. I guess our next best dodge was sending a pleasure trip of newspaper reporters out to Napoleon. Never paid them a cent; just filled them up with champagne and the fat of the land, put pen, ink, and paper before them while they were red-hot, and bless your soul when you come to read their letters you'd have supposed they'd been to heaven. And if a sentimental squeamishness held one or two of

them back from taking a less rosy view of Napoleon, our hospitalities tied his tongue, at least, and he said nothing at all and so did us no harm. Let me see — have I stated all the expenses I've been at? No, I was near forgetting one or two items. There's your official salaries — you can't get good men for nothing. Salaries cost pretty lively. And then there's your big high-sounding millionaire names stuck into your advertisements as stockholders — another card, that—and they are stockholders, too, but you have to give them the stock and nonassessable at that — so they're an expensive lot. Very, very expensive thing, take it all around, is a big internal improvement concern — but you see that yourself, Mr. Bryerson—you see that, yourself, sir."

" But look here. I think you are a little mistaken about it's ever having cost anything for Congressional votes. I happen to know something about that. I've let you say your say — now let me say mine. I don't wish to seem to throw any suspicion on anybody's statements, because we are all liable to be mistaken. But how would it strike you if I were to say that / was in Washington all the time this bill was pending? — and what if I added that / put the measure through myself? Yes, sir, I did that little thing. And, moreover, I never paid a dollar for any man's vote and never promised one. There are some ways of doing a thing that are as good as others which other people don't happen to

think about, or don't have the knack of succeeding in, if they do happen to think of them. My dear sir, I am obliged to knock some of your expenses in the head — for never a cent was paid a Congressman or Senator on the part of this Navigation Company."

The president smiled blandly, even sweetly, all through this harangue, and then said:
"Is that so?"

" Every word of it."

"Well, it does seem to alter the complexion of things a little. You are acquainted with the members down there, of course, else you could not have worked to such advantage?"

" I know them all, sir. I know their wives, their children, their babies — I even made it a point to be on good terms with their lackeys. I know every Congressman well — even familiarly."

" Very good. Do you know any of their signatures? Do you know their handwriting?"

" Why, I know their handwriting as well as I know my own — have had correspondence enough with them, I should think. And their signatures — why I can tell their initials, even."

The president went to a private safe, unlocked it and got out some letters and certain slips of paper. Then he said:

" Now here, for instance; do you believe that that is a genuine letter? Do you know this signature here? — and this one? Do you know who those initials represent — and are they forgeries?"

Harry was stupefied. There were things there that made his brain swim. Presently, at the bottom of one of the letters he saw a signature that restored his equilibrium; it even brought the sunshine of a smile to his face.

The president said:
"That name amuses you. You never suspected him? "

" Of course I ought to have suspected him, but I don't believe it ever really occurred to me. Well, well, well — how did you ever have the nerve to approach him, of all others?"

" Why, my friend, we never think of accomplishing anything without his help. He is our mainstay. But how do those letters strike you?"

"They strike me dumb! What a stone-blind idiot I have been!"

"Well, take it all around, I suppose you had a pleasant time in Washington," said the president, gathering up the letters; "of course you must have had. Very few men could go there and get a money bill through without buying a single "

" Come, now, Mr. President, that's plenty of that! I take back everything I said on that head. I'm a wiser man to-day than I was yesterday, I can tell you."

" I think you are. In fact, I am satisfied you are. But now I showed you these things in confidence, you understand. Mention facts as much as you want to, but don't mention names to anybody. I can depend on you for that, can't I?"

" Oh, of course. I understand the necessity of that. I will not betray the names. But to go back a bit, it begins to look as if you never saw any of that appropriation at all?"

We saw nearly ten thousand dollars of it — and that was all. Several of us took turns at log-rolling in Washington, and if we had charged anything for that service, none of that $10,000 would ever have reached New York."

" If you hadn't levied the assessment you would have been in a close place, I judge?"

"Close? Have you figured up the total of the disbursements I told you of?"

" No, I didn't think of that."

"Well, let's see:

Spent in Washington, say, . $191,000 Printing, advertising, etc., say, 118,000 Charity, say, . . . 16,000

Total, . $325,000 " The money to do that with, comes from— Appropriation, . . $200,000

Ten per cent, assessment on capital of $1,000,000, . . 100,000

Total, . $300,000

"Which leaves us in debt some $25,000 at this moment. Salaries of home officers are still going on; also printing and advertising. Next month will show a state of things !' '

"And then — burst up, I suppose?"

"By no means. Levy another assessment."

"Oh, I see. That's dismal."

" By no means."

" Why isn't it? What's the road out?"

" Another appropriation, don't you see?"

"Bother the appropriations. They cost more than they come to."

" Not the next one. We'll call for half a million — get it, and go for a million the very next month."

" Yes, but the cost of it!"

The president smiled, and patted his secret letters affectionately. He said:

" All these people are in the next Congress. We shan't have to pay them a cent. And what is more, they will work like beavers for us — perhaps it might be to their advantage."

Harry reflected profoundly a while. Then he said:

" We send many missionaries to lift up the benighted races of other lands. How much cheaper and better it would be if those people could only come here and drink of our civilization at its fountain head."

" I perfectly agree with you, Mr. Beverly. Must you go? Well, good morning. Look in, when you are passing; and whenever I can give you any information about our affairs and prospects, I shall be glad to do it."

Harry's letter was not a long one, but it contained at least the calamitous figures that came out in the above conversation. The Colonel found himself in a rather uncomfortable place — no $1,200 salary forthcoming; and himself held responsible for half of the $9,640 due the workmen, to say nothing of being in debt to the company to the extent of nearly $4,000. Polly's heart was nearly broken; the "blues" returned in fearful force, and she had to go out of the room to hide the tears that nothing could keep back now.

There was mourning in another quarter, too, for Louise had a letter. Washington had refused, at the last moment, to take $40,000 for the Tennessee Land, and had demanded $150,000! So the trade fell through, and now Washington was wailing because he had been so foolish. But he wrote that his man might probably return to the city, soon, and then he meant to sell to him, sure, even if he had to take $10,000. Louise had a good cry —several of them, indeed — and the family charitably forbore to make any comments that would increase her grief.

Spring blossomed, summer came, dragged its hot weeks by, and the Colonel's spirits rose, day by day, for the railroad was making good progress. But by and by something happened. Hawkeye had always declined to subscribe anything toward the railway, imagining that her large business would be a sufficient compulsory influence; but now Hawkeye was frightened; and before Colonel Sellers knew what he was about, Hawkeye, in a panic, had rushed

HIS AIR CASTLES CRUMBLED TO RUINS

to the front and subscribed such a sum that Napoleon's attractions suddenly sank into insignificance, and the railroad concluded to follow a comparatively straight course instead of going miles out of its way to build up a metropolis in the muddy desert of Stone's Landing.

The thunderbolt fell. After all the Colonel's deep planning; after all his brain work and tongue work in drawing public attention to his pet project and enlisting interest in it; after all his faithful hard toil with his hands, and running hither and thither on his busy feet; after all his high hopes and splendid prophecies, the fates had turned their backs on him at last, and all in a moment his air-castles crumbled to ruins about him. Hawkeye rose from her fright triumphant and rejoicing, and down went Stone's Landing! One by one, its meager parcel of inhabitants packed up and moved away, as the summer waned and fall approached. Town lots were no longer salable, traffic ceased, a deadly lethargy fell upon the place once more, the " Weekly Telegraph " faded into an early grave, the wary tadpole returned from exile, the bullfrog resumed his ancient song, the tranquil turtle sunned his back upon bank and log and drowsed his grateful life away as in the old sweet days of yore.

CHAPTER XXIX.

PHILIP SURVEYS THE ILIUM COAL LANDS

— Mihma hatak ash osh ilhkolit yakni ya hlopullit tztnaha boliht£ vlhpisa ho krshkoa untuklo bg hollissochit holisso afobkit tahii cha.

Chosh.

PHILIP STERLING was on his way to Ilium, in the state of Pennsylvania. Ilium was the railway station nearest to the tract of wild land which Mr. Bolton had commissioned him to examine.

On the last day of the journey, as the railway train Philip was on was leaving a large city, a lady timidly entered the drawing-room car, and hesitatingly took a chair that was at the moment unoccupied. Philip saw from the window that a gentleman had put her upon the car just as it was starting. In a few moments the conductor entered, and without waiting an explanation, said roughly to the lady:

" Now you can't sit there. That seat's taken. Go into the other car."

" I did not intend to take the seat," said the lady rising. " I only sat down a moment till the conductor should come and give me a seat."

"There ain't any. Car'sfull. You'll have to leave."

(316)

"But, sir," said the lady, appealingly, "I thought "

"Can't help what you thought — you must go into the other car."

"The train is going very fast, let me stand here till we stop."

"The lady can have my seat," cried Philip, springing up. The conductor turned toward Philip, and coolly and deliberately surveyed him from head to foot, with contempt in every line of his face, turned his back upon him without a word, and said to the lady:

" Come, I've got no time to talk. You must go now."

The lady, entirely disconcerted by such rudeness, and frightened, moved toward the door, opened it and stepped out. The train was swinging along at a rapid rate, jarring from side to side; the step was a long one between the cars, and there was no protecting grating. The lady attempted it, but lost her balance, in the wind and the motion of the car, and fell! She would inevitably have gone down under the wheels, if Philip, who had swiftly followed her, had not caught her arm and drawn her up. He then assisted her across, found her a seat, received her bewildered thanks, and returned to his car.

The conductor was still there, taking his tickets, and growling something about imposition. Philip marched up to him, and burst out with:

"You are a brute, an infernal brute, to treat a woman that way."

14 Perhaps you'd like to make a fuss about it," sneered the conductor.

Philip's reply was a blow, given so suddenly and planted so squarely in the conductor's face, that it sent him reeling over a fat passenger, who was looking up in mild wonder that any one should dare to dispute with a conductor, and against the side of the car.

He recovered himself, reached the bell rope, " Damn you, I'll learn you," stepped to the door and called a couple of brakemen, and then, as the speed slackened, roared out:

" Get off this train."

"I shall not get off. I have as much right here as you."

"We'll see," said the conductor, advancing with the brakemen. The passengers protested, and some of them said to each other, " That's too bad," as they always do in such cases, but none of them offered to take a hand with Philip. The men seized him, wrenched him from his seat, dragged him along the aisle, tearing his clothes, thrust him from the car, and then flung his carpet-b.ag, overcoat, and umbrella after him. And the train went on.

The conductor, red in the face and puffing from hie exertion, swaggered through the car, muttering "Puppy! I'll learn him." The passengers, when he had gone, were loud in their indignation, and

talked about signing a protest, but they did nothing more than talk.

The next morning the Hooverville Patriot and Clarion had this " item ":

SLIGHTUALLY OVERBOARD.

" We leam that as the down noon express was leaving H yesterday a lady! (God save the mark) attempted to force herself into the already full palatial car. Conductor Slum, who is too old a bird to be caught with chaff, courteously informed her that the car was full, and when she insisted on remaining, he persuaded her to go into the car where she belonged. Thereupon a young sprig, from the East, blustered up, like a Shanghai rooster, and began to sass the conductor with his chin music. That gentleman delivered the young aspirant for a muss one of his elegant little left-handers, which so astonished him that he began to feel for his shooter. Whereupon Mr. Slum gently raised the youth, carried him forth, and set him down just outside the car to cool off. Whether the young blood has yet made his way out of Bas-com's swamp, we have not learned. Conductor Slum is one of the most gentlemanly and efficient officers on the road; but he ain't trifled with, not much. We learn that the company have put a new engine on the seven o'clock train, and newly upholstered the drawing-room car throughout. It spares no effort for the comfort of the traveling public."

Philip never had been before in Bascom's swamp, and there was nothing inviting in it to detain him. After the train got out of the way he crawled out of the briars and the mud, and got upon the track. He was somewhat bruised, but he was too angry to mind that. He plodded along over the ties in a very hot condition of mind and body. In the scuffle, his railway check had disappeared, and he grimly wondered, as he noticed the loss, if the company would permit him to walk over their track if they should know he hadn't a ticket.

Philip had to walk some five miles before he reached a little station, where he could wait for a train, and he had ample time for reflection. At first he was full of vengeance on the company. He would sue it. He would make it pay roundly. But then it occurred to him that he did not know the name of a witness he could summon, and that a personal fight against a railway corporation was about the most hopeless in the world. He then thought he would seek out that conductor, lie in wait for him at some station, and thrash him, or get thrashed himself.

But as he got cooler, that did not seem to him a project worthy of a gentleman, exactly. Was it possible for a gentleman to get even with such a fellow as that conductor on the latter's own plane? And when he came to this point, he began to ask himself, if he had not acted very much like a fool. He didn't regret striking the fellow — he hoped he had left a mark on him. But, after all, was that the best way? Here was he, Philip Sterling, calling himself a gentleman, in a brawl with a vulgar conductor, about a woman he had never seen before. Why should he have put himself in such a ridiculous position? Wasn't it enough to have offered the lady his seat, to have rescued her from an accident, perhaps from death? Suppose he had simply said to the conductor, " Sir, your conduct is brutal, I shall report you." The passengers, who saw the affair, might have joined in a report against the con-

ductor, and he might really have accomplished something. And, now! Philip looked at his torn clothes, and thought with disgust of his haste in getting into a fight with such an autocrat.

At the little station where Philip waited for the next train, he met a man who turned out to be a justice of the peace in that neighborhood, and told him his adventure. He was a kindly sort of man, and seemed very much interested.

" Dum 'em," said he, when he had heard the story.

" Do you think anything can be done, sir?"

Wai, I guess tain't no use. I hain't a mite of doubt of every word you say. But suin's no use. The railroad company owns all these people along here, and the judges on the bench, too. Spiled your clothes! wal, 'least said's soonest mended.' You hain't no chance with the company."

When next morning, he read the humorous account in the Patriot and Clarion, he saw still more clearly what chance he would have had before the public in a fight with the railroad company.

Still Philip's conscience told him that it was his plain duty to carry the matter into the courts, even with the certainty of defeat. He confessed that neither he nor any citizen had a right to consult his own feelings or conscience in a case where a law of the land had been violated before his own eyes. He confessed that every citizen's first duty in such a case is to put aside his own business and devote his

time and his best efforts to seeing that the infraction is promptly punished; and he knew that no country can be well governed unless its citizens as a body keep religiously before their minds that they are the guardians of the law, and that the law officers are only the machinery for its execution, nothing more. As a finality he was obliged to confess that he was a bad citizen, and also that the general laxity of the time, and the absence of a sense of duty toward any part of the community but the individual himself were ingrained in him, and he was no better than the rest of the people.

The result of this little adventure was that Philip did not reach Ilium till daylight the next morning, when he descended, sleepy and sore, from a way train; and looked about him. Ilium was in a narrow mountain gorge, through which a rapid stream ran. It consisted of the plank platform on which he stood, a wooden house, half painted, with a dirty piazza (unroofed) in front, and a signboard hung on a slanting pole bearing the legend, "Hotel. P. Dusenheimer," a sawmill further down the stream, a blacksmith shop, and a store, and three or four unpainted dwellings of the slab variety.

As Philip approached the hotel he saw what appeared to be a wild beast crouching on the piazza. It did not stir, however, and he soon found that it was only a stuffed skin. This cheerful invitation to the tavern was the remains of a huge panther which had been killed in the region a few weeks

before. Philip examined his ugly visage and strong crooked fore-arm, as he was waiting admittance, having pounded upon the door.

"Vait a bit. I'll shoost put on my trowsers," shouted a voice from the window, and the door was soon opened by the yawning landlord.

"Morgen! Didn't hear d' drain oncet. Dem boys geeps me up zo spate. Gom right in."

Philip was shown into a dirty bar-room. It was a small room, with a stove in the middle, set in a long shallow box of sand, for the benefit of the " spit-ters," a bar pcross one end — a mere counter with a sliding glass case behind it containing a few bottles having ambitious labels, and a wash sink in one corner. On the walls were the bright yellow and black handbills of a traveling circus, with pictures of acrobats in human pyramids, horses flying in long leaps through the air, and sylph-like women in a paradisiac costume, balancing themselves upon the tips of their toes on the bare backs of frantic and plunping steeds, and kissing their hands to the spectators meanwhile.

As Philip did not desire a room at that hour, he was invited to wash himself at the nasty sink, a feat somewhat easier than drying his face, for the towel that hung in a roller over the sink was evidently as much a fixture as the sink itself, and belonged, like the suspended brush and comb, to the traveling public. Philip managed to complete his toilet by the use of his pocket-handkerchief, and, declining

the hospitality of the landlord, implied in the remark, "You won'd dake notin'?" he went into the open air to wait for breakfast.

The country he saw was wild but not picturesque. The mountain before him might be eight hundred feet high, and was only a portion of a long unbroken range, savagely wooded, which followed the stream. Behind the hotel, and across the brawling brook, was another level-topped, wooded range exactly like it. Ilium itself, seen at a glance, was old enough to be dilapidated, and if it had gained anything by being made a wood-and-water station of the new railroad, it was only a new sort of grime and rawness. P. Dusenheimer, standing in the door of his uninviting groggery, when the trains stopped for water, never received from the traveling public any patronage except facetious remarks upon his personal appearance. Perhaps a thousand times he had heard the remark, " Ilium fuit" followed in most instances by a hail to himself as "./Eneas," with the inquiry, "Where is old Anchises?" At first he had replied, " Dere ain't no such man;" but irritated by its senseless repctition, he had latterly dropped into the formula of, "You be dam."

Philip was recalled from the contemplation of Ilium by the rolling and growling of the gong within the hotel, the din and clamor increasing till the house was apparently unable to contain it, when it burst out of the front door and informed the world that breakfast was on the table.

The dining-room was long, low, and narrow, and a narrow table extended its whole length. Upon this was spread a cloth which, from appearance, might have been as long in use as the towel in the bar-room. Upon the table was the usual service, the heavy, much - nicked stone ware, the row of plated and rusty castors, the sugar-bowls with the zinc teaspoons sticking up in them, the piles of yellow biscuits, the discouraged-looking plates of butter. The landlord waited, and Philip was pleased to observe the change in his manner. In the bar-room he was the conciliatory landlord. Standing behind his guests at table, he had an air of peremptory patronage, and the voice in which he shot out the inquiry, as he seized Philip's plate, "Beefsteak or liver?" quite took away Philip's power of choice. He begged for a glass of milk, after trying that green-hued compound called coffee, and made his breakfast out of that and some hard crackers which seemed to have been imported into Ilium before the introduction of the iron horse, and to have withstood a ten years' siege of regular boarders, Greeks and others.

The land that Philip had come to look at was at least five miles distant from Ilium station.

A corner of it touched the railroad, but the rest was pretty much an unbroken wilderness, eight or ten thousand acres of rough country, most of it such a mountain range as he saw at Ilium.

His first step was to hire three woodsmen to ac-
company him. By their help he built a log hut, and established a camp on the land, and then began his explorations, mapping down his survey as he went along, noting the timber, and the lay of the land, and making superficial observations as to the prospect of coal.

The landlord at Ilium endeavored to persuade Philip to hire the services of a witch-hazel professoi of that region, who could walk over the land with his wand and tell him infallibly whether it contained coal, and exactly where the strata ran. But Philip preferred to trust to his own study of the country, and his knowledge of the geological formation. He spent a month in traveling over the land and making calculations: and made up his mind that a fine vein of coal ran through the mountain about a mile from the railroad, and that the place to run in a tunnel was half way toward its summit.

Acting with his usual promptness, Philip, with the consent of Mr. Bolton, broke ground there at once, and, before snow came, had some rude buildings up, and was ready for active operations in the spring. It was true that there were no outcroppings of coal at the place, and the people at Ilium said he " mought as well dig for plug terbaccer there;" but Philip had great faith in the uniformity of nature's operations in ages past, and he had no doubt that he should strike at this spot the rich vein that had made the fortune of the Golden Briar Company.

CHAPTER XXX.
SENATOR DILWORTHY INVITES LAURA TO WASHINGTON

— "Gran pensier volgo; e, se tu lui second!, Seguiranno gli effetti alle speranze: Teosi la tela, ch' io ti mostro ordita, Di cauto vecchio esecutrice ardita."

Tasso. " Belle domna vostre socors

M'agra mestier, s'a vos plagues."

B. de Yentadour.

ONCE more Louise had good news from her Washington — Senator Dilworthy was going to sell the Tennessee Land to the government! Louise told Laura in confidence. She had told her parents, too, and also several bosom friends; but all of these people had simply looked sad when they heard the news, except Laura. Laura's face suddenly brightened under it—only for an instant, it is true, but poor Louise was grateful for even that fleeting ray of encouragement. When next Laura was alone, she fell into a train of thought something like this:

" If the Senator has really taken hold of this matter, I may look for that invitation to his house

(327)

at any moment. I am perishing to go ! I do long to know whether I am only simply a large-sized pigmy among these pigmies here, who tumble over so easily when one strikes them, or whether I am really—" Her thoughts drifted into other channels, for a season. Then she continued: " He said I could be useful in the great cause of philanthropy, and help in the blessed work of uplifting the poor and the ignorant, if he found it feasible to take hold of our Land, Well, that is neither here nor there; what I want, is to go to Washington and find out what I am. I want money, too; and if one may judge by what she hears, there are chances there for a — " For a fascinating woman, she was going to say, perhaps, but she did not.

Along in the fall the invitation came, sure enough. It came officially through brother Washington, the private secretary, who appended a postscript that was brimming with delight over the prospect of seeing the Duchess again. He said it would be happiness enough to look upon her face once more — it would be almost too much happiness when to it was added the fact that she would bring messages with her that were fresh from Louise's lips.

In Washington's letter were several important enclosures. For instance, there was the Senator's check for $2,000— " to buy suitable clothes in New York with !" It was a loan to be refunded when the Land was sold. Two thousand — this was fine indeed. Louise's father was called rich, but Laura

doubted if Louise had ever had $400 worth of new clothing at one time in her life. With the check came two through tickets — good on the railroad from Hawkeye to Washington via New York — and they were "dead-head" tickets, too, which had been given to Senator Dilworthy by the railway companies. Senators and representatives were paid thousands of dollars by the government for traveling expenses, but they always traveled "dead-head" both ways, and then did as any honorable, high-minded men would naturally do — declined to receive the mileage tendered them by the government. The Senator had plenty of railway passes, and could easily spare two to Laura—one for herself and one for a male escort. Washington suggested that she get some old friend of the family to come with her, and said the Senator would " dead-head " him home again as soon as he had grown tired of the sights of the capital. Laura thought the thing over. At first she was pleased with the idea, but presently she began to feel differently about it. Finally she said, "No, our staid, steady-going Hawkeye friends' notions and mine differ about some things — they respect me, now, and I respect them — better leave it so — I will go alone; I am not afraid to travel by myself." And so communing with herself, she left the house for an afternoon walk.

Almost at the door she met Colonel Sellers. She told him about her invitation to Washington.

"Bless me!" said the Colonel. "I have about

made up my mind to go there myself. You see we've got to get another appropriation through, and the company want me to come East and put it through Congress. Harry's there, and he'll do what he can, of course; and Harry's a good fellow and always does the very best he knows how, but then he's young — rather young for some parts of such work, you know — and besides he talks too much, talks a good deal too much; and sometimes he appears to be a little bit visionary, too, I think—the worst thing in the world for a business man. A man like that always exposes his cards, sooner or later. This sort of thing wants an old, quiet, steady hand — wants an old cool head, you know, that knows men, through and through, and is used to large operations. I'm expecting my salary, and also some dividends from the company, and if they get along in time, I'll go along with you, Laura — take you under my wing — you mustn't travel alone. Lord, I wish I had the money right now. But there'll be plenty soon — plenty."

Laura reasoned with herself that if the kindly, simple-hearted Colonel was going anyhow, what could she gain by traveling alone and throwing away his company? So she told him she accepted his offer gladly, gratefully. She said it would be the greatest of favors if he would go with her and protect her — not at his own expense as far as railway fares were concerned, of course; she could not expect him to put himself to so much trouble for her

and pay his fare besides. But he wouldn't hear of her paying his fare — it would be only a pleasure to him to serve her. Laura insisted on furnishing the tickets; and finally, when argument failed, she said the tickets cost neither her nor anyone else a cent — she had two of them — she needed but one — and if he would not take the other she would not go with him. That settled the matter. He took the ticket. Laura was glad that she had the check for new clothing, for she felt very certain of being able to get the Colonel to borrow a little of the money to pay hotel bills with, here and there.

She wrote Washington to look for her and Colonel Sellers toward the end of November;

and at about the time set the two travelers arrived safe in the capital of the nation, sure enough.

CHAPTER XXXI.

PHILIP BREAKS HIS ARM. RUTH ASSISTS THE SURGEON

Deh! ben fora all' incontro ufficio umano,

E bed n'avresti tu gioja e diletto, Se la pietosa tua medica tnano

Awicinassi al valoroso petto.

Tasto.

She, gracious lady, yet no paines did spare To doe him ease, or doe him remedy: Many restoratives of vertues rare And costly cordialles she did apply, To mitigate his stubborne malady.

Spenser't Faerie Queene.

MR. HENRY BRIERLY was exceedingly busy in New York, so he wrote Colonel Sellers, but he would drop everything and go to Washington.

The Colonel believed that Harry was the prince of lobbyists, a little too sanguine, maybe, and given to speculation, but, then, he knew everybody; the Columbus River navigation scheme was got through almost entirely by his aid. He was needed now to help through another scheme, a benevolent scheme in which Colonel Sellers, through the Hawkinses, had a deep interest.

I don't care, you know," he wrote to Harry,

(332)

" so much about the niggroes. But if the government will buy this land, it will set up the Hawkins family — make Laura an heiress — and I shouldn't wonder if Beriah Sellers would set up his carriage again. Dilworthy looks at it different, of course. He's all for philanthropy, for benefiting the colored race. There's old Balaam, was in the Interior — used to be the Rev. Orson Balaam of Iowa — he's made the riffle on the Injun; great Injun pacificator and land dealer. Balaam's got the Injun to himself, and I suppose that Senator Dilworthy feels that there is nothing left him but the colored man. I do reckon he is the best friend the colored man has got in Washington."

Though Harry was in a hurry to reach Washington, he stopped in Philadelphia, and prolonged his visit day after day, greatly to the detriment of his business both in New York and Washington. The society at the Boltons' might have been a valid excuse for neglecting business much more important than his. Philip was there; he was a partner with Mr. Bolton now in the new coal venture, concerning which there was much to be arranged in preparation for the spring work, and Philip lingered week after week in the hospitable house. Alice was making a winter visit. Ruth only went to town twice a week to attend lectures, and the household was quite to Mr. Bolton's taste, for he liked the cheer of company and something going on evenings. Harry was cordially asked to bring his traveling-bag there, and

he did not need urging to do so. Not even the thought of seeing Laura at the capital made him restless in the society of the two young ladies; two birds in hand are worth one in the bush certainly.

Philip was at home — he sometimes wished he were not so much so. He felt that too much or not enough was taken for granted. Ruth had met him, when he first came, with a cordial frankness, and her manner continued entirely unrestrained. She neither sought his company nor avoided it, and this perfectly level treatment irritated him more than any other could have done. It was impossible to advance much in love-making with one who offered no obstacles, had no concealments and no embarrassments, and whom any approach to sentimentality would be quite likely to set into a fit of laughter.

Why, Phil," she would say, " what puts you in the dumps to-day? You are as solemn as the upper bench in Meeting. I shall have to call Alice to raise your spirits; my presence seems to depress you."

It's not your presence, but your absence when you are present," began Philip, dolefully, with the idea that he was saying a rather deep thing. 4I But you won't understand me."

No, I confess I cannot. If you really are so low as to think I am absent when I am present, it's a frightful case of aberration; I shall ask father to bring out Dr. Jackson. Does Alice appear to be present when she is absent?"

Alice has some human feeling, anyway. She

cares for something besides musty books and dry bones. I think, Ruth, when I die," said Philip, intending to be very grim and sarcastic, " I'll leave you my skeleton. You might like that."

" It might be more cheerful than you are at times," Ruth replied with a laugh. "But you mustn't do it without consulting Alice. She might not like it."

" I don't know why you should bring Alice up on every occasion. Do you think I am in love with her?"

" Bless you, no. It never entered my head. Are you ? The thought of Philip Sterling in love is too comical. I thought you were only in love with the Ilium coal mine, which you and father talk about half the time."

This is a specimen of Philip's wooing. Confound the girl, he would say to himself, why does she never tease Harry and that young Shepley who comes here?

How differently Alice treated him. She at least never mocked him, and it was a relief to talk with one who had some sympathy with him. And he did talk to her, by the hour, about Ruth. The blundering fellow poured all his doubts and anxieties into her ear, as if she had been the impassive occupant of one of those little wooden confessionals in the Cathedral on Logan Square. Has a confessor, if she is young and pretty, any feeling? Does it mend the matter by calling her your sister?

Philip called Alice his good sister, and talked to her about love and marriage, meaning Ruth, as if sisters could by no possibility have any personal concern in such things. Did Ruth ever speak of him? Did she think Ruth cared for him? Did Ruth care for anybody at Fallkill ? Did she care for anything except her profession ? And so on.

Alice was loyal to Ruth, and if she knew anything she did not betray her friend. She did not, at any rate, give Philip too much encouragement. What woman, under the circumstances, would?

" I can tell you one thing, Philip," she said, " if ever Ruth Bolton loves, it will be with her whole soul, in a depth of passion that will sweep everything before it and surprise even herself."

A remark that did not much console Philip, who imagined that only some grand heroism could unlock the sweetness of such a heart; and Philip feared that he wasn't a hero. He did not know out of what materials a woman can construct a hero, when she is in the creative mood.

Harry skipped into this society with his usual lightness and gayety. His good nature was inexhaustible, and though he liked to relate his own exploits, he had a little tact in adapting himself to the tastes of his hearers. He was not long in finding out that Alice liked to hear about Philip, and Harry launched out into the career of his friend in the West, with a prodigality of invention that would have astonished the chief actor. He was the most generous fellow in the world, and picturesque con-

versation was the one thing in which he never was bankrupt. With Mr. Bolton he was the serious man of business, enjoying the confidence of many of the moneyed men in New York, whom Mr. Bolton knew, and engaged with them in railway schemes and government contracts. Philip, who had so long known Harry, never could make up his mind that Harry did not himself believe that he was a chief actor in all these large operations of which he talked so much. Harry did not neglect to endeavor to make himself agreeable to Mrs. Bolton, by paying great attention to the children, and by professing the warmest interest in the Friends' faith. It always seemed to him the most peaceful religion; he thought it must be much easier to live by an internal light than by a lot of outward rules; he had a dear Quaker aunt in Providence of whom Mrs. Bolton constantly reminded him. He insisted upon going with Mrs, Bolton and the children to the Friends' Meeting on First Day, when Ruth and Alice and Philip, "world's people," went to a church in town, and he sat through the hour of silence with his hat on, in most exemplary patience. In short, this amazing actor succeeded so well with Mrs. Bolton, that she said to Philip one day:

" Thy friend, Henry Brierly, appears to be a very worldly-minded young man. Does he believe in anything?"

" Oh, yes," said Philip laughing, " he believes in more things than any other person I ever saw." 23*

To Ruth Harry seemed to be very congenial. He was never moody for one thing, but lent himself with alacrity to whatever her fancy was. He was gay or grave as the need might be. No one apparently could enter more fully into her plans for an independent career.

"My father," said Harry, "was bred a physician, and practiced a little before he went into Wall street. I always had a leaning to the study. There was a skeleton hanging in the closet of my father's study when I was a boy, that I used to dress up in old clothes. Oh, I got quite familiar with the human frame."

"You must have," said Philip. "Was that where you learned to play the bones? He is a master of those musical instruments, Ruth; he plays well enough to go on the stage."

" Philip hates science of any kind, and steady application," retorted Harry. He didn't fancy Philip's banter, and when the latter had gone out, and Ruth asked:

" Why don't you take up medicine, Mr. Bricrly?"

Harry said, "I have it in mind. I believe I would begin attending lectures this winter if it weren't for being wanted in Washington. But medicine is particularly women's province."

" Why so?" asked Ruth, rather amused.

"Well, the treatment of disease is a good deal a matter of sympathy. A woman's intuition is better than a man's. Nobody knows anything, really, you

know, and a woman can guess a good deal nearer than a man."

*' You are very complimentary to my sex." "But," said Harry frankly, "I should want to choose my doctor. An ugly woman would ruin me; the disease would be sure to strike in and kill me at sight of her. I think a pretty physician, with engaging manners, would coax a fellow to live through almost anything."

" I am afraid you are a scoffer, Mr. Brierly." " On the contrary, I am quite sincere. Wasn't it old what's his name? that said only the beautiful is useful?"

Whether Ruth was anything more than diverted with Harry's company, Philip could not determine. He scorned, at any rate, to advance his own interest by any disparaging communications about Harry, both because he could not help liking the fellow himself, and because he may have known that he could not more surely create a sympathy for him in Ruth's mind. That Ruth was in no danger of any serious impression he felt pretty sure, felt certain of it when he reflected upon her severe occupation with her profession. Hang it! he would say to himself, she is nothing but pure intellect anyway. And he only felt uncertain of it when she was in one of her moods of raillery, with mocking mischief in her eyes. At such times she seemed to prefer Harry's society to his. When Philip was miserable about this, he always took refuge with Alice, who was never moody,

and who generally laughed him out of his sentimental nonsense. He felt at his ease with Alice, and was never in want of something to talk about; and he could not account for the fact that he was so often dull with Ruth, with whom, of all persons in the world, he wanted to appear at his best.

Harry was entirely satisfied with his own situation. A bird of passage is always at its ease, having no house to build, and no responsibility. He talked freely with Philip about Ruth, an almighty fine girl, he said, but what the deuce she wanted to study medicine for, he couldn't see.

There was a concert one night at the Musical Fund Hall, and the four had arranged to go in and return by the Germantown cars. It was Philip's plan, who had engaged the seats, and promised himself an evening with Ruth, walking with her, sitting by her in the hall, and enjoying the feeling of protecting that a man always has of a woman in a public place. He was fond of music, too, in a sympathetic way; at least, he knew that Ruth's delight in it would be enough for him.

Perhaps he meant to take advantage of the occa sion to say some very serious things. His love for Ruth was no secret to Mrs. Bolton, and he felt almost sure that he should have no opposition in the family. Mrs. Bolton had been cautious in what she said, but Philip inferred everything from her reply to his own questions, one day, "Has thee ever spoken thy mind to Ruth?"

Why shouldn't he speak his mind, and end his doubts? Ruth had been more tricksy than usual that day, and in a flow of spirits quite inconsistent, it would seem, in a young lady devoted to grave studies.

Had Ruth a premonition of Philip's intention, in his manner? It may be, for when the girls came down stairs, ready to walk to the cars, and met Philip and Harry in the hall, Ruth said, laughing:

"The two tallest must walk together," and before Philip knew how it happened Ruth had taken Harry's arm, and his evening was spoiled. He had too much politeness and good sense and kindness to show in his manner that he was hit. So he said to Harry:

" That's your disadvantage in being short." And he gave Alice no reason to feel during the evening that she would not have been his first choice for the excursion. But he was none the less chagrined, and not a little angry at the turn the affair took.

The hall was crowded with the fashion of the town. The concert was one of those fragmentary drearinesses that people endure because they are fashionable: tours de force on the piano, and fragments from operas, which have no meaning without the setting, with weary pauses of waiting between; there is the comic basso who is so amusing and on such familiar terms with the audience, and always sings the Barber; the attitudinizing tenor, with his languishing "Oh, Summer Night"; the soprano

with her " Batti Batti," who warbles and trills and runs and fetches her breath, and ends with a noble scream that brings down a tempest of applause, in the midst of which she backs off the stage smiling and bowing. It was this sort of concert, and Philip was thinking that it was the most stupid one he ever sat through, when just as the soprano was in the midst of that touching ballad, " Comin' thro' the Rye" (the soprano always sings " Comin' thro' the Rye" on an encore — the Black Swan used to make it irresistible, Philip remembered, with her arch, " If a body kiss a body") there was a cry of " Fire!"

The hall is long and narrow, and there is only one place of egress. Instantly the audience was on its feet, and a rush began for the door. Men shouted, women screamed, and panic seized the swaying mass. A second's thought would have convinced every one that getting out was impossible, and that the only effect of a rush would be to crush people to death. But a second's thought was not given. A few cried "Sit down, sit down," but the mass was turned towards the door. Women were down ind trampled on in the aisles, and stout men, utterly lost to self-control, were mounting the benches, as if to run a race over the mass to the entrance.

Philip, who had forced the girls to keep their seats, saw, in a flash, the new danger, and sprang to avert it. In a second more those infuriated men would be over the benches and crushing Ruth and Alice under their boots. He leaped upon the bench in

front of them and struck out before him with all his might, felling one man who was rushing on him, and checking for an instant the movement, or rather parting it, and causing it to flow on either side of him. But it was only for an instant; the pressure behind was too great, and the next Philip was dashed backwards over the seat.

And yet that instant of arrest had probably saved the girls, for, as Philip fell, the orchestra struck up "Yankee Doodle" in the liveliest manner. The familiar tune caught the ear of the mass, which paused in wonder, and gave the conductor's voice a chance to be heard— " It's a false alarm !"

The tumult was over in a minute, and the next laughter was heard, and not a few said, " I knew it wasn't anything." " What fools people are at such a time!"

The concert was over, however. A good many people were hurt, some of them seriously, and among them Philip Sterling was found bent across the seat, insensible, with his left arm hanging limp and a bleeding wound on his head.

When he was carried into the air he revived, and said it was nothing. A surgeon was called, and it was thought best to drive at once to the Boltons', the surgeon supporting Philip, who did not speak the whole way. His arm was set and his head dressed, and the surgeon said he would come round all right in his mind by morning; he was very weak. Alice, who was not much frightened while the panic

lasted in the hall, was very much unnerved by seeing Philip so pale and bloody. Ruth assisted the surgeon with the utmost coolness and with skillful hands helped to dress Philip's wounds. And there was a certain intentness and fierce energy in what she did that might have revealed something to Philip if he had been in his senses.

But he was not, or he would not have murmured, " Let Alice do it, she is not too tall."

It was Ruth's first case.

THE END

Made in the USA
Las Vegas, NV
25 January 2024

84849130R00077